HIGH PRAISE FOR T
STEVE PERRY'S STORIES O
INCLUD

**The Man Who Never Missed, Matadora,
The Machiavelli Interface, The 97th Step,
The Albino Knife, and Black Steel**

"A crackling good story. I enjoyed it immensely!"
—Chris Claremont, author of *FirstFlight*

"Action and adventure flow cleanly from Perry's pen!"
—*Pulp and Celluloid*

"Heroic . . . Perry builds his protagonist into a mythical figure
without losing his human dimension. It's refreshing."
—*Newsday*

"Perry provides plenty of action [and] expertise about weapons and combat."
—*Booklist*

"Noteworthy!"
—*Fantasy and Science Fiction*

"Another Sci-Fi winner . . . cleanly written . . . the story accel-
erates smoothly at an adventurous clip, bristling with martial
arts feats and as many pop-out weapons as a Swiss army knife!"
—*The Oregonian*

"Plenty of blood, guts, and wild fight scenes!"
—*Voya*

"Excellent reading!"
—*Science Fiction Review*

BROTHER DEATH

STEVE PERRY

ACE BOOKS, NEW YORK

This book is an Ace original edition,
and has never been previously published.

BROTHER DEATH

An Ace Book / published by arrangement with
the author

PRINTING HISTORY
Ace edition / December 1992

All rights reserved.
Copyright © 1992 by Steve Perry.
Cover art by Royo.
This book may not be reproduced in whole or in part,
by mimeograph or any other means, without permission.
For information address: The Berkley Publishing Group,
200 Madison Avenue, New York, New York 10016.

ISBN: 0-441-54476-2

Ace Books are published by The Berkley Publishing Group,
200 Madison Avenue, New York, New York 10016.
The name "ACE" and the "A" logo
are trademarks belonging to Charter Communications, Inc.

PRINTED IN THE UNITED STATES OF AMERICA

10 9 8 7 6 5 4 3 2 1

This book is for Dianne, as are they all;
and for the Supper Club: Carol, Dick, Ann,
Bruce and Nancy

ACKNOWLEDGMENTS

There are always people who help. This time most of it was maybe not so direct but more in a collateral sort of way. We are talking here about aliens, Batman, politics, barbarians, brass bras, alternate China and good old moral support. My thanks for this to: Mike Richardson, Michael Reaves, Vera Katz, Dean Wesley Smith, Kris Rusch and Vince Kohler.

"Victory is certain when the enemy is caught up in a rhythm which confuses his spirit."

—*Miyamoto Musashi*

"Whoever conspires cannot find companions except among those who are discontented."

—*Machiavelli*

ONE _____

DEATH CAME FOR Bork's sister during the party.

On Muto Kato there was a ceremony designed to welcome babies to life, dating from the time when a local disease made human pregnancies difficult. It was not so much a religious thing as a social gathering that allowed people in those unhappy times a peek at the lucky family and, of course, the new baby. In the hundreds of years that had passed since the infertile period, the ceremony had become a tradition. It was called Baby Day.

Bork stood between his sister, Tazzimi, and his wife, Veate, who held their three-month-old son Saval Antoon. They were part of a crowd of perhaps ten thousand parents holding most of the babies born locally since the last such gathering. Eighty meters in front of them a raised platform held several dignitaries, one of whom was making opening remarks to the assembled.

Muto Kato's bright sun shined down temperately and the air was filled with the sharp gingerspice smell that came with spring on this continent. Flowers bloomed, trees greened thicker, the cycle of the seasons renewed itself. There might be nicer places in the galaxy, but not many.

The baby's maternal grandparents, Emile Khadaji and Juete, were supposedly crossing Daito's fairgrounds at that moment to join their daughter and son-in-law, as well as to meet for the first time Bork's sister. Taz had come all the way from Tembo and her job as a cool to see her new nephew.

Ten meters away from Bork, a man focused his attention upon them. Bork felt the gaze almost as a physical pressure, and he shifted his big frame but slightly to see the cause. At nearly two meters tall and a hundred and twenty-five kilos on this world, shifting his frame without drawing attention took some skill; fortunately, matadors had such training—you didn't get to be one of the best bodyguards in the worlds of men without learning a few dance steps.

The man was paying most of his attention to Taz, Bork saw, and that was unusual. Taz was a striking woman, sure enough, tall and muscular as were most mues of their kind, and certainly interesting to look upon. But with Veate standing there breast-feeding a sleepy baby, watching anyone else ought to be almost impossible. Veate was an Albino Exotic, and she commanded attention in the same way that a sudden explosion commanded it. *Every*body looked at Veate, some with more subtlety than others, but if the eyes worked and she was around, they would fasten their gaze upon her eventually.

Only, this guy was staring at Taz as though she were the most fascinating thing on the planet.

Something wrong with that.

Bork moved nonchalantly but carefully to put himself between the watching man and Veate. His wife seemed intent on listening to the speech and making sure their son was getting fed properly. She didn't glance at Bork, but she did put one hand out to lightly touch his arm, as if to make sure he was really there.

The man flicked a look at him, but resumed his watch of Tazzimi after no more than a couple of heartbeats.

Quietly Bork said, "Taz, there's a guy about ten meters to your left staring a hole through you. Anybody you know?"

His sister didn't appear to hear him, but she said, "Nope. Never seen him before. I figured he was just enjoying your wife's bare breast more than he ought to."

"Far as I can tell, it's you he's interested in."

The man took a deep breath. A fine sweat had broken out on his face.

"And he's gathering himself to move, too," Bork said.

"Yeah. Might be a problem."

"Left my spetsdöds at home. I don't wear 'em much these days."

"My service gun is under a peace seal at customs," Taz said. She thought about it for a second. "Maybe I'll just go get us something nice and cold to drink," she said.

"Good idea."

If the guy meant trouble, and if he were armed, better he should follow Taz away from this crowd of parents and babies. Bork didn't want to think about who might get hurt if some psychoballoo started shooting around here.

Taz headed toward the refreshment stands on the edge of the fairgrounds. She got about five meters away, turned toward Bork and said loudly, "You wanted greenfruit juice, right?"

"Right," Bork called back. He turned away and pretended to look again at the speaker up front. Adrenaline bubbled in him as he catalogued the man. He was average enough, not quite as large as Taz herself. She'd go maybe one hundred and eighty-three centimeters and eighty, eighty-two kilos here, he figured. The guy didn't have any obvious ethnic lines that leaped out at Bork. He was medium dark, somewhere about the shade of coffee-and-cream, dark hair chopped close. He wore baggy, bright blue two-piece matching shirt and three-quarter pants, orthosandals with paler blue stockings to the knees. He had a matching synlin personals bag slung over his left shoulder on a wide strap, and looked like any other local come for the celebration. Could be somebody's uncle or cousin, nothing to mark him as unusual, save his intense attention to Bork's sister.

When Taz was thirty meters away, the man casually ambled after her. Yep. Coffee Cream over there was trouble. He had the feel.

Bork let him cover five meters and glance back once to be sure he wasn't being followed. When Cream returned his attention to Taz, Bork said to Veate, "I'm going to the fresher."

She nodded, and switched the baby to the other side, drawing stares from the people around her as perfect breasts flashed whitely in the sunlight, shining like gravid pearls. "Is everything okay?"

"Yeah. No problem. Back in a couple minutes."

She knew something was up but she didn't push it. Bork appreciated that.

Bork quickly angled off, and took a parallel course somewhat behind Cream. He'd worn light gray to keep from getting too hot, but he felt a little sweat begin forming under his own loose-weave orthoskins.

Cream had one hand in the shoulder bag now, and Bork was fairly certain he was holding some kind of weapon.

The big matador edged closer to the man tailing his sister, moving precisely and silently.

Cream was intent on his target, speeding up a little, gaining on her.

Taz kept her back to her watcher, as if she hadn't a care in the galaxy past achieving the drink stand.

A few more meters and Bork would be in perfect position to staple the guy into a meaty knot if he even blinked funny. Unless that hand came out of the bag empty, Bork planned to arrange it so Cream was out cold before he hit the plastcrete.

When Bork was still three steps away, Cream pulled a gun from the shoulder bag and began to swing it up in line with Taz's back. She was five meters ahead, an easy shot.

Bork yelled, "Hey, you! Drop it!"

Cream jerked his attention away from Taz and started to turn, swinging the gun around to cover the noisy threat.

That was good. Bork slid into Arc of Air, a portion of the Ninety-seven Steps that covered a lot of ground in a hurry.

"Static it, Jobo!" Taz yelled. "Move and I'll blast you!"

Cream's eyes grew wide and wild and he twisted, trying all at once to stop his turn toward Bork, to regain his primary target, and to figure out what had happened. The gun—a satin-dull, blue-black carbon-fiber spring pistol—wavered and moved back toward Taz.

"Needle him, Morry!" Bork yelled.

"Lose the gun!" Taz screamed.

The guy's mental circuits must have overloaded at that point. Both Taz and Bork were moving in on him fast and he couldn't cover both of them. Bork was closer, but Taz was who he'd come to dance with, so he half-twisted, half-fell toward her, shoved the spring pistol out and started pulling the trigger.

He got off two rounds before Bork slammed into him and smacked his upper back with the heels of both hands in the third variation of Dark Shroud.

Bork had long ago learned that this particular sumito move was a very powerful attack, even from someone with normal physical strength; done correctly, it would almost always ground a human target.

It grounded him, all right.

The spring gun flew one way, the shoulder bag another, and Cream's legs snapped up from the knees hard enough to fling both sandals off and a good four meters away. He hit like a big rock falling off a cliff on a high-gee planet. Hard enough to raise dust from the solid plastcrete and to flatten his nose and abrade his face into a bloody mess. Whatever sense he had was knocked from him instantly. He wasn't going anywhere under his own power for some time.

Problem with being so big and potent was that sometimes you didn't throttle it down enough and you caused some real damage. Well, that was too bad. Guy should have thought about that before he thought to take a shot at Bork's sister.

"Taz?"

"I'm okay," she said. "He missed."

She came to stand next to Bork. She had scooped up the spring gun and now held it loosely pointing down at the fallen man. The gun was unnecessary.

Passersby began to gather.

"You don't know him, huh?"

"Nope. But he's a clever dongo, whoever he is."

"Yeah?"

She hefted the spring gun in her hand, looked at it, then at her brother. "This is mine," she said.

"That's fine, I don't have any use for it."

"No, I mean it's *mine*. This is my service pistol. My number, my initials, right there."

Bork blinked and thought about that for a second. "How'd he get it?" He nodded at the unconscious man.

"Now there's the question of the hour," she said. " 'How?' indeed."

When Emile and Juete arrived, the local cools had already hauled the unconscious would-be assassin away to the local medical kiosk for repair. Juete went to see her daughter and grandson. While Taz talked to the officer in charge of the investigation, Bork explained the situation as best he could to his father-in-law.

"Your sister have enemies who would follow her all the way from Tembo to Muto Kato?"

Bork shrugged. "I dunno. She's the assistant Chief of Investigators for High Crimes, whatever they are on Tembo. Could be she stepped on somebody's toes there. Goes with the job, she says."

Emile Khadaji nodded. As the legendary freedom fighter called The Man Who Never Missed, he knew about such things.

"Well, nobody was hurt, that's good. Anything we can do to help, Saval . . ."

Bork nodded. "Thanks, boss." It was an old habit; he hadn't really worked for Khadaji for years, but once upon a time a long way back, Bork had been a bouncer in The Jade Flower, the headquarters for the revolution that eventually toppled the Confed. Another lifetime. "I'll talk to her about it."

So Khadaji went to see his grandson and Bork went to see his sister and the local cools.

"So, you figure out who he is yet?"

The Katoan policeman had a belt reader scanning the ID cube taken from the fallen man, but he shook his head. "Fake," he said, waving the reader.

"Taz?"

She shrugged. "I didn't get a real good look at him before somebody sanded his face off," she said. She grinned. "Hell of a sidewalk tattoo."

Bork returned the smile.

"But it might be tied up with some trouble we're having at home."

Bork nodded, waiting.

"There have been some killings in the last six months," she said. "Rich and powerful people, humans, mues, men, women. A dozen or so we know about. Not just in Leijona where I'm based, but all up and down the east coast of Raion. Guy in Watu who owned a big villie plantation, couple of political types in town, the mayor of Shaba City, a timber export king down in Tibois, like that. Other than the fact they all earn more stads in a month than I'll see in a lifetime, they don't seem to have anything in common, except that they all got murdered after they were warned it would happen. We don't have shit for clues. Locked-room deals, most of them."

Bork nodded. "Even people with money get killed."

"Yeah, except that these people had some pretty good bodyguards who tried to keep it from happening."

"Any matadors?"

"No."

"Well, there you go," Bork said.

"Yeah, there you go. Thing is, these killers are beginning to worry a lot of people. I got put in charge of the investigation, starting right after I get back from my vacation here to see my brother and his new wife and nephew. I do pretty fair work most of the time. Maybe somebody doesn't want me involved."

"Well, if that's the best they can do they don't seem all that formidable to me."

"Oh, they are. This guy might not be connected to that, or maybe he just barely qualified or something. You, ah, interested in maybe doing a little consulting work, Saval?"

"You want me to go to Tembo?"

"You're one of the best bodyguards in the galaxy. If you can't help me figure out how to keep these toobies from slaughtering the local citizens, who else?"

"I dunno . . ."

"I would consider it a personal favor," she said.

That's when Bork knew how worried Taz really was. The Borks seldom asked for favors, even of each other.

Especially of each other.

He nodded. Bork had two families—one he'd been born to, another he'd chosen. Either one needed his help, he would give it. Family meant something to him. "Okay," he said.

That was that.

TWO

THE BABY WAS asleep, angelic in slumber: he had wispy, almost downlike white hair and he was paler even than his mother. You could see the tapestry of blue blood vessels under the translucent white of him, and his skin made the finest spidersilk cloth seem coarse. People said he looked like his father, but standing naked there in the dim nursery, Bork couldn't see it. Five minutes ago the baby had let out a small squawk and rolled over in his sleep. Bork had gotten there from his own bed before his child finished the turn.

He put one big hand out and touched his son lightly. At the touch, little Saval smiled reflexively.

Bork moved his hand back but stayed next to the crib, feeling for the thousandth time the weight of responsibility that came with being a father. It wasn't uncomfortable, the feeling, but there were ways it was heavier than a flexsteel bar loaded with plates. He had sometimes thought about it but never really figured he'd get to be a da. It was a whole lot different than he'd ever guessed. Here he was, a father, married to the most beautiful woman in the galaxy. Life sure was strange.

"He okay?" Veate said from behind him.

"Yeah." He continued to watch the baby.

Veate came to stand next to him. She slid one hand up Bork's bare arm and lightly squeezed his tricep. "You're going to get eyestrain staring at him like that."

"It's just so amazing, you know? I mean, he's a little person

and we made him. And he's so beautiful. I have to say, he's
the best-looking baby I've ever seen."

She laughed. "Well, if it isn't Bork the master of objec-
tivity."

He glanced at her. "What? You don't think so?"

"Are you kidding? I'm his mother. Of course he's the most
beautiful baby you've ever seen. He's the most beautiful baby
ever *born*."

Bork nodded. "Yeah, that's true."

She punched him. "You're an idiot, you know that?"

"Huh? How come?"

"Great big thing like you in here stupe-faced over a baby.
Some kind of tough guy you are. Sleel would fall down
laughing, he knew about this."

"Yeah? Last time I talked to Sleel, he said after seeing little
Saval he and Kee were thinking seriously about having one of
their own. This is a special kid here."

Veate leaned over and kissed his arm. "What am I going to
do with you? You get any prouder and you'll explode. Come
on." She tugged at him.

"Where?"

"Remember how we made this extraordinary babe?"

He grinned. "Vaguely."

"Vaguely? You thug!"

She started to move away in mock anger, but he picked her
up, as easily as a normal-sized man might pick up a small
child. He cradled her. "Hey, I'm old," he said. "Can't expect
me to remember everything."

"I expect you to forget your *name* before you forget lovemaking with me, Saval Bork!"

"Who? What did you call me?"

She pretended to pout. "That's better. Not good enough, but
better."

He carried her from the nursery to their bedroom.

Love wasn't about technique, Bork knew that, but if you
did love somebody, them knowing pretty much everything

there was to know about the physical aspects of it made it real interesting.

"Lie back," Veate commanded.

Bork did so.

"Lume control, one-quarter on the overheads."

The computer brought the lights up obediently.

"Lume control, pink spot, centered on the bed."

Her white hair and skin turned to rose quartz.

"It's better for you when you can see me, isn't it?"

"Yeah," Bork said.

She straddled him, but sat on his belly, her fine pubic hair, now shaded pink, tickling his navel. She put her hands on the thick muscles of his upper chest, leaned into them and massaged him, squeezing hard. He enjoyed the feel of her fingers digging into him. After a moment, she slid her hands up to his neck and worked the bands of muscle under his ears.

"Mmm."

She slid back a little. He felt wetness on his belly, smelled her pungent musk. The lightest touch of warmth pressed against the base of his erect penis.

"And you like to smell me, too, don't you?"

"Yes."

She leaned back a little more.

"Mmmmm."

He raised his hands and pressed them lightly against her hips, urging her to move yet farther back.

"No, you don't. Not yet. You aren't ready yet."

"Hell I'm not."

"Hey, who's the albino in this bed?"

He chuckled. "Got me. I can't even remember who I am."

"Hah! You don't get off that easy. I'm going to make you suffer."

But she didn't. Instead she raised herself up, touched him at the tip of his very much erect penis, then slid down slowly until she ensheathed him completely to the base. Without lifting herself again, she massaged him with internal muscles, clamping and relaxing, over and over again, until she brought forth from him a powerful orgasm.

"Oh!"

Veate laughed. "You still don't get off that easy, you thug."

His laughter joined hers.

Through some acoustical trick, Taz heard her brother laugh, even though she was on the opposite end of the house. Cooling duct or something, she figured.

She sat up and swung her bare legs over the side of the bed. She hadn't been able to sleep. Might as well do something useful.

She slipped a robe on and padded down the hall to the gym. Saval had a good set-up, as complete as many small public gyms. Even though he favored free weights over machines, he had, along with the couple tons of flexsteel plates and bars, a full ROM unit, a state-of-the-art computer-controlled SSA LS-21. Gym rats around the galaxy liked to joke that the initials for the Strength Success Associates Corporation who made the machine really stood for "Suffer, stupid asshole." The unit could measure tonus and nerve conduction close enough so that when programmed properly it would take a user exactly as far as she could go, no more, no less. It wouldn't let you overextend yourself; on the other hand, you couldn't slack your way past it.

The gym lights blinked on as Taz stepped inside. The far wall was mirrored, and she watched herself as she slipped out of the robe and stood naked in front of the LS-21. She was in good shape, she knew. Most mues of her kind were; it seemed a waste not to be, given the potential. HG engineering had given her great-grandparents thicker and heavier bone structure, a slight advantage in tendon leverage and attachments, and more muscle-building hormones than standard humans, as well as a faster metabolism. Great-grandfather and -mother had been designed for planets with a gee-and-a-half or better. Maybe the desire to use her body hard was built into her gene structure, she didn't know, but she did muchly enjoy working up a good sweat.

Saval was a bug about free weights, called them more "organic," but Taz preferred the machines. They were less risky than the heavy bars, even with the safety fields. The machines wouldn't let you go past your limits; the flexsteel didn't know what those limits were, didn't care.

The SSA stood there like a larger version of a child's girder construction set, a tall rectangle with cams, bearings, bars and handles that moved into place or pivoted out of the way depending on the exercises. She stepped into the machine. "On," she said. "Ten percent warm-up. Squats."

The machine weighed and measured her with its bioelectronic sensors, calculated and computed its results, and increased the field strength to respond to her movements at one-tenth of her capacity for the exercise ordered.

The crossbar came down and rested across her shoulders. Felt like about twenty-two, twenty-three kilos. That'd be about right; she could squat two-twenty, two-thirty for a triple. She took a couple of breaths and began to squat, facing the mirror, watching her doppelganger flash nudely back at her. Gods, her pubic hair was thick. Looked like some animal's furry black pelt down there. She grinned. At least there wasn't any gray in it yet, like there was on her head. A few strands at the temples shined through the blue-black. She had it pulled back in a low braid; she usually wore it tied or plaited short when she was working, but she sometimes liked being able to let it hang to her shoulders on her own time. Saval had more gray in his hair than she did, but then her da had gone gray before her ma.

—Two. Three. Four—

Her thighs warmed as she moved up and down, back kept straight, knees bending, upper legs going to parallel.

—nine, ten.

Her legs weren't quite ready yet, she decided. "Lunges," she told the machine. Obediently, it lightened the amount of weight. She followed the lunges with exercises for her hamstrings and calves.

When her legs were suffenctly heated, Taz moved to work her back, then her chest, shoulders and arms. After ten minutes

with the light weights, she had a thin sheen of sweat and was
ready for some serious work.

"Squats," she told the machine. "Maximum intensity, three
reps."

The bar across her shoulders grew heavy, gradually increas-
ing until it was almost three times her own body weight. She
felt the strain in her low back, and going down was a lot
easier than coming back up. Muscles in her thighs and buttocks
tensed, bulged and strained under the machine's heavy hand as
she rose, barely able to fight her way through the rep. Now the
sweat poured from her and the burn was painful, a deep, hot
ache that went to the bone.

She grunted at the bottom of the second rep, almost didn't
get past the sticking point as she trembled upward, and yelled
her way through it.

One more. She could do it, the machine wouldn't let her try
otherwise, but gods, she was tired! The sweat seeped past her
eyebrows and ran into her eyes. She blinked it away. Should
have worn a headband.

Down. Don't bounce at the bottom! Come on, up, up, up,
goddammit! You can do this!

She came up, a plant growing slowly toward the sun, a
glacier oozing over virgin winter ground. Christo, this was
hard, it was impossible! Fuck the machine, what did a machine
know? She couldn't make it—

Yes, she could. Move, move, *move*, dammit—!

Her bent knees straightened. She rose, reached the top.
Locked her legs.

"Jesu Damn! Off!"

The SSA turned the many kilos on the bar into air.

Taz stretched. Grinned. Well. So much for squats.

Time to do her back. "Rows," she said. "Eight reps at
maximum . . ."

Thirty minutes later she stood under the pulse of her shower,
letting the hot water wash away the sweat and some of the
fatigue. She ached all over, but it was a good feeling. She'd
been to her limits, and that was always a satisfying trip. She

knew what she could do if she had to, and that was better than
not knowing. She was a strong woman, stronger than most
ordinary men, and it felt good to take the muscles out for
a brisk walk. Now she could sleep. Saval was going to help
her figure out what to do about the mystery back on her own
planet; she was in good health, powerful, ready. How much
better off could she be?

What about Ruul?

Fuck Ruul.

You wish. That's the problem, isn't it?

Fuck you, too.

Her inner voice just laughed, high and girlish, a leftover
from the days when she was eighteen and just finding out
about real sex and love and first heartbreak.

So long ago, that seemed. Back when the galaxy was hers
to take, and any road was possible. Ah, if she had it to do over
again . . .

You'd do it the same way, wouldn't you?

She sighed. Yeah. Probably would. What the hell. She
hadn't made that much of a mess of it. Besides, if you liked
who you were, you had to honor how you got there. Looking
back over your shoulder too much was apt to make you trip
over something in today's path. You couldn't do anything
about the stupid mistakes you made anyhow, so why let them
drag you down?

Still, some memories were hard to shake. Taz climbed into
bed, fell into sleep, and some of the past seeped into her
dreams.

THREE _____

IT WAS A large chamber, nearly empty. In it the man Ndugu
Kifo; before him, a silk cushion with a small object upon it;
behind him, a suitcase-sized Ultralux vouch tuned to his
brainwaves, perched alertly upon its built-in tractor. Kifo
sat with his legs knotted in lotus, the bare wooden floor
cool under his naked buttocks and heels. Inside the Temple
of Despair it would seem still to someone not paying attention,
but when a man achieved a certain level of true stillness, his
senses opened. Sent the smells, feels, sights, sounds along their
pathways into an open mind, a mind that noted, catalogued,
then dismissed, unless the input had some . . . relevance.

The beams overhead ticked, wood obeying the laws of ther-
modynamics and physics, expanding from the hot sunshine
beating down upon the city of Leijona, contracting from the
coolers within the temple. Not important.

Traffic rumbled past, noises muted by the thick walls, but
still producing subtle vibrations. No matter.

The vouch hummed electronically to itself, constantly monitoring Kifu's physical and mental telemetry. A small matter.

In the hall outside the closed meditation chamber a student
sweated, bacteria thriving in the altered salts of his perspiration, their microscopic life and tiny works making him smell
sour with nervousness. A faint remnant of incense lingered,

clinging to the fine-grained black walnut planks, wood that had a hundred years of careful hand polishing and honing so it was almost thincris-smooth. Kifo identified the stink of sweat and the more pleasant incense, noting the bitter-but-sweet tang of *musté,* a local inkwood the poets liked to claim was dark as original sin.

Neither did these things matter.

When he opened his eyes, his vision matched in its clarity his other senses. On a cushion of diamond-grade ghostsilk from Rangi ya majani Mwezi lay the Sacred Glyph. It was a flat gunmetal blue-black against the pale material, a cloth ranked as the finest ever done by the best weaver the Green Moon had yet produced. The covering of the cushion had cost more than a rich man's home, yet the silk, too, was nothing.

But the Glyph. Ah. The *Glyph* mattered.

It was the holiest of all relics in any religion, made by the Gods Themselves, and outside of the Few, no one knew it existed. In the eighty years since its discovery, no member of the Few had ever revealed his or her knowledge of the Sacred Glyph to any outside the order. To even speak the name aloud anywhere save the electronically shielded and regularly swept meditation room was worth instant death, administered by any within earshot. To fail to strike down such a transgression was itself worth death. Only those initiated into the Very Few— never more than nine, never less than six—were considered trustworthy enough to learn of the existence of the Sacred Glyph, and only the Unique, the Leader of the Few, knew more than that.

The previous Unique, Ndugu Maumivu—Brother Pain—had taught Kifo all he knew of the mysteries even as he lay dying, kept alive by money-powered medical machines only just long enough to finish his instructions. Kifo was the sole man living who knew the secrets; more, he had himself added to them, divining greater depths, and his death, did it come suddenly and unexpected, would put an end to the knowledge. The Unique must take care that such a thing did not happen. Thus the vouch, standing vigilant, ready to defend Kifo's body from illness or injury at any instant.

Kifo smiled at that thought. For a man whose holy-nom meant "Brother Death" to be protected by the acme of galactic civilization carried with it a certain irony he appreciated.

The smile faded. No time for such thoughts, not when he was about to take in hand the Sacred Glyph. He banished the humor from his mind, composed himself, took a deep breath and allowed most of it to escape. Reached for the Glyph.

It didn't look particularly impressive, though some of the more sensitive among the Very Few had said they could feel the Glyph's power from across the room. It looked something like a human foot sheared off cleanly below where an ankle would join with it, the toes fused into a smooth plane. True, the ball and arch were somewhat more pronounced than real ones would be; there were indentations along the sides, the butt was thicker than a heel would be in proper proportion; the top was smooth, a flat plane with a slight incline from the back to the front. The Glyph was half a centimeter longer, perhaps, than Kifo's thumb, and as big around at the widest as his large toe. Hardly an impressive relic, as these things went. It would be virtually invisible if viewed against the Burning Bishop's pectoral jewelry; would hardly turn anyone's gaze away from the Trimenagist's Gold Triangle; would certainly get lost in the least of the glittering detritus from Tut's Tomb.

Ah, but even so, the Sacred Glyph was unlike any of these ornaments, unlike any talisman or focus for any other religion in all the galaxy. Because the Sacred Glyph *worked*. Kifo himself had discovered after years of meditations the final key.

Kifo reached forth, took the Glyph into his hand, felt it slide into proper position as if on its own. It had been designed for the hands of the Gods, of course, but a human's grasp found it grippable enough. His index finger curled under the plane of the toes, his middle finger in the arch, his ring finger wrapped itself around the indented heel. His thumb naturally lay upon the smoothness of the top.

It was like holding a carved chunk of ice. It sucked energy from his fingers. No matter what the temperature in the room— and the Very Few over the years had tested it through a range a hardy man could barely survive—the Sacred Glyph was always this way. It felt cold at twenty below, it felt cold at forty above. Always.

Now that he held it, he was ready.

"Brother Mkono," he said. He did not raise his voice, but the student outside was listening, waiting. Before the word finished echoing in the corridor, the student would already be running to fetch Mkono, appointed Third among the Nine.

The door opened a moment later and Mkono entered.

He was big, Brother Mkono, two meters tall, a hundred and fifty kilos, spawned by parents created for heavy-gravity worlds. He wore the loose, draped robe of the order, but under it he was a physically perfect specimen and even the voluminous folds could not hide the power when he moved. He was a mountain of a mue, and perhaps he should have been named something that reflected it, but his holy-nom spoke to his function and not his form. Mkono meant "hand."

Among the Few it was the Hand who went forth to deal justice. Among the Few—and among the enemies of the Few.

"I have a mission for you," Kifo said.

Brother Mkono closed his eyes and nodded, once.

In his own hand, the Sacred Glyph seemed almost to pulse. Cold it was. Cold as death.

Customs was embarrassed. The woman in charge of the peace sealer unit kept shaking her head and looking away, unable to meet Taz's gaze.

"We've checked and rechecked, *Amaniafisir* Bork."

When Taz had arrived on the planet, they'd called her "Po," the more common and somewhat less than respectful designation used on the streets for cools. That was before they fucked up and lost her pistol, of course. Now they were falling all over themselves to be polite. *Now* the customs agent used the honorific, addressing Taz as "peace officer." In their shoes, she would be real polite, too.

"No one entered or left the vault after lockdown, and the seals were clean when the computer threw the bolts. The seal alarm beeped at 2306, but the simadam monitoring assumed it was a computer glitch—he was *at* the door station, it was closed, and it's the only way in or out. The vault door is a quarter-meter squashed-steel-sandwich plate with stun gas inserts and full electronics. It never moved, according to every alarm system we have and a guard's sworn and verified visual. The walls, floor and ceiling are all made of ten-centimeter-thick carbonex and there are no signs of tampering with any of them; we've had them inspected with an electron deepscan. It's impossible that anybody got in there."

Taz pulled her pistol from under her jacket, where it rode comfortably in her orthoflex holster. Held the weapon pointed up at the ceiling. Waved it a little.

The customs agent colored. Shook her head again, spread her hands and fingers. She had to be thinking that Taz thought her people were fools or liars. And she wouldn't have been wrong, had not the cools on Tembo recently found themselves making similar explanations.

Taz holstered the weapon. Whoever this guy was, he was involved with the stuff going on back on Tembo, she was certain of that. The mysterious deaths, getting past locked doors and alert guards, it had to tie in.

So far, the local cools hadn't gotten anything out of the guy, either. Hadn't spoken a word.

Galactic regulations made it possible to get a scan, if all the proper legal niceties were observed. Electropophy and related invasive techniques were easy to abuse, so after the Confed went down, Republic laws concerning such machineries had been tightened. Careless brain-drain could leave somebody a mindless husk, and the public should be protected from such things. Taz thought it was a good idea in principle, but she also wanted whatever this guy knew pried out of him any way it took. While more than a few felons had swung at or shot at her over the years, it sure didn't endear this guy to her that he was among them. Besides, he had answers that would help her solve the murders on her homeworld, she was fairly certain of it.

Taz left the customs office and went out into the sunshine. Almost immediately, Saval arrived to retrieve her from her meeting. His flitter fanned to a stop at the curb, but didn't settle to the plastcrete, bobbing a handspan off the road on the air as might a cork on a calm pond. The passenger door gullwinged up. He'd been watching for her, she realized, and now he kept the repellors running. Careful, her brother.

"How'd it go?" he asked, as she got in. She noticed he was wearing his spetsdöds. She'd never actually seen him shoot, but if half the stories were true about how good the matadors were with those little back-of-the-hand dartguns, they could use them to swat flies at close range. She felt safe enough with her own pistol snugged over her right hip, but she didn't mind that Saval was armed.

"Apparently the thief was Merlin the Magician," she said. "Invisible, able to walk through walls, and faster than the half-life of a gotcha-chronon particle."

"Hmm."

"That a professional opinion?"

He returned her smile.

"Where are we going?"

"Jail," he said. "The boss talked to some people before he and Juete left. Speeded up things some. They're going to do a scan on your dance partner in about an hour. We can watch, you're interested."

"Oh, I'm interested."

The chamber was not much different from a standard inter-rogation and medical exam room, Bork saw. Form-chair, diag-nostic bank, cabinets, a sink. But the man in the chair was restrained, pressor field clamps pinning his wrists and ankles and hips. His head was free to move, the scanner being a fairly wide induction field that was not affected by motion. With a competent tech running the gear, they could peel him like an onion; he couldn't run and he couldn't hide. Next to the prisoner, a tech adjusted controls on the medical scanner.

The viewing window was cleared, though it could be opaqued or mirrored as needed. Bork stood next to Taz; a young and attractive blonde woman rep from Legal Aid stood on the other side of her, wearing puce skintights and holding an inducer; two cools in blue and gray work uniforms leaned against the wall behind the Legal. One was the officer in charge of the Crimes Against Persons section, the other the Medical Procedures Commander.

"You about ready, Lu?" the MPC asked.

The tech next to the prisoner nodded. "Yeh, we can fire it up any time."

"Telemetry?"

A voice from the speaker on the wall said, "Recording. Baseline and feed are green and green."

"Okay, Lu, give us a nice, clean insertion and for-the-record ID."

"Extruding," Lu said.

The MPC leaned toward the young woman Legal. "This is your first one of these, right?"

"Yes."

"Well, we start by pulling the guy's ID, a name, cit number, occupation, like that. The scanner strums a dendritic chord that makes the brain call up what we want. Real simple stuff. Hooks him like a fish on a line." He put a hand on her shoulder and nodded at the prisoner, then smiled at her. She smiled back.

Bork felt a small grin tug at his lips. Watch yourself, kid, he thought. Pretty soon the MPC'll be asking you to his cube so you can see the great holoproj he's got installed on his bedroom ceiling. Just lie right here, hon, and you can see it perfectly. Here's an idea—what say you get out of those hot old tights and let me rub your back for you . . . ?

Well, she was an attractive enough woman, she didn't have any problems showing it off, he could see why the MPC was interested. But Bork was spoiled. Nobody compared to his wife.

The man in the chair jerked his head from side to side; his eyes went wide, he bared his teeth. He growled, the sound coming clearly from the speaker, then said something Bork didn't understand.

"Something's wrong," the CAP said.

The MPC dropped his hand from the Legal's shoulder and stared. "Lu, what's happening in there?"

"Got a block," Lu said. "I'm compensating—"

The prisoner opened his mouth, clacked his teeth together hard. Repeated the word he'd said before.

"What language is that?" the CAP said.

"Sounds like Tembonese," Taz put in. "Maybe Numish."

"I'm getting a spike—" Lu began. "Oh, shit!" he said.

"Lu—?"

"He's flatlining, chief!"

"Fuck!" The MPC ran to the door. Three seconds later he ran into the interrogation chamber. He moved the tech aside and fiddled with the instruments. "Goddammit!"

The Legal blinked, puzzled. "What is it?"

"I think maybe this fish just slipped off the hook," Taz said quietly.

They were scheduled on a short-hop ship that would connect them with the starliner *Bellicose* for the trip to Tembo. The man Saval had called Cream was alive and in the jail's hospital but he wasn't going to be helping solve anything. He was brain-dead, checked out, nobody home. His lungs worked and his heart beat, but his mind was a ruin, destroyed by an implanted block the scan had triggered. Taz knew such things existed; even on a backrocket world like Tembo the police had come up against them. Usually the implants were nanomechanical or some kind of fast viral or explosive charge that would wipe or destroy certain areas of memory. Cream's block was different, hypnotic or something else undetectable by ordinary checks. The single word he had spoken, duly recorded by the telemetric computer, had been "Moja," and according to the translation program, had meaning in sixteen of the archived languages or dialects to which the computer had access. If Cream had been, as Taz suspected, speaking Tembonese, then the term meant, depending on how one used it, "lone," or "single," or "one." In some of the other languages the word could have been "power," or "evening," perhaps "party," or even "earlobe."

Moja. Could have even been the guy's name.

Not a whole fucking lot of help, that.

Taz finished packing her travel bag. Looked around the guest room in Saval's place, saw nothing she'd missed. She drew her pistol, popped the magazine, and checked to see that it was fully loaded, the battery and capacitor diodes green. The magazine was a blue code, the entire chunk of plastic and each dart a bright and unmistakable azure. That meant each needle collected a less than lethal electrical charge as it zipped through the muoplastic barrel, somewhere around seventy-five thousand volts with moderately low amperage. The needle would punch through clothes or even lightweight body armor to deliver its charge to bare skin or muscle, and the juice was almost always enough to knock a roegg off his feet. Blues were what the Leijona police were allowed in their duty weapons. Like most of the cools she knew, Taz had a couple of magazines of reds tucked away. A normal man or mue shot with a red needle wasn't going to get up on his own afterward.

She reholstered the pistol. This whole thing kept getting nastier and nastier, and she didn't have a good feeling about it. Not like she could do much other than what she already doing. At the very least Saval was going along. That was something.

She slung her bag. Time to go. Saval was down the hall, telling his wife goodbye in the way Taz had heard them communicating almost every night since she'd been here. She grinned. Well. Nobody had ever accused the Borks of being antisex.

She moved toward the door. Maybe she'd have time for lunch while she waited for Saval and Veate to finish.

FOUR

FROM LOW ORBIT Bork thought Raion looked something like a lopsided boomerang, fatter on the bottom than the top, thick with greenery. Taz had told him there were four major land masses on the planet, the continent of Raion being the second largest. The convex curve of the land was to the east, and even though much of the southern portion was obscured by clouds, it appeared that a range of fairly high mountains ran the length of the west coast. As the boxcar dropped in its spiral to the spaceport in Leijona, Taz pointed out other features on the seat's holoproj viewer.

"That's the Mafalme Ocean to the east, the Gulf of Pagotono to the west. The Tabik Coastal Range stops a lot of the weather, so there is some desert between them and the more temperate side of the island. Most of the civilization is on the east coast. Leijona is the biggest city, million and a third population, Shaba City is next with half that—to the south on Mkia Bay, see there? That's Shaba. Tibois is a timber town, and pretty much the southernmost civilization on the east side of the island."

Bork nodded, letting the names soak into him. He had a pretty good memory, if he thought stuff was worth keeping, and since this was going to be work, everything about this world was potentially useful. Emile used to teach them at the Villa that you never knew what tiny scrap might save your

27

neck, so it was best to file it all away.

"We're coming in from the south, over Ini Bay," Taz said a little later. "The Rubani Spaceport is just offshore from Central City in beautiful downtown Leijona." She waved her hands over the holoproj and a map lit the air next to the nosecam view. Ini Bay was shaped sort of like a foot in a sock, with a bump on the front of the ankle. Leijona lay along the western shore of the bay, cupping it like a fat crescent. The middle of the city was at the confluence of two rivers.

"There are the Zonn Ruins," she said, pointing at the 'proj.

Even under full magnification, there wasn't much to see at the boxcar's height. Dark lines against the greenery.

"I didn't know you had any of those on your world," Bork said.

She shrugged. "We knew they were there, but the Confed kept them off limits to civilians. I understand they're all over the galaxy, but the Confed kept them mostly hidden, too. You know anything about them?"

It was Bork's turn to shrug. "Not much. Some long-dead aliens supposedly built them. I've never been to any of the ruins, only know what I've seen on the ent- or edcom casts."

"They're in pretty good shape for being half a million years old. Impressive to see up close. We get some time, maybe we'll run out there," she said. "After you help me solve these murders."

Bork leaned back in his seat, feeling the hardfoam strain under his weight. He wore the matador uniform now, the dark orthoskins and spetsdöds. Since the baby had been born, he'd mostly done local security consulting, and more often than not had been in biz clothes and unarmed. Muto Kato was a pretty peaceful world. Good place to raise kids.

Of course, he'd stayed in shape. Went to the range now and then and shot a few magazines, kept the skills up. It wasn't the same as being in a shoot-or-get-shot situation, though, and was a long, long way from the revolution. Last time he'd been in any real danger was when Sleel had needed a hand with that crazy nobleman on Rift. Reminded him, he'd have to call Dirisha and Geneva pretty soon, he owed them a com. They were training a police force on a new wheelworld somewhere in Delta last he'd heard. Sleel would know.

But he didn't think there would be any real problem on Taz's planet. A few local murders didn't stack up against some of the bad spots he'd been in.

It felt good to get home, Taz thought. As she and Saval made their way through customs—here she had some clout and they weren't bothered—she noticed some of the stares. She was a fairly large woman and used to drawing curious looks, but Saval made her seem quite ordinary and even small. People would glance at him, then away, then back again, as if seeing a big cat escaped from some zoo. His years with the matadors had given him a smoothness when he moved, a kind of grace that she admired. Oh, she was strong enough, more powerful than an average basic-stock man, and she had learned some useful fighting tricks from her years as a street cool, but she wasn't much of a gymnast. Saval almost glided when he walked, very little friction evident in his stride.

A blue-and-blue waited where the pedway met the street, and a uniformed officer Taz vaguely recognized stood leaning against the side of the vehicle. The officer was in work tans, short-sleeved khaki shirt and knee-length pants with thin, matching osmotic socks flowing into darker tan flexboots. He wore the garrison hard cap, and the usual gear on his belt: pistol, a reel of memory cuffstrap, shockstik, override keycard, com. He snapped upright when he saw them, and Taz knew he'd had been sent to collect them. The Watch Commander had supplied a ride. How nice.

" 'Lo, Chief," the officer said.

Saval looked at her.

"Even the assistant chief gets the title," she said. "This is Peace Officer Jolerie," she said, spotting the man's name on his badge. "Po, Saval Bork, my brother. And if you remember your training from the academy, you might have noticed he's a matador."

Jolerie nodded once at Saval. "M. Bork." He looked back at Taz. "Chief, the Supervisor sends his best and hopes you had a nice vacation."

"Why is it I hear a 'but' attached to that?"

"We just found another one," Jolerie said. "Got the com not half an hour ago. The labbos have secured the scene and the Supe wants you to take a look at it before anybody else tromps around in it."

Taz shook her head. "Welcome home," she said.

"Sorry, Chief, I didn't kill him."

"Maybe. We'll see." She turned to look up at Saval. "Well, don't say I let you sit around doing nothing to earn your money."

"I get paid?" he said. He grinned.

"Get in the flitter, big brother. Somebody might mistake you for a bus and try to put their luggage in your mouth."

The crime scene was wound with flashing ribbons, plastic strips that alternated orange and red pulses to warn off the curious and threaten punishment for trespassers. Taz led the way and the uniformed cools parted in front of her without asking for ID.

The building was low, almost a squat rectangle of cast plastcrete designed by somebody with taste and a lot of money to spend on it. The entire front was decorated with a bas-relief sculpture that cleverly included the door and windows as part of the design, and the mural told a story of natives dealing with gods and magic and a lot of bad weather, from what Bork could tell.

"Nice artwork," he said.

"It was done by Fabrini Senh Buel."

"I think I've heard the name."

She laughed. "He's the highest-paid artist in the entire galaxy, Saval, he got more for this mural than you and almost everybody you know put together will make in the next ten years. He has a waiting list he won't live long enough to do half of, and his staff won't even return your calls unless you have half a billion stads in your personal accounts."

"Yeah, that's the guy."

"That's what I like about you, brother; you're so easy to impress."

Armed men and women in different uniforms than the tan and sandy tropical wear of Taz's department paced in front of the building.

Taz said, "Bevin's private guards. He's got—he *had* fifty of them. Lot of ex-military and ex-cools among them."

"Bevin being the dead guy?"

"Yep. Tibois Bevin, named for his grandfather. The family owns half of the Kimanjano Rainforest, made their money in wood products, timber, exotic papers, livestock feeds. His grandfather built most of the town of Bully Bay, which the locals later renamed 'Tibois' in his honor."

They reached the door. The private guards nodded at them. Bork watched the men move, decided they were not too bad. But somebody had gotten past them.

Inside, more local cools, more bodyguards.

Taz and Bork took a lift up three levels.

A man nearly as tall as Bork but maybe a third as heavy stood outside a door, blinking as if somebody was shining a bright light into his eyes. He wore a stretchwhite coverall that hung loosely on him. Didn't see that very often.

"Missel," Taz said.

The gangly man blinked at her. "Where have you been, Taz? WC says that Supe says I can't run the drill until you get here. Jesu Buddha, woman, evidence is evaporating and breaking down in there!"

"Damp your drive, Missel. This killer doesn't leave tags."

"Not before. This time, maybe. Go, go!"

He reached down and touched a control on a chunk of metal with heat sinks along one side. Bork felt a blast of warm air splash against his face. An airwall, to seal the room once the door was opened.

The entrance slid wide as Taz palmed the admit. She looked inside for a moment, then stepped across the threshold. "Behind me, Saval."

As Bork moved, the tech said, "You aren't going to take this human tank in with you? Jesu, Taz—!"

"This is Saval Bork," she said. "My brother. He's a matador, Missel, he knows about this kind of stuff."

"He's got feet like cargo carriers!"

"I'll try not to step on anything important," Bork said. He knew tech-types. He would bet money that Missel's next words would be something about everything being important at a crime scene.

"Everything is important at a crime scene!" Missel said.

Bork smiled.

"Do you want us to stand out here in the hall all day discussing this while your evidence decays or do you want us to get in and out so you can run the drill?"

"Go, go, go!"

Inside, Taz said, "He's really not a bad guy."

"I used to get along with Sleel before he met Kildee," Bork said. "No problem."

They were in an outer office, and to look at, nothing was amiss. As they moved, Taz handed Bork a com button from her belt. He pressed the speaker into his left ear.

"Assistant Chief Bork making inspection of the Tibois Bevin homicide site. Who's first on the scene?"

A female came on the com. "Officer Trager."

"Okay, you're in the barrel. Tell me a story, Trager. Give me an outline, we'll get the names and titles later."

Moving slowly and with care, Taz worked her way toward the inner office, the door of which was open.

Bork catalogued what he saw around him. Plush carpet, some kind of animal fur analog, a dishwater blond color and centimeter-thick nap. Not cheap. The furniture was organoplast, fully mechanized and computerized. Paintings on the walls, some flats, some holoprojics. Probably not copies, either. Lots of money showing here.

"Bevin was in his office, working," Trager said. "Door closed, only two ways in or out, both locked from inside. Secretary and bodyguard, three of them, parked at the main entrance in the outer office; three guards outside the connecting door to a hall that leads to the fresher. Three *more* guards outside the fresher door into the hallway. He was alone in the room."

"Windows?" Taz said.

"Full wall, view of Vilas Park. Denscris plate as thick as your wrist, comp-control polarized against photon or lasers. Can't be opened, not a scratch on it."

"Keep talking."

"An alarm went off. The guards called to Bevin, didn't get an answer, overrode the door's lock. Didn't wait for the simadam to clear the system, two of them were knocked cold going in before somebody coded the door field off.

"Bevin's body was on the floor. Except for his head. *That* was in the middle of his desk." She sounded crisp, but Bork caught a hint of something in her voice. Squeamishness. Revulsion. Something.

There was a com and computer terminal on the secretary's desk, a form-couch and chairs on either side of the inner office door. Indirect lighting. A chem and smoke detector was mounted in the door frame, and a poison and probably a hard-object scanner pick-up was inset flush into the frame. Somewhere there would have been an operator checking the sensors.

"Zap field inside, too?" Bork asked.

A moment of silence.

"My brother," Taz said. "He's working with us on this."

Trager's voice again. "Yes. Variable field, state of the art, automatic in the door if a weapon is detected, manual override on Bevin's desktop. All he had to do was wave his hand and anybody anywhere in the room but his chair would get zapped cold."

"Unless maybe the attacker was in an insulated groundsuit," Bork said.

"And *invisible,*" Taz put in. "Even a ninja in a shiftsuit couldn't open the door and sneak in without somebody noticing. And a groundsuit makes you look like you're wearing an over-stuffed chair."

Bork didn't speak to this. If you were good enough, you could rascal almost any machines. If the computer was blanked and the guards were bribed, the scenario was possible.

"We've already run fast truthscans on the guards and secretary, deepscans to follow. So far, our people tell us, nobody is lying."

Interesting, Bork thought. But not certain. Anybody who was sharp in fugue could beat a shallowscan. It took a lot of skill and practice, but it could be done.

They reached the door. Blood had pooled on the carpet, much of it soaking in, but some of it jutted a sticky, congealing finger almost to the entrance. There was a bloody footprint halfway to the desk. The room had a funny smell, not just the metallic odor of spilled blood, but something sharper.

"Looks like somebody threw up on the desk," Taz said.

Bork nodded. That was the sour stench he detected.

In life, Tibois Beven had probably been a handsome man. Bork estimated he'd been a fit sixty or seventy, hair naturally gray, features clean, either by nature or surgery. His body, sprawled in a fetal pose on the rug, was attired in a silk suit that revealed a certain amount of care as to its appearance. Not fat, not too lean, fairly sthenic.

Bevin's eyes were open, fogged somewhat as they dried, staring into infinity. But his mouth was closed and his expression was almost neutral, no fear, no surprise. A certain amount of blood formed a small puddle under the cleanly cut neck on the desk, but the severed head appeared remarkably neat otherwise.

"Somebody with a real sharp knife or a real strong arm," Bork said.

"Both," Taz said. "If the pattern is the same. The first one we found was so clean we figured it was a laser or vibrowire did the decapitation, but the lab found a few steel molecules.

Could be a sword, they figure, that might give the leverage."

"Interesting."

"Yeah, ain't it. Okay, Trager, what else you got for me?"

"That's it, Chief. We're running beegees on the guards and secretary—she was Bevin's mistress, along with two others we've found out about so far. His wife was offworld, visiting a daughter on Little Numa. His son was setting up a solar converter in the Nojina Swamp. The usual enemies, mostly business competitors. One threat, unsigned, same as the others."

Taz nodded. Looked at Bork. "Welcome to the house of mystery, Saval. Let's get out of here. I'll buy you some lunch and we can work on this."

She gave him a slight smile, and he knew the line was for the listening Trager's benefit. Chief Bork wasn't anybody's *picaflor*. But Bork already knew that. They'd been children together, and even then, Tazzimi had been somebody to reckon with.

FIVE

BORK WAS TWELVE, and he didn't much like his eight-year-old sister Tazzi tailtagging along behind him, but there wasn't a whole lot of choice. Da was off work, drinking too much, looking for something to be mad at, so it was bring her along or leave her there for him to smolder at. When Da was working, he was the best father you could want—took them places, did fun stuff—but when he was waiting for a job to happen, he got mean. It wasn't personal, Ma said, but it was hard to take it any other way when his big hand smacked you for something you didn't do.

So they were on the docks, Bork and Revoo, his buddy, and Tazzi all bright-eyed and curious and buzzcut black fuzzy head right behind them. The Confed liner had put its boxcars down at the offshore terminal and the old fanner ferries were hauling the tourists in to see the wonders of Hadiya's Sin City. Hadiya was the fourth—no, the fifth world Bork could remember living on, they'd been on Three Fingers, Tatsu, Baszel, and of course, Ohshit. Twice they'd gone back for jobs on Ohshit, which was really named #313-C, but which got the nickname from what offworlders usually said when they first got a good look at the place.

When you are a heavy-gravity mue, the big planets like #313-C are where you get the most work. Da Bork was strong, the strongest man his son had ever seen, that was for sure.

It was scary when he was in a bad mood; he could punch holes in walls and move flitters by himself, but it was also something that made Bork proud. A week past, Da had tossed a rubbish cannister across the street when it had gotten in his way, and Revoo was still talking about that. He and Bork together had barely been able to move it, much less pick it up and fuckamucka *throw* it like it was nothing.

"Here comes the ferry," Taz said. "What are you going to do? How do you pick somebody? Can I help?"

"Yeah, you can help by shutting up," Bork said, irritated at her. "Revoo and me, we'll spot one who looks real lost and we'll follow them for a little while. Then we offer to help them look around. For two stads. You just be quiet, you copy?"

Taz nodded, her head bobbing rapidly. Bork turned away and tried to pretend she wasn't there.

The ferry settled to the water's surface, the fans cycling down. The engine sounds muted to a drone, the collateral wind splash dropped to a breeze. The conveyor jacked out to the dock, looped itself on, and the offie tourists stepped onto the belt and began moving off the ferry. They had money, otherwise they wouldn't be traveling, Confed rules being what they were. Even here in the middle of a bored zone like this, there were troopers with carbines slung, standing by to make sure nobody tried to climb the mountain of regs the wrong way. Da didn't much like the Confed and some of that filtered through to Bork, but he didn't really understand all that much about it. Nobody had ever bothered him personally and Bork sometimes thought about joining the military and being a soldier. As an HG mue, he could apply for an exemption to the draft and probably get it—there were places in the galaxy where they needed all the help they could find, and the Confed would rather have him hauling crap than waving a gun. Yeah, he was a shrimp compared to Da, but he was gonna get bigger someday, maybe as big as his father. Gonna have muscle to spare. Even so, he could choose to go into the service; they always needed more troops, so they said. It was a thought.

"Look at that one," Revoo said. He was used to doing this,

he didn't point, but Bork caught the drift and saw who his buddy meant easy enough. A short fat man in purple glowsilks waddled off the conveyor, blinked against the warm summer sunshine. They were close enough to see the man's eyes darken as his droptacs polarized. He stuck a thin rod into the air, and Bork realized it was an umbrel-field set to cut the UV and much of the heat beating down on the tourist. Had to set the guy back what Da made in a week, that field. Money.

"Yeah, copy that," Bork said.

The three of them flowed slowly into the fat man's wake, staying back far enough to avoid stepping on his heels, close enough to keep from losing him in the outrush of the crowd from the ferry.

Other children who'd finished or skipped edcom for the day jockeyed for position around various tourists. The one good thing about such a stillwater like this was that there were usually enough tourists to go around. If somebody took the one you wanted, you could find another one easy enough. A bigger guy or somebody with a gang behind him wanted your offie, you smiled and slid away. If you were bigger or had more clobber on your side, then it was up to the other guys to shear off. Simple enough.

Apparently the gangs had other offies in their sights today; nobody gave Bork the wave-off.

"We're clean," Revoo said.

"Looks like."

"What does that mean?"

Bork turned to his sister. "You don't worry about it, twaddle. You just seal it and stay right behind me."

"Okay, Savvie."

"And don't call me Savvie. It's 'Saval.' I could leave you at the cube with Da next time."

She looked as if somebody had slapped her, and Bork felt a quick flash of guilt. Tough boy. Make the little girl cry. "Okay, I won't, never mind. But keep quiet, all right?"

Her smile came back. "Sure, Savvi—I mean, Saval."

"You through with primary edcom?" Revoo said. "Can we

make a run at the offie, or you got more lessons for the smooth twaddle here?"

"When he gets to the pedway, yeah," Bork said, trying to maintain a sense of control. Embarrassed by his sister.

They moved in closer, so that when the fat offworlder reached the spinstep for the pedway, they were right behind him. "Hey, citizen," Revoo said, "need a guide?"

The fat man hesitated at the spinstep. Turned to look at them. Smiled, showing lots of wrinkles around his eyes. Happy kind of guy, must smile a bunch, Bork thought.

"Fuck off, street lit. I don't need scum like you trying to squeeze my stad account."

Whoops.

Bork and Revoo glanced at each other. Sometimes you got a bad one. When that happened, you just backed out and away. More where he came from, they hurried.

"Problem here, citizen?"

Bork turned slightly and saw a Confed trooper. Right next to them. Not just a trooper, an officer; he wasn't carrying a carbine, he had a holstered handgun on one hip. Definitely time to leave. Bork edged back. Put out one arm to move Taz with him.

"Yes, as a matter of fact. These little turds are trying to suck on my credit cube. Isn't there a law against that or something?"

The officer smiled and nodded. "I think we can find something to get you breathing room, citizen."

With that, the officer reached out and grabbed Bork's tunic front, twisted his fist into the cloth, and pulled Bork almost clear of the ground.

He had started to grow some height in the last few months, but Bork's weight—clothes, boots and all—wouldn't have added up to sixty kilos. The Confed officer, while not nearly so large as his da, was easily forty kilos bigger than the young Bork, much of it muscle. Before Bork could even think, the man backhanded him across the face, a hard slap that snapped his head to the side, stunning him.

Time went into a holding pattern, slowing, twisting, puzzling. What—?

"You don't dogheel citizens on these docks any more, swill, you hear me?" At the finish of the backhand his hand was naturally cocked for the second slap. Under his uniform, the officer's deltoids flexed as he tensed and started the hand coming back.

Bork saw it, but through a red and throbbing haze.

So slow . . .

Bork was also vaguely aware that Revoo was twenty meters away and speeding up, laying fast track and not looking back.

Another whack like the first one might cost teeth. Or knock him completely unconscious. Amazing that he had so much space to think and *notice* all these things, but at the same time was unable to move to *do* anything about them. Like there was a cut circuit between his brain and his body. He couldn't move, couldn't even blink—

Halfway to Bork's face, the officer's hand stopped.

Then the man screamed.

"Ahh! Shit—!"

In a moment of clarity unlike any he had ever experienced, Bork saw the reason:

Taz, wrapped around the man's right leg like a clutch-spider sucking a syrup cane. Biting him on the back of the thigh. The cloth tore under her teeth, the flesh parted, blood welled—

The officer let go of Bork's tunic. Reached down for Taz with both hands. Bellowed wordlessly.

Solidly back on the surface of the dock again, Bork reacted without thinking. He jumped at the soldier, both his hands extended. He hit the man square on the chest with all his weight behind the shove. The officer was twisted and the impact was enough—he tumbled, hit hard on his left side.

Bork grabbed Taz's arm. "Come on!"

She released her grip on the officer. Scrambled away from him. They ran, with Bork half-carrying her by one arm.

"Little bastard shitheads—!" the officer yelled. "Come back here!"

But Bork dodged through the crowd, darting in and out of the startled outworld tourists as if they were standing as still as trees. In five seconds they were out of the officer's sight. In ten seconds, clear of the docks.

A minute later, having put the maze of van delivery and trash collection alleyways between them and any possible pursuit, Bork stopped to catch his breath. Oh, man—!

Taz was crying. She wiped at her mouth, clearing the little bit of cloth and blood from it.

"You okay?" he asked.

"Yeah."

"Why are you crying?"

"That man hit you."

"Well, I'm okay. Don't cry now."

"I bit him."

"Yeah, that's right, you did."

He looked at her. Revoo, his best friend, rocketed the second the Confed officer had reached for Bork. Vapor-trailed and never looked back, and Bork had to wonder if he would have done the same had the officer grabbed Revoo instead of him. But little Taz, the tagtail twaddle, had grabbed the guy and sunk her teeth into him. Just like that, no questions, nothing, to help her brother. That meant something, something important. He was only twelve, but he understood that.

"You did okay, Taz."

"Yeah?"

"Yeah. You shouldn't be biting people, you know, but it was the right thing to do this time. I won't forget it."

"You won't tell Da?"

"No. It's between you and me. Our secret."

She grinned at him, and he rubbed her head, feeling the short burr of it under his hand, realizing something had changed. From the instant his sister had latched onto the Confed officer's leg, things weren't ever going to be quite the same between them again.

It was a lesson about family he would never forget.

SIX

KIFO SAT LOTUS, waiting.

The entrance to the meditation chamber opened. Kifo did not look up but he felt the other man's massive form move across the wooden floor, heard the old boards protest the passage. Mkono, Kifo thought, was an instrument upon whom the gods had writ boldly—and large.

Without speaking the big man sat. Knotted his legs, thick, but supple, into adept's pose. Waited.

Fifty heartbeats came and went. A hundred.

Two hundred.

Finally Kifo said, "There is now one less obstacle in the path of the Plan. The gods are pleased with their Hand."

A faint glimmer of a smile flitted across Mkono's face. He inclined his head a few millimeters, eyes closed.

The gods had not spoken of Mkono's mission; they did not converse with their servants directly in that manner. Neither had Mkono spoken of his success; still, the logic of it was simple enough: had Mkono failed, he would not be here. If the Hand believed that Kifo had some way of seeing that which he ought not to be able to see, so much the better. The Unique was supposed to be exalted, at least a little.

"Your work is not yet done, but for now there comes a pause."

The bigger man nodded again.

"Train yourself well, Mkono. The gods save the hardest for the end. They will provide themselves a real challenge."

"I shall not fail to meet and overcome it."

Kifo kept his face carefully neutral. Mkono would be the most formidable of opponents, even without the help of the gods; with their blessings, it was hard to imagine how he could be defeated. He had once seen Mkono launch a simple strike in practice, his fist moving only a few centimeters to punch thick padding on the chest of a strong man, with two more strong men bracing him from behind. Mkono's blow had knocked all three sprawling. Mkono was a worthy instrument, the greatest in the temple's history, perhaps, honed to deadly sharpness, totally dedicated.

The Plan moved toward completion and Kifo had confidence that it would come to pass. But the gods did not fancy easy victories. If there were no chances they might lose, they would not enter the game. And failure would be due to the instruments chosen, for the gods themselves did not err, save deliberately to give the game an edge. Mkono was willing to do his part. Kifo must see to it that any errors in the Plan were not his own doing, or suffer for it. A risky business indeed, for failing one's gods meant damnation; of course, that too was part of the allure. To dance on the keenest sword's edge without being cut was a powerful drug, addictive on its own even without the righteousness of the gods' bidding as a spur.

Kifo did not wish his own victories to be too easy. Then again, neither did he wish to fail.

In silence Brother Death sat meditating across from Brother Hand, considering all the possibilities. Their number was myriad, but not infinite, and therefore comprehensible.

And what a man can comprehend, he can achieve.

SEVEN ─────────────────────────────

A DEEP AND esoteric life-philosophy was not Taz's main concern. She considered herself a pragmatist, dealing with the day-to-day realities of life. True, she knew that happenstance, luck, could run either way. Fortune was fickle by its nature, impossible to control. One moment you might be walking arm-in-arm with your close friend *bon chance,* the next second the sky could fall, and you'd be caught flatfooted, watching your friend sprint away, laughing her ass off. Such things were to shrug about, if you survived.

Good luck decided to take a quick hike, Taz realized, as she and her brother arrived in The Oxidized Owl.

The Owl, a local restaurant and pub, was always crowded, no matter what hour of the day or night. The reasons for this were simple enough: they served good food and drinks in large quantities and both were cheap. The owner, Noe Teng Bicho, was a more than somewhat gaudy sex-changer from PrimeSat in Centauri. Born male, subsequent surgery and viral/hormonal revision had transformed him into a her, right down to a womb-implant that could, should she ever desire it, produce a child. With a little help, of course. Everybody called the owner of the Owl "Pickle." Curious, Taz had asked around and found that it had to do with a kind of vegetable made by soaking something called a cucumber in some kind of brine solution. The resulting product was shaped vaguely like a penis, which didn't really

help much, unless you had been into Pickle's private office
and seen what she kept in a jar on her desk. It was still fairly
esoteric even so, unless you knew that the pale pinkish-blue
thing in the jar had once been attached to Pickle herself.

Even during the most crowded times, there were always
tables kept free for the local police. Having cools in the
restaurant guaranteed that the most rowdy crowds would stay
relatively calm, and if you were a cool, you could eat free.
Taz had sometimes taken advantage of that, though not often,
given how reasonable the prices were. If Internal Investigations
intended to hang her for graft, she'd be in a line that included
the Supervisor and the head of Eye-eye, not to mention half
the street POs working.

So there'd be room for her and Saval, that wasn't the bad
luck, even though the place was mostly packed and dozens of
hopefuls milled around outside waiting for openings. No. The
falling sky was, *Ruul* was there, holding court at the best table
in the chi-chi looky-here corner reserved for celebrities.

Fuck him.

You wish.

Fuck you, too.

Saval stood like a thousand-year-old hardwood tree as Pickle
herself bustled up. She was an attractive woman, vibrantly alive,
maybe thirty-five T.S., and she looked at Saval with a gaze that
reminded Taz of feeding time at the vulp exhibit.

"Hel-*lo,* tall, wide one. New in town?"

"Hello, Pickle," Taz said. "This is my brother, Saval, from
Muto Kato. Saval, Noe Bicho, Pickle to her friends."

The restaurant owner wore green and red whispersilks that
revealed as much as they hid, held in place by static charges
that changed polarities every so often to play show and tell
with other parts of her. The cloth sang faint, breathy musical
chords in minor keys as it moved. Her hair, red and green to
match the silks, danced to similar charges. Her body was good,
she worked out, and the effect was certainly erotic. The outfit
and hairstyle had to set her back a chunk equal to two weeks'
of Taz's pay, easy. Maybe three. Pickle could take her pick

of a thousand men on any given night with whom to share her favors, with another five or ten thousand wishing for a chance just to make the short list.

"Are you this big where it doesn't show?" Pickle said. She put one hand on Saval's arm. "Heysoo Damn, honey, you wearing armor under those 'skins? Oh, my, I think I'm in *love!*" She slid her hand up Saval's arm, then down again. "A hard man is so good to find."

"He's married—" Taz began.

"Sweet cheeks, that never bothers me in the *least.*"

"—married to an Albino Exotic, Pickle."

The woman blinked, looked away from Saval at Taz. "Shit, Chief, you really know how to hurt a girl, don't you?" She turned her gaze back to Saval. "You a monopoker, big man? Exclusive contract?"

"Yes."

"An Exotic; figures. Damn. All the good ones are taken. Well, if you get lonely while visiting our lovely planet, just touch the com and call my name and I'll be there before you get undressed." She waved one hand. "Herzio, get Chief Bork and her brother a table, and a bottle of that *qar* vine in the rockroom, my treat."

With that, Pickle flounced away in a flash of skin and silk. Before she took two steps, however, she turned back. Smiled. It was the expression of a savage queen condemning somebody to torture; you could cast it and sell it to scare small children. "I'll tell Ruul you're here, Chief."

Ouch.

Your point, Taz conceded with a nod. Saval is a grown man; he could have protected himself. Shouldn't have mentioned his wife.

Pickle twisted the bitchy smile a hair, collecting her due. She loved to win, but if you were a good loser she was usually merciful. Maybe she wouldn't say anything to Ruul.

The waiter led them to a table, and Taz was most careful to avoid looking at Ruul as she and Saval sat. The bottle of vine arrived within thirty seconds. Taz touched a menu button

on the tabletop and a small doubleside holoproj glimmered to
life as the wine waiter poured for them.

"What's good?" Saval asked.

"Everything. Not a bad entree on the list. The local meat
beast is called sweef, kind of a cross between porkers and
cattle, big ugly suckers, but it makes a nice steak. The fish'll
be fresh; Pickle has a buyer at the docks every morning.
The spearfish is good, the shallow tack better. Veggies are
all complementary to the main course; the chef's got good
taste."

He nodded. "I'll try this one. The Slab."

"You'll draw a crowd. That's almost two kilos of meat."

"I'm hungry."

They grinned at each other.

"So," he said, after the waiter had come and gone. "This
thing with you and Ruul serious, or what?"

She nearly choked on her wine. Managed to put the glass
down without spewing the stuff all over the table. Swallowed and shook her head. "How the fuck did you do that?
We've been together since we touched down, unless you've
got a source in the fresher. Somebody telling you tales while
you piss?"

"No. Just paying attention. I saw your expression when
Pickle mentioned the name. Saw her trot off to the corner
where that guy is making fifteen people laugh. Watched you
look at every face in the room like a working po *except* the
guy in the corner."

She smiled, a small one. He was her brother, but they
hadn't spent a lot of time together in the last twenty years. If
the other matadors were this sharp, then they would be folks
to reckon with, sure enough. She'd heard the stories, but it was
different to see the focus turn upon you for a demonstration.
She was impressed.

She said so.

"And it's none of my business," he said.

She shrugged. "It's no big secret. Ruul is in entertainment.
Has his own 'cast, he's an actor, comedy. Very funny man,

but also got some depth. Very popular in the local system, moderately rich, can pick from a long list of people to run with. Last year somebody killed his niece. Turned out to be an accident, at least in the sense the killer wasn't aiming at her, she was in the wrong place, wrong time. Ruul and I met when I did the investigation. One thing led to another. We spent some time together. It didn't work out, that's pretty much it."

Saval nodded.

There was a lot more to it than that, of course.

They talked about the murders until the food came. A few people turned to watch Saval's order when it went past, to see who thought they could put down that much meat in a sitting. Taz had ordered the fish, and while it wasn't nearly so much as Saval's, it was probably nearly a half kilo of tender whiteness in a *sremea* sauce rich enough to make you get fat by looking at it. She had just popped a big forkful of the fish into her mouth when somebody came up behind her. She saw Saval notice before she heard the voice.

"Hello, Tazzi."

Her heart froze, her brain locked in neutral. She practically inhaled the mouthful of fish to get rid of it. Turned. Saw him there. Ached as her heart restarted and throbbed much too hard.

"Hello, Ruul."

He looked good; he always looked good. Even if he wasn't the funniest man she'd ever met, he'd still get invited to parties just to brighten up any room he was in. Tall, a little taller than she was, slim, naturally blond, face full of smile lines and character that went all the way into his soul. Eyes too blue to be real, but they were. And, goddammit, he was glad to see her. That was the worst part of it, every time. And if he'd said, Tazzi, you want to go to my house and roll around and destroy the furniture with me? she'd be up and moving before the echoes of his voice died, wouldn't even wave goodbye. Of course, he wouldn't say that. Not now.

"Ruul, this is—"

"Your brother," he finished. "Pickle told me. Not that anybody could miss it. You two split the genes pretty close. Hello. I'm Ruul Oro. Very honored to meet you."

Saval nodded. "Saval Bork," he said. His voice was calm, almost grave. He might be a matador and he might be good at hiding stuff from strangers, but Taz caught a hint of something in his tone. He didn't rise or offer a clasp or palm-down, but he was civil enough.

Taz and Ruul looked at each other. The rest of the place went away for her. A long time passed. Half an eon, at least. Finally he said, "Well. I've got some people, I have to get back to them. I just wanted to stop and say hello. It's good to see you again, Tazzi." He looked away from her. "And to meet you, M. Bork." Looked back to Taz. "Com when you get a chance. Or come by, anytime. The doors still have your code."

"I wouldn't want to walk in on anything," she said. God, her voice was stiff.

"You wouldn't. There's nobody else. I miss you."

With that, he turned and walked away, moving through the crowd watching him with an acrobat's grace, apparently oblivious to the admiring stares.

God *damn* him! How could he *say* that? It was not fair!

She felt herself trembling. Reached for her wine to try and cover it.

"Want me to bite him?"

She blinked. "Huh?"

"Remember when you were eight? The Sin City docks on Hadiya?"

Abruptly, she did remember. Smiled at the recollection. Gods, she hadn't thought about that in *years*. That stupid Confed officer.

"Not right now," she said. "But maybe later."

"Anytime, twaddle."

He dug back into his steak. Gave her as much privacy as he could.

It wasn't a cure, but it made her feel better. Like a patch pressed against an open wound, it didn't make it well, but it helped stop the bleeding. Good old Saval. About as perfect as an older brother could be. She was glad he was here. Always there when she really needed him.

Now, if she could solve a series of impossible murders and get in order her relationship with a man she loved but who wouldn't sleep with her any more, she'd be just fine.

Probably fat, after eating this fish, but otherwise just fine.

EIGHT

TAZ HAD A house twenty minutes from the police station by flitter. The place was surprisingly large; three private sleep chambers, a fresher for each, plus assorted communal rooms and a kitchen, as well as a garage for her personal flitter, half of which was a gym.

As she showed Bork around, he said, "They must pay cools pretty well here."

She laughed. "Not really. I'm in debt to my hairline to pay for this. We came in along the Eusi River Expressway, so you missed the scenic route through Mende Town, our local slum. City officials have been trying to clean it out for years but something always happens to stop it. If you limber your arm up a little, you can toss a rock and hit the left hind leg of the place—'mende' means 'cockroach,' and that pretty much describes the place. Real estate that snuggles against the roach's backside is a lot cheaper than the hillsides overlooking the bay."

"Ah."

"Don't worry, I've got a pretty good alarm system. But you would have noticed that when we came in."

Bork nodded.

He put his travel bag in the sleep chamber she offered him, and they went to sit in the biggest of the common rooms. The

chairs were nonmechanical, overstuffed, and comfortable for
somebody Bork's size.

"So. What do you think about the killings?"

He leaned back. "Locked-room stuff almost always turns
out to be done by insiders. A bribed guard, security monitor,
somebody selling codes, like that."

Taz nodded. "Yeah, that's how we figured it at first."

"But not now?"

She shook her head. "We've strained the brains of the
guards, secretaries, friends, lovers, and so far gotten null.
You saw the latest one. I'd bet a thousand stads to a toenail
clipping everybody we touch will come up clean, even on the
deepscans."

"You have enough money and clout, you can get around a
deepscan."

"Sure, *if* the operator is open to baksheesh or a higher-up
wants to diddle with results. We have our share of bent cools,
but we aren't that corrupt."

"Then you haven't scanned the right people yet."

"Yeah, that's what we figure. Problem is—how do we find
the right ones? Take the second case. Woman killed was Leona
chu bahn Sikon, a rich humanist. No enemies. Two bodyguards
outside her bedroom on the ninth floor of a residental plex.
No way in or out save through the door they watched. No
windows. The guards tested truthful when they said nobody
came or went, but she was chopped up like the others, head
here, body there. If what the guards said was true, it was
impossible. Just like when my gun got lifted on your planet.
It doesn't compute."

"When you eliminate the impossible, whatever is left, no
matter how unlikely, has to be the answer," Bork said. "Emile
used to quote that at us when we were training in defense scenarios. Some famous investigator said that, Watson Hemlock
or somebody."

"Fine in theory," she said. "But we've had our own people
working during three of these assassinations and we ain't
eliminated shit. Our computers fuzz when we feed them info;

we have almost no physical evidence. How are we going to figure out where to grab hold of these things when they're as slick as lube on thincris plate?"

"Next time you get a threat, I'll park myself next to the client," Bork said. "Maybe get a look at what's sneaking under the door."

Later, when Taz was sleeping, Bork went for a workout. She'd converted half her garage into a gym, and it was outfitted fairly well, except there weren't enough free weights. Taz liked the machines, and while Bork preferred plain flexsteel bars and plates, he could make do. He'd stripped to hardskin gloves, headband and a groin strap, and he had a thick towel over one shoulder.

The murders were interesting. He'd never come across anything quite like them, though the matadors had a common file where they dumped records of assassination attempts upon various of their clients. There was a case where a man had been killed inside a locked and guarded room on Spandle. But that had turned out to be an induced suicide. Somebody had coated a drawer handle with a tailored psychedelic derm chem that soaked through the client's skin when he touched it. The chem drove the guy crazy and he dived off the desk onto the floor and broke his neck.

It probably wasn't real likely the guy Bork had seen earlier in the day had chopped his own head off and then cleverly hidden the weapon afterward.

Bork adjusted the controls on Taz's ROM gear, stepped into the device and allowed it to test his tonus.

A couple of warm-up sets and he began to work out in earnest. He began with legs, and when the machine said he'd reached his limits, he overrode the safety and added five more to his kiloage. The machine could see muscle density, could determine nerve conduction, but no machine could yet measure spirit.

A soft voice repeated, "Warning, you have exceeded your limitations," as Bork went down to parallel, then slowly strained against the bar across his shoulders to come up. It was hard.

The mechanical aspect of it was beyond him, according to the device designed to know such things.

Bork did three reps.

Then he grinned at the computer voice when it said, "Warning, systems malfunction. Please call your dealer for repair. Your operating program is in error."

Sorry, machine, Bork thought. But he really wasn't sorry. He'd always liked the fable of John Henry and the contest with the steam engine. He was aware that he was among the strongest men or mues in the galaxy. There had been times when he'd known for sure he was the most powerful person on a particular planet—there were records kept of certain endeavors, weightlifting being a common enough sport on most worlds. If he could push more than the local record, that was pretty much self-evident. It was a mild curiosity in him, though, not one he put much energy into. Strength, like intelligence, was a variable thing. One day you might beat a guy, the next day he might beat you. At noon the puzzle might be beyond you, at dinner the answer easier than snapping your fingers. At any given time there might be a pool of fifty or sixty people, mues surely, who could move more weight than could he; then again, maybe he could outlift them. So he might not be the strongest guy in the galaxy, but then again, maybe so. In any event, it gave him a certain perverse pleasure to make the machine blink when he went past its boundaries.

The battle on Tembo was confined to Raion and most of the action, such that it was, to Leijona and the surrounding countryside. Tembo was a frontier world, sparsely populated, and the Confed presence consisted of a few companies, mostly conscripts and a few career officers. Even after the small infection of revolution grew into a killing plague, it came late to Tembo. The career men mostly saw which way the winds of change were blowing and stacked their weapons and commands. Confed policy wouldn't allow any significant number of local boys and girls to person the garrisons, for fear they wouldn't behave like soldiers when they knew or were related to the locals they might have to shoot at. Still, a lot of the troopers had been onplanet for years, and they had commerce and person connections with the natives. The trouble with an occupying army is that it will eventually be absorbed by the culture it resides within, and some of that had happened on Tembo. It was hard to point a carbine at the man who served you drinks with dinner every time you got liberty, or the woman you'd been sleeping with for a year, or the brother of the man married to your quad's sub-loo.

So, when the voices grew louder, the local Confed troops mostly behaved like people and not soldiers, which was a failure for the military but a victory for humanity.

Not all of them put down their weapons, however.

Since the Confed frowned upon an armed populace, there weren't a lot of folks with guns. Sure, there were permits available, but mostly those were for hand wands or stunners or sublethal dart guns, spetsdöds and the like. And the few people who had those licenses tended to be fairly individualistic types who would protect themselves and their families if attacked, but not offer organized resistance to an army.

That left the cools.

That was why Tazzimi Bork found herself holding her service pistol in sweaty hands, her back against the rough permaplast exterior wall of a flitter repair shop on the southern edge of North Docktown, waiting to shoot it out with a military quad approaching her position. The magazine and loads in her pistol were reds. If she had to shoot, it would be to kill. Killing a Confederation soldier was a galactic crime, and depending on the circumstances, worth full brain-strain or lengthy incarceration.

"Yeek, Taz, you set?"

She glanced across the alleyway at Jerlu. If he looked as nervous as she did, they must be a pair to see. He clutched his shotgun to his chest and his face was beaded with sweat, his tan uniform soaked through where his flesh touched it.

"Yeah. Set."

Taz was a cool, she enforced the laws of the city and the

country, and such laws did not normally come into conflict with Confed regulations. Being as how the Confed frowned with greatly wrinkled brow on any planet daring to naysay it in any way. They enforced the stuff that concerned them, left the rest of the local regs alone. Still, it was a dilemma. While she'd never considered herself political, what the Confed did and stood for was wrong. She'd seen the replay of the 'cast where the black woman matador had called for a revolution. They'd never met, but she knew the name. Knew too her brother Saval would be right in the middle of it, and whichever side he had chosen, for whatever reason, she would not fight against him. Saval was sharp, he had an IQ that tested out far above the average, though he took pains to pretend it was otherwise. If he'd signed on with these folks, he had thought long and hard about it before he'd done so. Da was gone; the mining disaster had taken him with nine hundred others. That had crippled Ma; all that was left was a hollow, almost mindless shell, living with her only sister and well on her way to the final chill. Saval was what family she had, save for her mother and aunt, and if he thought this was a good idea, then that was good enough for Taz.

The quad jogged along, not expecting trouble. They weren't wearing armor or electronic gear that she could see, but they carried their carbines unslung, held at port arms where they could bring them into play quickly. Taz took a deep breath, let it out, inhaled through her nose again. Shifted her grip on the pistol's stickygrip, slipped her finger inside the trigger guard. Thumbed the safety print plate twice to toggle the weapon into firing mode. Glanced at Jerlu again, nodded.

Once she'd made the choice, she found there were a lot of other POs who were in agreement. Three-quarters of the force, it turned out. She'd suspected the rebels had a lot of sympathy, but hadn't guessed it to be quite so high. Or so high up. The Supe himself, nearly all of the WCs, most of the ranked officers. And they were glad to have her declaration.

When it finally shook loose, maybe three-quarters of the Confed troops said 'Fuck it,' and shucked their weapons. But there was a core of those who were loyal or venal or something, a couple of hundred soldiers altogether, who moved to take control of the planet Tembo. Not many, but they were better armed and knew tactics and strategy in a way most civilians did not. Fifty troopers with two hovertanks and medium-heavy weapons occupied the Rubani port, so offworld traffic was under their control—at least insofar as normal boxcar drops and lifts went.

The remaining troops moved to take classic objectives—broadcast and com centers, food distribution points, local transportation plexes, river and highway access, seaport docks.

Taz and Jerlu and five others had been sent to North Docktown to keep the agroplex clear. It was not the most important spot in the city, but a lot of food was imported through the agroplex, and whoever controlled it would have an advantage. Regardless of who was in power, people had to eat.

Taz and Jerlu were the sentries. They had short-trans com sets, basically an ear button and mike, but they had to assume the military could monitor the standard opchans with their scanners, so any transmissions had to be short and fast, even with compscramblers working. Taz and Jerlu had to warn the five-person team heading for the harbormaster's control office if trouble showed up, and they had to delay it long enough for the team to get in place. The HCO was fairly defensible from the inside, so whoever got there first would have a big advantage.

A quad had one less member but a lot better firepower than the five-person team of cools with sidearms and shotguns. In a stand-up, the Confed boys would most likely win.

"I got the two in front," Taz said.

"Copy," Jerlu said.

"I'll call the team now," she said.

He merely nodded. She could see he was afraid, could smell his fear. Or maybe that was her own nervous sweat she smelled.

"Team, company, one quad, flitter shop," she said. She hoped somebody was paying attention, because if the quad got past her and Jerlu, it would be the team's problem.

Taz could hear the quad's boots thumping now. The sound grew louder. The four soldiers would pass right by the alley-way on the narrow street, moving from right to left across her field of vision. Any second.

"Heads·up!" she called to Jerlu.

He brought the shotgun up, flicked the sighting laser on. Swallowed loudly enough so she could hear it.

She didn't trigger her own built-in laser sight. The quad would come past at maybe ten meters away, max. She didn't want to take the time to put the dot on the target; she would do better with a barrel index. She hoped.

The first trooper moved into view.

"Go!"

Taz pushed away from the wall, snapped her pistol up and pointed it like her finger at the trooper. Pressed the trigger, as if she were at the range and had all the time in the world. But her nervousness told; she kept firing the gun even as the man fell, following him down, half a dozen shots.

The rest of it went both slow and fast. The other three troop-ers, two men, one woman, appeared as if thrust by rockets. Taz swung her pistol up from the still-falling man and toward the second man, but it was like moving a heavy weight through gel; she couldn't believe how slow it was.

Jerlu's shotgun went off. Some of the unburned propellant sprayed onto Taz's neck and face, stinging where it touched bare skin. The sound was like a bomb, bounced and funneled from the walls over them in a hard wave. The woman trooper's face disappeared, wiped clean by the heavy metal shot that sleeted into her.

Taz's pistol thrummed and whumped, spewing deadly mis-siles at her second target. The trooper was trying to stop and turn, and he managed neither well, but he did point his carbine in her direction.

The tiny red dot of Jerlu's laser sight danced in slow motion and came to a vibrating semistop on the carbine of Taz's target. What was he *doing*—?

The little red spot was like an electron's orbit. Taz had all the time in the galaxy to see it; it reminded her of nothing so much as a small child playing with a flickstick at night, waving it in a tight, squashed circle so fast that a human eye made it into a line and not dots. The persistence of vision, they called that, Taz remembered.

The shotgun spoke again, and the carbine shattered into plastic and spun fibers and crystal.

"Wrong one!" Taz heard herself yelling.

The last trooper in the quad had more time to work with, and he used it. A short burst from his carbine stitched up from Jerlu's right hip to his sternum, ten or maybe a dozen rounds on full auto. Blew fist-sized holes through the cool's back, shoved liquefied bone and globs of muscle and internal organs through the holes as the explosive rounds went off inside him.

Taz screamed something, she would never know what, and pulled her pistol toward the trooper, still firing. She wasn't counting shots; the spring gun held eighteen rounds in the triple-stacked magazine and she was putting them into the air as fast as she could pull the trigger.

By the time she lined up on the trooper, he was almost lined up on her with his carbine. Her pistol fired a final time and ran dry just as she saw his startled face over the end of the barrel.

It was enough. The needle caught him somewhere unseen and he crumbled, his weapon firing, chipping craters in the wall behind her a meter over her head.

Jesu Christo!

She had fired all eighteen shots, pulled the trigger each time, in something under maybe three seconds. Six shots a second. She'd never been that fast in practice before.

The troopers were all dead or dying. Jerlu was certainly dead.

Taz sagged against the wall. When she breathed in, it was a sigh, almost a sob.

"Hey, point?" came a voice from her earphone.

She took another breath, let it out raggedly. Forced herself

to as much calmness as she could muster. She had never fired
at a living person before, only lacs in practice. But she'd just
killed three people and nearly been killed herself. She had to
pee so bad she thought she was going to explode. She might
just pull down her pants and squat right here. Piss on the walk.
Nobody would care if she did, why not?

"Point?"

"Clear," she said. But gods, she had to pee . . .

Her full bladder woke her from the dream, and Taz rolled
out of bed and the dream, headed for the fresher. She could
see how old people might start wetting the bed. She had been
going to urinate in her dream and there must be a fine line
between knowing you were asleep and dreaming and thinking
you were in some appropriate place to spring a leak.

Saval's being here must have triggered the memories of the
revolution. She couldn't really consider herself a heroine or
anything, but she had drawn blood, been part of it. She and
her brother had never talked about it before, not in any depth.
Maybe this was a good time, during his visit here, to see
how he'd handled being shot at and shooting back. To see
if sometimes he dreamed about the things he had done.

She went back to bed, took a while to fall asleep again.
If she dreamed again, she did not remember it when the
morning came.

NINE

SNAKE ROAD BEGAN at the outback edge of South Leijona and meandered to the southwest in a lazy S-curve through an old-growth forest spared by the treecutters and now a national park. The road could easily have been named for its shape as viewed from the air; could have been, but was not. In the early years of the colony on Tembo, more serpents lived in this region than did everywhere else on the planet combined. In those times there thrived Bloat Adders, green, orange and blue Neons, Black Tigers, Birdheads, Queen-and-Jacks, Water Rollers, Hilt Ring Asps—and scores of other legless reptiles from a few centimeters long and thin as spaghetti to ten meters and thick as a big man's thigh. From harmless to dead-before-you-hit-the-ground toxicity if one bit you. Snake Road had been a herpetologist's orgasmic dream, a place where an active scientist could spend years simply identifying and cataloguing new species.

Many of those species were gone now, killed out of fear or for their unique hides or simply by passing vehicles and the press of civilization, but hikers were still advised to carry repellors when walking along Snake Road and warned to be careful even with the electronic protectors. A man squatting to defecate in a stand of flametrees had been bitten on the buttock last month by a doubtlessly surprised Grassmaster and had died before his companions could com for aid. And a tourist heading for the ruins only last week stepped on a *kitani,* a variant of the local Linen Snake, and lost his foot from the poison despite immediate first aid and aggressive medical treatment begun within five minutes of the strike. Civilization might be able to fling humans across the galaxy in ships that bent the fabric of space and time, but it still paid to watch where you put your feet when walking in snake-infested bush.

Kifo smiled at the thought as he walked along the edge of the plastcrete road. The morning sun was halfway to its midday perch, but the humid air was still considerably cooler than the body temperature it would achieve in the afternoon unless one of the local rain showers stymied it. Pollen and mold and other plant detritus hung fecund in the air and the smells were tropical and damp. He was far enough away so the airwash of passing vehicles didn't bother him much, close enough to stay out of the chemically stunted brush that lined the pedestrian path. He carried a repellor, of course, the small device even now uttering silent but jangling and harsh electronic pulses that supposedly made the average reptile wish to hurry and seek its fortunes elsewhere. And his vouch rolled along behind him on its rugged and fat all-terrain silicone wheels. The vouch was Healy's top-of-the-line model and could, so Kifo had been told, climb a wall or a tree with special grapples to reach its master should the need arise. The little suitcase was also supposedly full of antitoxins proof against any known venom the local slitherers carried.

The repellor and the vouch were helpful, of course, as was the wide-beam hand wand secretly built into his walking stick, but Kifo did not really think any of them were necessary. The gods would hardly allow their Unique to be taken down by a common snake or passing cutpurse unless they were mightily displeased with him, and he didn't think he had given them any reason for such displeasure.

It never hurt to check, though. Which was why he hiked the ten-kilometer stretch between the outskirts of South Leijona and the Zonn Ruins. He could have ridden, of course, but walking allowed a man the time to put himself in the proper mental and spiritual state before reaching his destination. The ruins were the reason that the Snake Road had been built, and rightly so. The stupidest tourist was impressed at the sight of the remains of the Zonn culture even when thinking of the vanished race as merely aliens. To one who knew the truth, the ruins were much, much more. They were holy, for the Zonn had been and were more than simply a long-vanished race of strange beings who had gone from the galaxy before man had crawled out of the water on his homeworld. Gone where, no one knew. But a few men did know one thing of monumental importance:

The Zonn were gods.

The Zonn had attained heights men could not hope to reach; the Zonn had risen as far above humans as humans were above the snakes in this forest. Men were as nothing to them, which was why Kifo's church was called the Temple of Despair, why he was named for death, his brothers and sisters given similar, less than joyous names. Because men were dogs to Them, and only through demonstrating loyalty could men gain even the smallest bit of reflected glory. It was sometimes not an easy thing to deal with, man's relative status in the scheme of things, but at least there was the knowledge of where one stood. Better to know one's place, even if it were low. Along that path lay security; a great strength lay buried under the trail—one did not have to be *responsible*. Somebody else was in charge, and that lifted a great deal of weight from mankind's shoulders—provided one was lucky enough to be aware of it.

A passing hovertruck blew grit up from the hard surface in a fine spray; some of it stung the side of Kifo's face, got into his eyes. He blinked the dust away, but even that small a discomfort was enough to hurry the vouch closer.

"No," Kifo said. "Override. I don't need medical attention."

The vouch dropped back two meters.

Yes, men were as the dirt beneath the feet of the gods, but some men were less so. Those who gave the Zonn their proper due, those who respected and worshipped them, paid

proper obeisance, those who formed a dedicated line behind
the Unique, the believers who knew their place, they were
better than the rest.

We are better.

Too, there were some men who were less even than the dirt.
Those who impeded the will of the gods, those who blocked
the path, knowingly or not, those who refused to bend the
knee to a force that could, if it wished, smash them like the
worthless rodents they were.

Of course, the gods would not sully their hands with such
work; rat-killing was so far beneath them.

That's what dogs were for.

"Morning!" a walker going the other way called out.

Kifo glanced at the man, a short and heavyset balding local,
tanned and smiling. "Morning," he called back. He waved his
walking stick as the man drew closer.

"The ruins are beautiful today," the fat man said. "Yesterday's rain has washed everything clean."

Kifo nodded. Smiled. The fat man had no idea of what the
ruins really represented. And he was not among the chosen to
ever know, either, but still Kifo smiled. He was not intolerant
of some things. Ignorance was not in itself evil. With a few
words, he could offer the man a status he could never hope
to achieve on his own, could break through his shell of not-
knowing and haul him out into the light, did he but choose
to do so. But, no. He did not wish to offer that pearl to this
swine. He could almost feel sorry for the hiker. No, ignorance
was not necessarily evil, but it certainly *was* a lack, and why
disturb this man's foolish bliss, unfounded though it was?
There were three kinds of people in the galaxy: those who
worked for the gods, those who worked against them, and
those who did neither. The first must be cared for, the second
removed, and the third group was of no interest. Dogs were
supposed to worry about the rats in their master's compound,
not those in the far fields, was this not so?

Ahead of him a panicked shrew scurried out onto the pedestrian walkway, right behind it a red treesnake, gaining. Kifo

watched with interest as the snake, moving much faster than he would have thought possible, lunged and sank its fangs into the shrew. The little mammal spasmed, went rigid, then limp. After a few seconds the snake dislocated its jaws and began to swallow the shrew.

Kifo moved a bit nearer, treading carefully so as not to make too much noise.

The snake turned, the shrew half-eaten, and regarded the man. Perhaps it was his size, or maybe the vibrations from the repellor. Whatever, the snake slithered away into the bush quickly, winding its coils over the hard surface like a sine wave on a holoscope. In two seconds it was gone.

Kifo smiled. Some lesson here, he supposed, but he couldn't quite put a finger on it. Ah, well. Perhaps later when he sat to meditate it would come to him.

He continued his walk toward the ruins. Behind him the vouch hummed to itself and tagged along, ready to do its job at any hint of need.

When Taz padded out of the fresher from her shower, the call light was lit on her com, on the personal number. Someone had called while she was showering. She was pretty sure it wasn't anybody from work; they'd have used the priority code. She regarded the light for a moment. Turned away from it.

She dressed. Silks under her loose-weaves and flexboots. She tucked her short double-charge backup hand wand into her boot pocket, put on her belt and holster, but left the spring pistol on the night table. Stared again at the com and its tiny blue light. Chewed at her lip. Picked up her pistol. Began to leave the sleeproom. Stopped at the doorway, turned back, moved to the com. Sat on the bed and stared at the light for ten seconds.

"Fuck it," she said, reaching for the control.

"Hello, Tazzi. I love you."

The recording chip beeped once, indicating the end of the message, then gave her the date and time stamp. The caller hadn't identified himself, but there was no need.

Ruul. God damn him. She'd *known* it would be him.

This was going to have to stop. She couldn't stand it. Her heartbeat was too fast, her breathing too shallow, she felt as if she were in a fight-or-flight situation, her hormones flowing in danger mode. Damn, damn. She sat and made an effort to slow her breathing. When she was calmer, at least on the surface, she stood.

In the kitchen, Saval prepared breakfast: soypro links, eggs, toast, cereal, fruit, juice.

"Hey, I'm the host," she said. "I'm supposed to fix the meals."

"I got here first. What the hell, I can cook as well as the next man."

Taz looked at the meal. "Better than most, actually," she said.

They ate, and Taz didn't say anything about Ruul's call.

"So, what's on the agenda for today?" he asked, as he polished off the last of what had to be a dozen eggs.

"Well, there's not much direct investigating we can do until we get lab results or more input. It's about time for my monthly weapon qualification. I thought we'd go to the range and do that. Give me a chance to see if you can hit the side of a warehouse with those toys you carry." She waved at Saval's spetsdöds.

He shrugged. "Sure. I'm not in Geneva's class or even Emile's, but I might be able to keep you up with you."

Taz grinned. Saval was in for a little surprise at the range. She'd been combat pistol champion for the Leijona police force the last three years, had scored third in the planetary peace officer games last summer. And would have tied for first had not a magazine malfunction cost her six points during the final round shoot-off. She'd never mentioned any of this to Saval before.

"Hey, I'm just a small-talent local cool," she said. "With a beat-up spring pistol. I hardly ever practice."

He chuckled. "And your wrist is sore and your eyes are tired and you've been sick, too, right?"

Her laugh joined his. Good old Saval. Still sharp as a needle. "Come on, brother. Let's go places and shoot things."

The police range was in the training center near the west Kubwa River Bridge, only a few klicks from the station. It was state of the art, full holoprojics, with a full-time range master and two line officers. Most of the police agencies onplanet used the place for matches and qualifications, but there were a couple slots open when Taz and Saval arrived. She signed them in, was assigned an alley and issued a couple hundred rounds of practice ammo by the RO. Saval also collected some blunt-nosed loads for his spetsdöds.

"It's a pretty good setup," she told Saval as they moved toward the alley. "You can program the targetcomp to provide from one to a hundred attackers, any scenario you want to input, hostages, cover, whatever. The qualification runs require passing scores on five standard streetsits, with perps at ranges from point blank to fifty meters. Got some armed better than you, some in protective gear, like that. Probably stuff you could do in your sleep."

"Been a while since I did anything other than plinking at plastic cans," Saval said. He exchanged his chemical dart magazines for the practice rounds.

She smiled. "Right, and *your* arms are sore, too?"

They both laughed.

The alley was short and narrow, smooth and hard walls tapering from a square large enough to allow three people to stand side by side next to a small armored box that caught the funneled shots. With the holographics lit, the scene could be any size.

Taz switched her spring gun's magazine for the indoor target loads, holstered the pistol. "You want to warm up, shoot a few practice sessions?"

"Not unless you do," he said.

"Let's try it cold. You don't get to practice on the street."

She smiled to herself as she moved to stroke the computer to life. She knew the five standard runs real well, Saval didn't,

so she had an advantage right off. But hey, he was supposed
to be the best, right? After she beat him she would put the alley
on scramble mode so neither of them would have an edge, just
to be fair.

"I'll set things so we're shooting at identical scenarios. You
take the right, I'll do the left. Five setups."

"Okay," he said.

"What's the effective range on those things?"

"Well, they will shoot to fifty meters okay. I don't know if
I can hit anything that far away."

She finished the computer sequence. "Got ten seconds,"
she said. She moved back to stand next to her brother. She
wouldn't see his targets from her angle, only her own, so she
wouldn't be distracted. The first round was a simple one. A
shop interior in good lighting, one perp popping out from
behind cover—exactly what cover was different each time
the thing ran—with a handgun. You had two seconds max
from the time the attacker showed until he started firing, and
if he fired first, you lost, because the computer never missed
at close-range encounters. Average combat distance of this run
was seven meters, sometimes closer.

Since they were both using chemically augmented hand
weapons, any hit on a target would count the same—you
scored as much for a hand as a head—so the only things
you had to worry about were missing and time. If you shot
your opponent before he could shoot, you won the round. If
you didn't, you lost. Simple.

Her half of the alley shimmered and turned into a clothing
shop. Racks of coats and coveralls came into being, grew
solid-looking. Taz shook her hand a little to relax it, moved
it away from her body toward the holstered gun over her
right hip.

A short, squatty man with wild eyes leaped out from behind
a display of vat-leather capes and thrust a slug gun toward Taz.
Screamed at her: "Die, fucker!"

Taz snatched at her spring pistol, the uncounted hours of
practice over the years making the movement smooth and fast.

She was concentrating on the attacker, but was aware enough of the unseen Saval on the other side of the holoproj to hear the cough of his spetsdöd.

He shot before she even *touched* her own weapon.

Damn!

It didn't delay her draw more than a half second, though, and she snapped her pistol out and fired, hitting the attacker solidly on the chest. He moaned very realistically and crumbled.

The scene held for five more seconds, then flicked off.

The next run began to fade in. She glanced over at her brother before the holoproj blocked her view. He wasn't smiling; his face was serious.

Taz didn't reholster her gun. Since the spetsdöds were glued to the backs of Saval's hands with plastic flesh, he didn't have to draw, he just pointed his index finger and *pap!* there went the shot. If she wanted to beat him, she'd have to keep her gun out; otherwise he'd have a quarter, maybe a half second on her every round.

Yeah, well, in a one-attacker run, maybe that quarter second would make the difference, but in the later scenarios, thing got a little more complex. The second involved six attackers; the third had two with hostages as shields, two without; and the fourth had five guys in helmets and torso armor, so a body shot wouldn't count—you had to hit an arm or leg. And the last run threw six gunmen at you at ranges from in your face to fifty meters, in various combinations, and if you didn't stop and aim at the long-range guys, you'd miss, so that snap shot from the hip wouldn't help much.

A woman slipped around the corner of the warehouse and pointed a shotgun at Taz—

Taz shot her—

As the woman fell, a man rolled out from behind a trash masher, stayed prone and partially covered by the masher's rollup ramp, and aimed a pistol at her. As she swung to shoot him, another attacker screamed, jumped from the low roof, ran at Taz with an upraised knife—

Taz ignored the knifeman, shot the pistoleer, then punched her spring pistol into her other hand in a double grip and put a pair of shots into the last one's face. He fell, skidded to a halt right next to her feet. The first times she'd fired this scenario, years ago, the screaming knifeman had distracted her long enough for the pistoleer to get her. That hadn't happened in a long time. Six for six . . .

While the 'proj was still lit, she ejected her magazine, pulled another from her belt and shoved it into place.

The rest of the exercise went well. Taz got faster during the final runs. She missed all the hostages—that was always embarrassing, to hit one of them, even if it didn't matter with sublethal ammo—took out the bad guys cleanly. The fifth scenario was the most dangerous, and this time started with the closest attacker followed immediately by the one farthest away, then the mid-rangers. Adjusting from point blank, to fifty meters, then twenty meters in less than three seconds was tricky, but she was on top of it, and didn't miss a beat.

As the final run popped off, Taz looked at the timer on the floor by her feet. The five standard qualification runs were cumulative. The computer started the clock when an attacker appeared, stopped it when he was hit. You could miss and still outshoot the bad guys, provided you could get off a second or third shot fast enough. She hadn't missed any this session. The slowest you could go and pass was thirty-six seconds. The average speed for a qualification series was around twenty-eight. The record, set nine years ago by a cool Taz was certain had been circulating bacteria-aug or some kind of nerve-booster chem, was eighteen point two seconds. Her own personal best was nineteen-five, that the best time of three runs, after a week of intensive practice.

This run was at twenty point oh two seconds.

She smiled widely as she holstered her piece. A half second off her best, not bad for cold. Not bad, hell, it was fucking terrific.

She looked over at Saval, who was replacing the magazines in his spetsdöds. "How'd you do?" she asked.

He shrugged. "Not too good. Shooting never was my real strength."

Taz was prepared to be generous as she stepped over to look at his timer. To admit to her little secret of being combat champ, to offer to scramble the codes so they could start out even. But her smile went away when she looked down at the electronic numbers floating a handspan over the floor between his boots.

Seventeen seconds flat.

Damn!

He looked at her, and couldn't hide the little grin, though he tried. "Maybe when I get loosened up, practice some, we can try it again."

"You're a dick, you know that?"

He gave up trying to hold the smile.

"You just beat the fucking record by almost a full second and you have the nerve to stand there and shuck embarrassed at me. I ought to hit you!"

"Sorry," he said.

"You lie." But she grinned as she said it. She knew about karma. It served her right, thinking she was going to put one past him. She'd shaded the odds in her favor, and still he'd won. That was appropriate. And also impressive. If what he said was true, that there were other matadors who could outshoot him, that was even more impressive. And he hadn't missed once, either.

Jesu Damn.

"Let's go," she said. "I think you've had enough practice for today."

TEN

WHILE TAZ TALKED to the lab people regarding their findings in the latest locked-room killing, Bork found a com booth in the lobby. He checked the time zone schedule converter program and found that it would be late afternoon on the part of Muto Kato where his wife and son were. He fed his credit code into the unit, accessed the White Radio net, and called home.

It took about three minutes for the system to accomplish its magic, and when the holoproj blinked on, he found himself grinning at Veate light years away.

"Bork!"

The transmission delay was short, Muto Kato being a long way off. For some reason nobody could explain, White Radio worked better at longer distance than it did close up. Delay at fifty light-years was less than at ten LY.

"Hi," he said. "How's everything?"

"I'm glad you called. We're lonely. You wait right there."

She moved from the screen, and Bork was treated to a view of his main communal room at a cost, according to the running tally in one corner of the holoproj, of about a stad a second. A ten-minute conversation would total about six hundred standards. Talk, when it was between stellar systems, was not cheap. He and Veate wouldn't be having any deep philosophical discussions at this price.

After what Bork guessed would cost his account forty stads, Veate returned with little Saval.

"Say hello to your father, brat."

The three-month-old albino baby could not speak, of course, but he could see okay. He smiled. Gurgled.

Bork's chest got tight. Not enough room for all the pride. "Hey, kid." Then he frowned. "How come you're calling him a brat?"

"Because he is, that's why. He's smiling at you like oleo wouldn't melt in his mouth but he kept me awake all night. You have to come home; I can't do anything with him. He's a daddy's boy."

Little Saval waved his chubby fists excitedly, smiled and made another noise at the holoproj.

"I miss you both," Bork said.

"Yeah, you big thug, we miss you, too. But I'm serious about the brat. Listen, I want you to sing him that song you do to put him to sleep."

Bork glanced around. The lobby of the cool station was fairly busy, POs going back and forth, civilians, even a few arrestees. "What, now?"

"Yes. I'll record it so I can play it back to him later. Maybe we can fool him with a holoproj at bedtime, too."

"Uh . . ."

"Look, Bork, I stayed home with your son so you could go play, and you *will* sing to him so I can get some rest. Do it."

Bork grinned. Well. If it would make her happy. He turned the booth dampers up to keep the sound from filtering out into the lobby. Sang the song. Cost about a hundred and fifty stads but hey, it was only money. The best-looking and brightest baby in the galaxy was certainly worth it.

Bork finished the song and leaned back. Came the sound of applause. He turned and saw Taz standing in front of a dozen cools, all of them clapping and grinning at him.

"The dampers are all shot in these booths," Taz said. "Hi, Veate! I'm trying to keep him out of trouble."

Bork blinked at his sister. And blushed.

• • •

At the end of Snake Road there was a trail that switchbacked down a rocky incline. The planetary agency in charge of the upkeep of national parks had installed guardrails along the trail, but left the rest of it alone. The path had been worn flat and smooth over the rocks by the passage of millions of feet, and there was little worry that plants would overgrow it.

As Kifo walked, his vouch tooling along behind him, he found himself part of a procession of people going to see the ruins. A dozen or so walkers were ahead of him, strung out in groups of two or three; at least that many more followed him, ambling down the switchbacks toward the first viewpoint just around the next curve in the trail. From where he now was the ruins were not visible, merely a vast expanse of tall and thick woods, a mottled green carpet that lay over the land all the way to the horizon.

Kifo rounded the sharp curve and as always, his breath caught, his throat clenched, and he was nearly overcome with awe as he beheld that which had been built by the hands of the gods Themselves.

Here the gods had dwelled, in a city made of a substance harder than diamond and stronger than any material men could produce. Five hundred million years past the Zonn had built their city, and while the roofs and doors and interiors were gone, the larger walls remained standing, untouched by the natural elements of weather. Five Major Walls still stood, ten meters high, half a meter thick, with two dozen shorter and thinner Inner Walls connecting them. During the revolution a group of rebels had chosen to hide in the ruins, and the Confed committed the worst of sins by attacking them there. Even as enduring as they were, two Major and six Minor Walls had been knocked askew in the bombing. Kifo was certain that the Confed's action had been the pivot upon which the revolution had turned: desecrating the home of the gods had surely guaranteed the fall of the Confederation.

He stood there, staring, aware that he had been joined by others stopping to take in the view. The Five Walls were

impressive, dull, midnight blue-black against the green back-
drop, dark and brooding giants. Scientists had done computer
projections; electronic and viral-molecular brains had tried to
reconstruct what the city must have looked like when whole,
but most of the projections made no sense. At least not to
human minds.

Kifo smiled. Can a dog understand its master's house?
Hardly.

He stared at the ruins, impressed again, though he had been
here a hundred times. Kifo knew the ruins better than the lines
on his own palm, knew the shapes and dimensions, the joinings
and connections, those things other men could know. But there
was more that the Unique knew, more than any man alive
could possibly know.

Kifo put his right hand into his pocket and touched the
Glyph he carried there. The talisman felt cool as it always
did to his touch, and a faint ripple of energy spread into his
fingers.

The vouch millimetered forward.

"Stay, foolish machine. I am in no danger."

Not yet. Soon, perhaps. Though he was certain he had not
failed the gods in any way, there was no way to be sure. The
true answer to that question lay down there in the ruins.

Kifo turned away from the view and continued his walk
down the trail.

The labbos had come up with precious little, nothing that
help Taz directly. Maybe if they had a suspect, one they could
match with some of the loose molecules scooped up by the
nanocops, but you couldn't stop every person on the street and
demand tissue and pheromone samples.

It would have been nice if the perp had left something a
little more concrete at the scene.

Yeah, like his ID cube and maybe a map to where he was
staying.

Saval was in the fresher, composing himself after his adventure in the lobby. Taz grinned. Hard to figure a guy like her

brother. She knew he was smart, had an IQ up on the edge
of genius. She'd seen the setting on her workout gear after
he'd finished using it, and according to those records, he was
stronger than anybody she knew on this planet. Then he'd
outshot her at the range, outshot *everybody* who'd ever used
the place, done it cold, no practice. And *then,* then, he'd sung
a lullaby to his kid, in a voice that would shame a professional
opera singer. Blew the stereotype of the big strong mope right
out of the sky.

Her com chimed. She pulled the tiny unit from the patch on
her belt. "Yeah?"

"Personal communication holding," the routecomp's tiny
chipvoice said.

"ID of caller?"

"Ruul Oro, number six-four-five-zero—"

"Record it," Taz cut in. Her voice sounded harsh. "I'm
unavailable at the moment."

"Acknowledged," the computer said.

She stood there rubbing the com with her thumb as Bork
returned from the fresher. "Everything okay?"

She looked at him. "Yeah, why wouldn't it be?" She tucked
the com back onto her belt.

She was going to have to talk to Ruul sooner or later, she
knew. That idea scared her much worse than the killer she was
hunting.

There were guards at the Zonn Ruins, though hardly anybody
could understand why. The Walls themselves were impervious
to almost anything a tourist might do to them. True, an explosion
of sufficient force might damage the material, but anything short
of that was pretty much a waste of effort. Paint or ink or gluestat
graffiti all wiped off with a damp cloth no matter what kind of
applicator was used. You couldn't cut the stuff with any kind
of knife—metal, vibro- or molecule chain. The Walls absorbed
lasers without damage or even undue heating. Maser, ultra-
sound, tachychroma, plasma, none of them did any significant
damage. It was unlikely a tourist could even transport a device

with sufficient energy to cause any real harm, unless they had access to military-grade weaponry, and if they did have such access, why would they do such a thing? Even the walls the Confed had knocked down were still in complete sections, no chips lying about.

There was always a chance that somebody poking around the ruins might find an artifact small enough to steal, of course, though this was not one of the ten major sites where such things had been discovered.

Then again, the Sacred Glyph *had* come from these ruins. Yes, the Few were chosen to receive it, under the direction of the Zonn, but who knew but that other such objects were still hidden here, awaiting the proper time to be revealed?

Directly after the fall of the Confed, the previous Unique, Brother Pain, had been instrumental in convincing certain governmental authorities to cause guards to be posted at the ruins. Bribes, threats, blackmail, whatever it took, all had been applied properly and justified, rationalized as needed so that the ruins would be watched with care. Great care, for every guard who had been hired in the years since the first had been a member of the Few. With enough money, many things were possible, and the Few had *more* than a few valuable holdings on Tembo. Timber property in the south, rental buildings in the city, interest in a couple of copper mines, a pharmaceutical plant in Mende Town. When you joined the Few, were selected from the chaff, what was yours became the property of the Temple. It was cheap admission to the house of the gods, and after a certain amount of money was achieved, it took on a life of its own. The Temple of Despair was not poor. Considerable care had been taken to keep that fact secret; dozens of accountants spent their days hiding it, shuffling files, renaming corporations, legal smokescreens, illegal transfers, whatever it took. The end, after all, justified the means. To be one of the Chosen Few meant that human laws became as nothing.

Kifo sat lotus in a shaft of the dwindling sunshine, waiting for night. The ruins were closed at dusk, tourists shooed away like bothersome flies by the guards, half a dozen of whom combed and recombed the entire area until it was free of the unfaithful. The guards would pass by Kifo, nod politely instead of bowing, in case there might be a stray watcher still around, as they went about their business. Once the place was dark, once the tourists were gone, then Kifo would begin *his* business.

Between the Third and Fourth Walls, a quarter of the way from the southernmost end of the Third, was the Gods' Chamber. This consisted of three Minor Walls formed into a squared-U shape, once a room it was thought, with a fourth wall covering the opening of the U.

What had happened to the fourth wall, indeed, what had happened to all the vanished walls, was a scientific mystery. Of them there was no trace, no rubble, nothing buried under the ground, no sign that they had ever existed. It was another question that puzzled the scientists, but not Kifo in his role as Unique. The gods gave, the gods took away, and if they chose to snap their digits and make disappear something as simple as a wall, then it was surely a thing of no great importance.

That the gods had allowed their Chamber to remain *was* important to the Few. For within the confines of the partial room, miracles were possible. Even the densest of tourists, the most unaware among them, could feel *some*thing did they tarry in the Chamber too long. For one who was among the Few, much more was possible. For the Unique holding fast to the Sacred Glyph, there existed the ultimate:

Communication with the very Zonn Themselves.

Ah, yes, there were stories that in one of the other ruins there existed a complete Gods' Chamber, bound against time and space on all four sides, wherein even an unbeliever could speak to and hear from the Zonn. Some said this was on Bocca, some said it was on Zena, some even said it was on Kontrau'lega, in the very heart of the Omega Cage. Ordinary men, so it was said, who went into and stayed in this chamber for more than a few minutes quickly went insane. Their minds were broken so badly they could never be repaired.

Kifo smiled at the thought. Unbelievers, and as such deserved no less.

Perhaps such a chamber existed, but if it did, it mattered not to Kifo. He was the Unique, he had the faith and training *and* the Glyph, and he could bespeak and hear the Zonn well enough here in these ruins.

And before the sun had settled comfortably into its night's rest, Kifo would do just that.

Despite the heat of the tropical afternoon, he felt a chill frost him, raising blains over his chest and shoulders. Communing with the gods was not something to be undertaken lightly. Best he calm his body and mind and still his soul before the event. He had done this holy work thrice before and each time had been most arduous. A misstep while dancing with the Zonn could be fatal. Best he be ready.

ELEVEN

THE OWL WAS, as usual, packed. A waiter led Taz and Saval to a double table in one of the quieter nooks, and Pickle arrived while they were still in the process of sitting.

"Hel-*lo,* big man. Oh, and you, too, Chief."

Taz decided not to get in Pickle's way if she wanted to flirt. Dueling the Owl's owner was generally a no-win proposition—even if you zapped her, she would bite you on the way down. Taz had no desire to be bitten again, not after last time.

"So," Pickle said to Saval, "are you ready to go somewhere and screw my brains out? Or here on the table, right now?"

Subtlety was not Pickle's greatest talent.

"Uh, I don't think my wife would like that much," Saval said. He wasn't Machiavelli's brightest pupil when it came to indirectness, either.

Pickle brought out her best pout and tried it on him. "You're no fun at all."

"Sorry."

She smiled, the pout vanishing instantly. "You know, I believe you really are. God, Chief, he's so *sincere*! I love him." She turned back to Saval, licked her lips, vamped a little. "You won't mind if I keep asking?"

"Uh, no."

"Good. Try the hammerfish and fried kaizis, the fish was still swimming around this morning and the kaizi was in the ground up to an hour ago."

She flounced away.

Saval smiled a little, shook his head. "Funny woman," he said. "She used to be a man?"

Taz stared at him. Damn, she wished he'd quit doing that. "How did you know? She'd be crushed if she found out you could tell."

He shrugged. "Dunno for sure. Just feels like it. Female pheromones too strong, maybe. Probably dusted."

He would know about that, being married to an Albino Exotic. "See if you can keep the table while I run to the fresher," she said.

"I'll try."

As she walked away, Taz thought about the possibility of somebody taking the table from her brother. That was enough to make her chuckle out loud.

But once inside the fresher, in a private stall, the humor evaporated. It felt as if there was a block of solid nitrogen in her belly, and her bowels suddenly twisted into frozen Gordian knots. She pulled her com from her belt and stared at it.

You don't have to call, she told herself. Nobody is making you do it. You can stick the com back on its patch and go back to your table, nobody will know.

I would know. Dammit.

She lit the com with a double press of her thumb. "Ruul Oro," she said. Her com had the code.

He could be rehearsing or taking a shower or hang diving off the cliffs next to his house. His mansion. Or he could be in bed with somebody or on a toilet or doing any one of a dozen other things that would prevent him from answering a call. A lot of people wanted to reach out and connect with Ruul Oro the comedian, the media light, or the just plain great-looking man. He had secretaries and assistants and hired security to screen and shortstop the masses. It was the first time she had

called him since that night at his place and she wouldn't have
been surprised to find that it was difficult or impossible to get
him—

"Tazzi!"

No such luck. And his computer had read her call code, so
she couldn't discom without his knowing who it was.

"Hello, Ruul."

"God, I'm so glad you called."

"I thought you might be busy."

"It can wait."

She stared at the com as if it had suddenly become a deadly
serpent, curved and hollow fangs ready to sink into her flesh
and fill her with poison. Here was the damning part of all this.
He *was* glad she had called. She could hear it as clearly as a
monk's bell in some quiet mountain zendo; the truth of it rang
so clean as to be undeniable.

Damn him for being so fucking glad!

"I got your message," she said. "Just like all the others.
Listen, Ruul, you're going to have to stop calling me like
that."

The silence stretched between them, and the excited parti-
cles and waves carrying the energy over space and through
time went slow, went mute and stalled to dead stillness, waiting for further instructions from their masters. It couldn't have
been very long, the silence.

Couple million years, maybe.

"Is that what you really want?"

Another eight or ten million years marched past, each fucking second of every fucking minute distinct, unique, quite
apparent.

"Tazzi?"

"Goddammit, Ruul—!"

"Come and see me," he said. Every bit of his talent and
skill in front of people flowed through those four words. She
could feel the power much as she had once felt the winds of
a hurricane beat against her, streaming her hair, flagging her
clothes. Stroking her skin . . .

"Please," he said. "We need to sit down and talk about this again."

"No, we don't," she said. "We've already said it all."

"Please, Tazzi."

She felt herself trembling, saw the com shaking in her hand. Why didn't he just leave her alone? Why was he continuing to torture her this way? Damn him—!

"Tazzi, I—"

"Don't say it," she cut in. "Don't say it."

"Will you come?"

She took a deep breath to smash him with her denial. The word "No!" was never going to feel so clean and fresh in her mouth.

"All right," she said. Blinked at the com in horror. Jesu Christo! She couldn't believe it! She couldn't have said that; it was impossible!

"Thank you," he said. "Tonight?"

She was numb, injected by the serpent's fangs, the chemicals filling her. Dying. Would that she could pass away before the next words came out of her. Hurry—!

But—no. "Okay. Tonight."

She discommed. Held the unit in her hand and looked around at the inside of the stall. It was unreal, as if she had suddenly been dropped into the middle of a psychedelic dream. The gray everlastplast panels and their extruded flanges and hinges seemed almost to glow with unnatural light. The slunglas bidet was too white, the ceramic floor shined up supernally at her.

God. What had she done? She had lost her mind!

Back at their table she didn't say anything to Saval about her conversation. He must have noticed that she was a lot paler and more subdued than when she left for the fresher, but he didn't speak to it. The fish and fried root nodules could have been wonderful, probably were, but for Taz it was like chewing raw and unseasoned soypulp, tasteless, odorless, bland.

She was going to see Ruul. At his house.

What the hell was she going to do?

• • •

Bork saw how shaken his sister was when she returned to their table. Had she run into somebody in the fresher? Only a couple of people had left the unisex unit, both of whom looked innocuous enough, and he kept glancing that way to see if anybody else had been inside with Taz, but it didn't seem as if they had. Something had rattled her, though.

Well. If she wanted him to know, she'd say something. She wasn't his baby sister any more, she was an adult and had been taking care of herself for a lot of years without his help. He was curious, but he wasn't going to pry.

The fish was great, and the fried potato things just about as good. Whatever else Pickle was, she set a pretty fine table.

Taz pushed her food around her plate, eating with a definite lack of gusto. She'd always been a big eater, all the Borks had been. He remembered watching her consume an entire *mbwa* cutlet once when she'd been thirteen, on a dare. Two kilos of dense meat, highly seasoned with hot spices and thick sauce. She'd thrown up later, but she'd enjoyed every bite of the meal while she was eating it. Whatever was bothering her must be fairly major that she would find no joy in the dinner before them.

He popped a chunk of the fish into his mouth. Well. She would tell him or she wouldn't. No point in his being worried about it.

As he chewed the delicious fish, he found he was still a little worried about it anyhow. He'd known Tazzimi longer than anybody else in his life, she'd been there since he was four, and if there was anything he could do to help, he wanted to do it.

But it was her move. If he'd learned nothing else in his years, he'd learned that there were times to move and times to sit still. Knowing when to do which was a fairly big lesson. Right now felt like it was time to wait, to watch, to keep his mouth shut. Except for eating this hammerfish. And to be polite, he'd have to tell Pickle how good it was.

Or, given how *she* was, maybe not. Maybe just tell the waiter to tell her.

But it was good, sure enough.

As the dusk thickened and darkened, a sauce with night added slowly to it, Kifo sat on a tree stump just outside the Gods' Chamber. His repellor kept the tropical insects buzzing outside the force field's range of a meter or so. The top of the stump, which had once supported a tree that must have been twenty meters around and probably almost a hundred meters high, was covered with thick green moss that cushioned the bare wood under his backside.

Kifo had already installed a temporary program in the vouch, to keep it from scooting in after him when he went into the chamber. Certainly the little machine would feel his mental agitation once he went into Communion, and while he appreciated the vouch's doglike devotion to his safety, it would hardly do for it to start injecting chemicals to calm him at the wrong moment.

True, there was an override circuit in the vouch that wouldn't let things get past a certain point. If death came close enough to claim Kifo, the vouch would seek to do battle no matter what he told it. Of course, if the Zonn wanted their subject dead, no bioelectronic viral/molecular computer on wheels would be able to stop it. Still, it was built to try, and over the years Kifo had come to feel a certain kind of affection for the vouch, even though it was only a biomechanical and not truly alive. People could do that, anthropomorphize almost anything. Hello, vouch. And how are we today?

A moment of humor to break the solemnity, that was good. Soon enough things would be a lot more serious.

A guard approached.

"The tourists and scientists have all left, Unique."

"Good. Check once again and report back."

The guard bowed slightly and hurried away. Kifo could have entered the chamber then, he knew. The guard would not have come had he not been sure of what he reported; still, there was no hurry. And though he was the highest of the chosen, the Unique of the Few, Kifo felt a tremor of fear dancing in him, slight, but there. He took a deep breath, let it escape, took another. It was not every day that a man spoke to the gods, and even though he knew in his heart and mind that he was a good servant, that in itself might not be enough. There were stories of those who had considered themselves worthy, who had been without apparent flaw, and who had displeased the Zonn in some manner when in Communion. Men whose minds had been snapped like twigs, who had been retrieved gibbering and totally insane, gone to a plane from which they never returned. Kifo thought he was pure enough, but who could say what a *god* thought?

He hoped his fear was not so strong that it would shine through and cause him grief. But if it was the will of the Zonn that he be struck down, then so be it. He was a dog, and they were the masters, and that was as it should be.

Like a man chosen to placate an angry volcano, Kifo sat next to the edge of his destiny. The guard would return soon, and whatever would be, would be.

TWELVE

MIXED EMOTIONS DIDN'T even come close to describing how Taz felt as she dressed. She stared at her mirror. Her hair was too long; it needed to be trimmed. She hadn't been working out enough; she was getting soft. How had Ruul ever found her attractive? She was ugly, too tall, too much muscle, too hairy; Christo, she was a fucking warehouse on legs.

The dark blue orthoskins, she decided. Dark would hide her better. And the new flexboots—

She blinked at her reflection. Dammit, woman, you're going to go tell the man to leave you alone, to quit calling you, to get on about his life and stay out of yours, not to knock him flat with your beauty. You shouldn't care a bug's ass what he thinks of what you look like!

Shouldn't. No, you definitely shouldn't.

Her reflection smirked at her. *Uh-huh. And who do you think you're fooling here, Tazzimi Bork? Not me. Not for a Spandle second. I know what is in the drawer.*

Fuck you.

It's in the drawer, right where you left it.

Taz stared at the drawer on the left side of the dresser. To avoid thinking about what lay therein, she thought instead about the dresser, and how she had come by it.

The dresser had been an extravagant purchase, she'd had it for years, ever since the first week she'd joined the peace force. It was carved of a dark red fruitwood called *namna ya tundo dogo,* which was a local variant of cherry, save that the fruit produced by the trees was blue-black and the size of small apples. She'd spotted it at an outdoor market in Mende Town, and an old man blotched with sunlight and age stood next to it, smoking a smelly pipe. There were dozens of other booths, but there was just the one piece and the old man—he had to be a hundred T.S., easy—in his stall, nothing more.

After she'd paid her rent, she had all of three hundred stads left to her name, but she had a job and wanted to celebrate it. The dresser was low, had a mirror on the back, a slot for a chair, was rounded and polished to a dull shine, and she'd lusted after it on sight. It was the most beautiful piece of furniture she'd ever seen. A simple design, no knobs or loops or twirls or stuck-on decorations. Simple, functional, but it had to be worth five or six times what was in her account at the very least.

Still, she couldn't not ask.

"How much?"

The old man smiled, revealing dazzling teeth that must be coated with the dental equivalent of nofric to stay so bright against the influx of greasy brown smoke from that awful pipe. Must be burning some kind of dung in the thing, it stank so bad. "How much do you have?"

"Not enough."

"But that is for me to decide, is it not? How much?"

"Three hundred standards."

The old man raised an eyebrow.

Yeah, I'd be insulted, too, grandda, I'd carved this and somebody waved that piddly amount at me.

"Only three hundred?" he said.

She pulled her credit cube, stroked it. A tiny one-side-only holoproj flickered dimly in the bright sunshine so it was visible to her alone. She turned the cube around so the old man could see the number. "Three hundred and two stads and four demistads, to be exact."

"Ah, well, that is another matter," he said, shining his odorous smile at her. "I could not possibly let this piece go for a mere three hundred, but for three hundred and two and four tenths, it is yours."

She blinked at him. "You serious?"

"Of course."

There was in her a sudden desire to transfer the money, to grab the dresser and run. If the old man was that stupid, *some*body was going to take advantage of him and she truly did love the piece. Then again, she was a newly minted cool, a peace officer, and to cheat the old man like that didn't seem right. Maybe he didn't know how valuable it was. Maybe somebody had left him to watch the store while they went to pee or something.

"It's worth a lot more," she said.

"I could take it to the market at Central City and get two thousand for it from a rich buyer," he said. "Three thousand, if I wanted to haggle. It is worth perhaps twice that offworld, and even after export taxes, I would clear four thousand."

She didn't understand. "If you could get five or six thousand stads for it, why in hell would you sell it to me for three hundred?"

"Three oh two point four," he said. "Do you have any money other than that in your credit account?"

A highly personal question, one he didn't have the right to ask. But she was intrigued. "Well, no."

"Have you food supplies enough to last until you get paid again?"

She admitted that she did not.

"Then if you give me your three hundred and two and four tenths, how will you eat?"

She shook her head. "I dunno. Scrounge somehow. Maybe sell something else I own."

"You would skip meals to own this dresser."

"Yeah, sure. Look at it." She touched the top lightly.

The old man's smile increased. "In Central City, a fat merchant or lumberlander would offer me much more money, but the amount would be but a tiny fraction of their wealth, a drop from a monied ocean. You are willing to give all the money you have. Surely you see that this is a measure of real value?

"Too, I saw your face when you saw this dresser, saw light up in it the *reason* I make such things. Money is nothing. I have more than I can spend. Your face reflects back to me what I put into the dresser. You will care for it, cherish it, enjoy it, is this not so?"

Taz grinned. Looked at the dresser, then back at the old man. She stroked the smooth wood softly, as he reached out and touched the opposite side at the same time. "Yeah," she said. "You bet."

"You and I, we have just made love, and this chunk of wood is the conduit of that energy. Such things are priceless. Money? Pah! When you look at this dresser, you will sometimes think of the crazy old man named Moyo with the smelly pipe and you will smile. And perhaps you will someday pass this poor wooden object to your child, and perhaps tell her the story of the old man. And maybe your daughter tells your grand-daughter and *she* tells your great-granddaughter, and on and on and a thousand years from now, Moyo is long dead, Moyo is dust, but so in a small way, he still lives.

"An artist wishes his work to be appreciated. If you walked away now you would be still be the true owner of this piece, it was made for you. But I will take your money and you will take my creation and we will *both* be richer for it, no?"

And he smiled and she smiled and so it was.

Nearly every week after that, Taz went to the market to see Moyo. They became friends, she was invited to his studio, got to know his family and some of his friends. Twenty-four years she knew and liked him. He worked right up until the day he died, keeled over next to a chair that he'd finished only minutes before. Moyo the artist passed away at the age of a hundred and thirty-three, and somebody suggested that a ceremony be held in his honor. He was well liked at the market in Mende Town. An announcement was made.

Taz had attended. As had nearly twelve thousand other people. Somehow, it didn't really surprise her, but still:

Twelve thousand people.

And nobody had anything but good to say about the artist. Dead, maybe so, but Moyo was going to be around for a long, long time . . .

Taz shook her way loose from the memory, found that she was smiling. Ah, old man and smelly pipe. What a joy.

That, however, was then. It was the now that concerned her at the moment.

She slid the drawer open. Reached inside. Withdrew the small plastic device. It was smaller than a pack of flicksticks, rectangular, a flat black with a single button on the side near one end. On the other end was a truncated cone the size of her little finger's tip, a tiny hole in the center. That was the nozzle. The button was the control. You just had to point the nozzle and touch the button and the device would spray the most potent pheromone the local black market could obtain. Invisible once it was on, odorless save deep in the olfactories, supposedly an analog duplicate of what Saval's wife could emit when excited. Guaranteed to attract a normal human or mue better than anything else money could buy.

A pheromone pump. It was Saval's comment about Pickle at the restaurant that made her think of it. It was easy enough to put in a com to one of her street people. It was in her mail slot when they'd gotten home.

There hadn't been enough problems with them on Tembo to draw the notice of the Planetary Legislative Body, so possession of such a device here wasn't against the law. Transportation on Republic ships *was* against the Galactic Penal Code, and worth a fat fine and possible imprisonment. Taz supposed that the pump *could* have been made onplanet, which would mean that she wasn't abetting criminal activity. She hadn't asked. It was only a matter of time until somebody seduced the wrong person, however, and pheromone pumps would be stuck on a schedule of proscribed chems.

That law wasn't going to happen tonight, though.

Taz turned the pump in her fingers, looked at it. If she had any sense, she would drop it back in the drawer and shut it away. Better still, drop it in the disposal and be done with it. Yeah, it had cost a week's pay, but she'd gotten better about tucking stads away over the years; she wouldn't miss it that much.

Time stumbled again, something she was getting used to seeing lately. When it recovered its footing, Taz stood along with it.

And put the pheromone pump into her belt case.

Bork was coming back from the gym, pumped and sweating, heading for the shower when Taz appeared in the hall. She was dressed in a dark outfit, her hair washed and combed, her face clean.

"I—I've got to go out for a while," she said.

"Sure."

"Make yourself at home."

"No problem."

"I'm not sure when I'll be back."

He nodded. "Okay."

"See you."

"Move safe, Taz."

After she was gone and he'd finished his shower, Bork went to check the time zone computer. Even if it was the middle of the night, maybe he'd call and leave a message for Veate and the baby on the house comp. All of a sudden he was feeling real lonely.

Kifo sat in the middle of the Gods' Chamber, the night hanging humidly over him like a damp sheet. The vouch prowled back and forth in front of the opening to the chamber; were he ascribing human characteristics to it, Kifo would have said it was frustrated.

The guards were posted throughout the ruins with instructions to come for him at dawn did they not see him sooner, but not before. The insects buzzed, the vouch hummed, and

the sounds of his own heartbeat seemed loud in the darkness.
Kifo pulled the Glyph from his pocket and held it in his hands,
taking comfort from the familiar coldness of it. It had been
more than two years since last he'd entered Communion. In
daylight in the city, that seemed like a short time, a blink of
an eye. Here and now, it seemed too long past to help him. He
had achieved much during that time, moving as he saw fit, but
there had been some failures. Most recently the matter of the
policewoman who had gone offworld. True, the one sent for
her had been selected in haste and trained in yet greater haste,
Mkono being busy elsewhere. But it was a small enough glitch,
easily rectified. Surely the gods would not fault him fatally for
it? What gnawed at Kifo more than the failure was the worry
that perhaps he should have simply let well enough alone. The
woman was adept enough, but had he let her continue to
to fumble around on her own, she would have likely failed
to stop his plans. Now there was that offworld hired guard,
the matador. He had heard about them, and there lay another
worry—

Came a faint tapping at the door to his mind. A thread of
inquiry slithered tentaclelike to the entrance.

One could never predict how the gods would come, each
time had been different. The first time they had thundered
at him like malignant demons, cursing and hurling bolts of
energy that made lightning seem pale and dim. The second
time they had whispered so softly he could barely hear them.
The third time they had done some of both, plus other things
he could not put a name to.

Whither which who who who?

Testing him, for he knew they knew very well exactly
who he was. Your servant, he formed in his mind. Come
for instructions.

Hie aaiiee who which which here now? came a second
voice, distinct from the first.

Kifo had his eyes open, and ghostly lights played in the night
air, soft greens and blue twinning together, flowing from the
walls liquidly, oozing like heavy vapor to swirl around him.

Calls speaks calls listens listens! another voice said.

Yes, Kifo thought, I am listening. Sing to me your songs, Great Ones, speak to me of what must be done.

Key key key keykeykeykey! yet another of the Zonn chimed in.

Kifo rubbed the Glyph. Yes, I have the talisman. I have learned the lessons you gave me last time.

Open open open!

Free free free freefreefree!

Complete! Complete!

These were things the Zonn had said before. He thought he understood some of them, but he wasn't sure. The refrain "Complete" was always part of what they had to say, and while he thought it meant his work in the temple, he was unsure. It felt as if it somehow meant more—

A vision of himself at fourteen, stealing fruit from a stand and being chased by the vendor, flashed through his mind, as vivid and real as the day it happened. He could feel the sweat of fear staining his clothes, the smooth plastcrete under his flexible running shoes, hear the vendor's angry yells. Every sensation was as fresh as a newborn still wet from its mother's womb. The smell of the vegetables too long in the sun, the rotted and spoiled produce stacked in the battered aluminum composting bins, yesterday's fish heads and guts and scales near the disposal drains that chopped them fine then piped and fed them to the neowheat fields a hundred kilometers away. So real—

The city vanished and Kifo found himself in the Mende Town brothel where he'd sold himself for two years before he'd become one of the Few. The woman with him was rich, too beautiful to have to pay for her pleasures this way, but she enjoyed certain kinds of degradation she perhaps could not find in the expensive homes of other rich people. Kifo was but a nineteen-year-old whore when he reasoned this. Foolish child not to know better.

"Yes," she said, "yes! Put it there, hard—harder, oh, oh, oh, it hurts—harder!"

He obeyed, ramming himself into her. Wondering what the cook would fix the whores for dinner as the rich woman screamed under his thrusts. Still, it felt good—

And now he was in the temple and the slap across the face Brother Pain gave him was hurtful but deserved, for he had questioned doctrine—

And now he found himself sinking the ceremonial knife into the throat of one who had betrayed the temple—

The air shifted, fluid with color that gleamed into the night, flowing, settling, forming a rainbow panoply, clothing him in light. The Armor of the Gods. It might eat him alive, but it would protect him from without.

In in in in ininininininin—!

Live live live live—!

Mine mine mine!

The Zonn sang and screeched and foamed and invaded Kifo, and he became one with them.

When the dawn was but an hour away, Brother Death stood, possessed still of the gods. Stood and walked to the nearest of the Zonn's near-invulnerable walls. Then walked into the wall and vanished from the face of the planet.

He was back in what passed for a few seconds in the normal world, stepping from the blue-black wall as if it were no more than a curtain of air. The gods had departed, returned to where they dwelled, but the face of their servant was not quite what it had been. And the light that danced behind his eyes carried in it a faint but unmistakable sheen of madness.

Now he understood. Now knew what he had to do. The gods had grown impatient. He knew what to do, but he also had to hurry.

Before another year passed, the gods would again walk the worlds. Kifo had been chosen to be the door through which they would arrive. No man had ever been given a greater honor. The gods could do anything they wished.

Even raise a dog to be one of them.

Kifo would become a god!

Unless, of course, he failed. In which case he would suffer damnation and tortures beyond imagination for ten million times ten million years.

When the madness faded from his eyes, Kifo could even find some humor in his situation. Such stakes! Godhood or eternal punishement.

Such a choice, was it not?

He laughed so loud that the vouch came bustling up to him as he walked from the chamber, and the guards ran to see what had happened.

Such a choice.

THIRTEEN _____

THE GUARD AT the gate to Ruul's estate waved Taz through without a second glance. His employer had obviously told the man she was expected.

Once inside the high fence, Taz coaxed her flitter slowly along the winding flatway to the house's front entrance. It truly was a mansion; you could put five of her house into it and have room left over, and that didn't count the garage. She didn't know how much he made or how much he was worth, but she'd once seen Ruul turn down an offer of thirty thousand stads for a one-night performance, an hour's work. He had plans to go hiking that day, he had said, and he'd really been looking forward to the walk.

Jesu Christo, Ruul, she'd said, you sure have a hard life.

Yeah, it's tough, all right. Want to screw?

She smiled at the memory. The smile faded as she dropped the flitter to the surface. Dust blew up and settled as the fans slowed, their soft whine dropping in pitch then to silence as they stopped. Got very quiet then. She could hear the insects chirping in the clipped lawn and carefully tended bushes and trees. Hear the water flowing over the miniature falls in the amphibian ponds. And a din edging a distant walk with electric clippers.

Taz gripped the pheromone pump tightly in her left hand. Do it or not, she thought. Shit or get off it. Decide—

The door to the mansion opened and Ruul stood there, outlined against the lights inside. Tall, slim, beautiful Ruul, wearing a couple thousand stads of hand-sewn gold silk, shining brightly as his family name. The shirt and pants draped precisely on him, his face reflected the colors, his hair damn near matched the outfit. His feet were bare. Ah, god, he looked perfect. Had he worried over what to wear? Or had he just thrown on what had first come to hand when he opened his giant closet and looked?

Fuck it. She pushed the button, pointed the nozzle at herself.

The pheromone pump hummed. It ran for two seconds, then sputtered, hissed, ran dry and clicked to a stop. She'd used the whole charge. The chemical was designed to react to human skin, oils, perspiration. Plenty of that last for it to mix with. It would become hers, the chem, augmenting her own hormones, and she wouldn't be able to smell it any more than she could smell her own breath.

She stepped from the flitter, trying with every bit of muscle control she had to make it appear smooth and effortless. He'd always liked that about her, that she was strong and relatively graceful. Look at what you are missing, Ruul. I'm worth something.

She walked toward him, smiling. Fuck, she was nervous, yeah, no doubt about that, but she was glad to see him. There was another part of the handicap, part of this whole shitty situation. He wanted her, she wanted him, why couldn't it be that simple?

"Hello, Tazzi."

"Ruul."

"Please, come in."

She saw his nostrils dilate slightly, saw his eyes widen a hair. Imagined she could feel his sudden and unexpected surge of lust.

Suffer, dickhead. You deserve it.

She felt a pang of regret almost instantly. She didn't want him to suffer. Well, yes, okay, she did a little.

It was a dull mind that couldn't hold a couple of totally contradictory concepts at once, wasn't it? After all, love and hate leaned on each other from opposite sides of a very thin line. Too thin to see sometimes, invisible to the touch. Ah, god, Ruul. Why are you so goddamn *stupid* about this?

He turned and she followed him into the house.

Someday, Bork thought, as he looked at his naked body in the mirror, someday your strength is gonna fade. One morning you'll get up and set the weights on the bar and it won't move. Age catches up with everybody in the end.

Bork turned away from the mirror. Yeah, and someday the universe is going to undergo heat-death, too. Why worry if you couldn't do anything about it?

He grinned. Be nice if it were that easy, wouldn't it? Don't worry, because it doesn't do any good anyhow. Right. The major life lessons are always simple—but seldom easy. Big difference.

He went to do a few stretches. Time was when he could bend over and put his palms on the floor and press into a handstand; now he could barely manage to get his hands flat at all and he had to rock into it to make the straight press. The trick with muscle was to balance the strength and flexibility. He could walk the pattern okay and move as much weight as he ever could—so far—but he was stiffer than he'd been at twenty. Not a lot, but some, and it needed attention. Seemed like only yesterday that he'd been twenty, but it had been a while. More than a quarter of a century, actually.

Damn. Had it really been such a long time?

Yep. Sure had.

Bork reached for the ceiling, arched his back, bent forward. Well, he had traveled a lot of light-years and done a lot of things, he couldn't complain. Been in love twice; a lot of people didn't even get once. And he was stronger than Da had been. It might not mean much to anybody else, but it did to Bork. There came a time when he could have shown it to his father, demonstrated graphically that what the old man considered his greatest power was not so great. That his son, whom he had kept in line with slaps and backhands all his life, had surpassed his father. In that electric moment, Bork had realized that embarrassing the old man would have been sweet, oh, yeah, really sweet—but also the wrong thing to do. That it was sometimes better to have strength and *not* use it. He'd always felt pretty good about that day.

He was not like his father, even though they looked alike, had very similar physical frames. Bork was proud of his physical strength, of the ability to pick up something heavy and move it when other men or mues couldn't, but it wasn't all he had. There was Veate and little Saval, and he'd do better by them than his own da had by his wife and kids, or fall over dead trying.

His back creaked as he raised from the stretch. He laughed. He hoped he wouldn't fall over dead just yet.

The argument started and sped down the familiar roads, racing across territory Taz and Ruul had covered all too many times before. She knew his comments before he spoke them; he had to know hers. Her anger rose, hot fluid piped in under high pressure, flooding her hollow places, turning her insides rage-red. Both their volume controls went up, slowly but inexorably, so the calm and reasoned voices quickly racheted into shouts. They had started out sitting on the couch, the couch made from the lizard-leather hides of giant cloned-dinosaurs raised on the Mason Reptile Farm, the couch that had cost enough to keep a middle-class cit family in high style for a year.

Now they both stood, facing each other across a meter of agitated, hostile air.

"—believe you won't even fucking *consider* it! I'm not your goddamned father and you aren't your mother!" he yelled.

"—you can't buy fucking everything, rich man, I'm not for fucking sale and I won't fucking do it—!"

And all of a moment he shut up and she shut up and she felt such a surge of pure lust bubble up in her that her breath stuck. She couldn't even *breathe* she wanted him so bad! But he wouldn't, they'd gone down *that* goddamned road too many times, too, she knew every centimeter of it—

"I—oh, *shit!*" he said. "Oh, shit."

She stared at him, hearing something she hadn't expected in his voice. Something she'd hoped for, but didn't really think would happen.

He sighed and practically leaped at her, arms stretched wide.

Yes!

Her reactions were good. She met him halfway.

He found her mouth with his, thrust his tongue between her lips. She chewed on it, not hard enough to draw blood, but enough for him to feel it.

He tore at her clothes, she at his. The golden silk of his shirt ripped next to the cro-tab, the cloth parting under her fingers as she slid her hands over his chest, around his back.

They dropped to their knees and she fell backward so he could peel her orthoskin pants off. With the pants still tangled around one boot, he bent and licked her clitoris; nibbled, all lips, and she screamed with the intensity of the sensation. The room seemed filled with flying clothes, panicked moths seeking to flee from a suddenly too-hot fire. Oh, god, she couldn't get enough of him in her arms, she kept urging him to her, moving her hands up and down, feeling, massaging, her voice matching her hands in a soft croon: "Yes, yes, there, oh, yes, that, oh, oh, yes—!"

When he moved to untab her boot, she grabbed his erect penis and pulled it into her mouth, making wet noises as she slid her lips almost to his base. He vibrated like an off-center machine trying to balance on an unstable base.

"Oh, fuck!" It was more a moan than anything.

You got that right.

"I won't last," he said. "Come here."

They twisted, turned, she felt the rough patterned leather scratch her buttocks as she moved and opened wide to receive him. He fumbled, missed, and she caught him and guided him into her. Wet? Any slicker and he would have slid right past her and onto the floor.

He thrust, sank to his limit, pulled back and began pumping with a frantic, urgent drive. He *was* close—

"Oh, god!" he said, as his climax wracked him.

Taz smiled over his shoulder as she hugged him to her, wrapped her legs across his back, her heels pressed to his sides. That was quick. How long had it been for him? She could reach her orgasm later, he was very good about that, but it wasn't necessary just now. In this moment, she was fulfilled, holding him like a lover, feeling as tender as if he were a child.

"Oh, Tazzi. I love you."

"I know," she said. "I know. It's okay."

But even in her triumph, she felt a sliver of guilt stick a sharp point into her soul, a bit of shame running down and staining the window of brightness there. She had won. But she had also cheated. The victory that should have been as solid and hard as steel rang hollow. She had seduced him and gotten what she wanted, but nothing had really changed, had it? When the morning light shined on them, he would feel ashamed at his weakness and she would feel guilty at having played to it, and it would be the same as it had been before. She knew him too well to believe otherwise.

But fuck it. That was in the morning. Might as well enjoy what the night had left in it. She kissed his neck, petted his back, and rocked him in the oldest and most wonderful of cradles, in the most ancient man-and-woman dance. Sang wordless things to him, and moved in the best of all rhythms. Felt him recharge and knew that for the moment, at least, he was hers.

Through the dwindling night the flitter carrying Kifo sped toward his temple. The driver must have been awed at what he had seen in Kifo's face, for he had not spoken to the Unique. Next to him on the seat, even the vouch seemed subdued.

Well they should be. It was not given to many to look upon a god in the making.

Kifo stroked his personal com. "Brother Mkono," he ordered the com.

The voice replied almost instantly, sharp, clear, awake even at this hour. "Yes." No question in the word, but a readiness. Mkono was the best Hand the Few had ever possessed, no doubt of it.

"We have much to discuss," Kifo said. "The gods have made themselves very clear to me this night. Our work must be doubled and redoubled."

"I am the Hand. I do what must be done."

Kifo smiled. Of course.

FOURTEEN

Taz FELT WORSE than she'd thought she would. As she guided her flitter out through the gates of Ruul's estate, it was as if a block of lead filled her belly, a solid indigestible lump that wanted to come up but could not. It held her to her seat like a pressor field. She felt as if she were a thousand years old and sick for the last five hundred.

After two hours of lovemaking, she and Ruul had fallen into a worn-out sleep, arms and legs twined, woven together in an exhausted but highly satisfied knot. But when she'd awakened just before dawn, he was gone. He was not in the fresher, nor was he close enough so that he responded to her nervous query.

It was then the dense metal chunk started growing in her. Yes, he had weakened, given in, done what he said he would not do, and yes, there had been a spark of joy in her at making him do it. But now the morning-after price must be paid, and there was no one to pay it for her.

Taz slid from the bed and went to the fresher. Stepped into the shower, ordered it to full, and was blasted by eight spiral-rigged nozzles of hot water. The needle spray cleaned her body well and quickly enough.

Too bad it couldn't clean her conscience so easily.

She washed her hair with Ruul's special shampoo blend, took her time under the blowers until she was dry. Padded

"Then that's all we can do."

Bork didn't say anything. If somehow all this security failed to stop an assassin, it would be pretty amazing, all right. But if somebody got past it, they still had to get past him. Nobody had done that in a long time.

Well. He guessed they'd see.

FIFTEEN

THE KNOWLEDGE OF the matadors was extensive and, like the plants in M. Jorine's greenhouse, continually growing. When a matador went up against a tricky opponent, when some new bit of arcanery was thus learned, often it would be communicated to the computers at Matador Villa. Graduates had access to most of the files and, since information about their profession was most likely to come from others practicing it, it paid to check the updates now and then.

Bork hadn't been particularly active of late, but he was dutiful about logging into the matador systems and keeping up with new developments. The attacks on Sleel by the toobie who'd kidnapped Kee, well, Bork had heard that story straight from Sleel himself. Such was the reason he had changed the loads in his spetsdöds. His dexter darts carried a variant of shocktox, about the same potency but enough changed in formula so somebody immune to the regular version would be real surprised. The sinister gun carried armor-piercing rounds with the same electrochem variant. Sleel had used explosive ammo on his final job as a matador, but Sleel was less worried about killing people than Bork was. The disadvantage to AP was that you could only carry a few shots per magazine, plus if you shot somebody *not* wearing armor, you might kill them. Even something as small as a spetsdöd dart could punch a nasty hole in an organ or vessel at AP speeds; flesh offered less resistance than spiderplate or armorweave. Bork didn't want to kill anybody, he could help it.

Then again, he didn't want anybody to kill his client, either. So, the compromise. Better safe than sorry.

Taz was outside on the ground, his client puttering among her flowers, and all systems were secure. The old lady was right there in plain sight, ten meters away. Still, Bork felt a tiny flutter in his belly, not uncomfortable, but definitely there. Something weird about all this, and it made him a little nervous. He had been in a lot of hassles in his life, some small, some big, and he hadn't lost one since he'd become a matador. Nor for ten years before that, you didn't count sparring or shooting matches while training at the villa. He was pretty confident of his abilities. But still.

He moved a few steps closer to his client, his gaze scanning the surrounding rows of rosebushes. Something was off here. He didn't want to be caught asleep at the controls when it went down.

Kifo arranged for the Eighth Wall Segment's hovertruck to be serviced, system harmonics tuned, sufficient fuel onloaded. The mechanics were of the Few, the shop owned by the Temple, but even so, security was paramount.

An hour later, the call came. The Segment's vehicle was in readiness. As was Mkono.

Here was the other big part of the secret the Few had kept from the rest of the galaxy, the Zonn Wall Segments. There were nine of them, each the size of a door or larger, and though some would cry "Stolen!" they had been liberated by Kifo's predecessor when the truth of what the Sacred Glyph might be had been suspected. It had taken daring and a certain amount of risk, for dealing in Zonn artifacts was frowned upon greatly by the fallen Confed and its replacement Republic. Each segment had been acquired with the utmost caution, garnered from four different offworld ruins, not the local ones, and those who might have said where and to whom the artifacts had been delivered were no longer alive to relate the tale. Discovery would have been a major problem for the Temple, the ruination of hopes for the return of the Gods.

Lying upon the bed in his personal cubicle in the temple, Kifo smiled. He had felt full of power the last few days since his visit with the Zonn. Powerful and potent, even to the point of sexual arousal. As he thought this, an erection throbbed against his belly. Sex was for him relatively rare. Mostly he was too busy to think after it, but when it came upon him, he would not allow himself to be distracted by its urgent pressures. Release was the simplest way to deal with it.

He sat up, waved his hand over his com unit.

"Send whichever of the sisters is on *tunira* to me," he said.

"At once, Unique," came the reply.

The founders of the Temple had realized that men and women had certain urges and to deny them was to deny reality. So, lower-rank brothers and sisters were assigned, on a rotating basis, the honorable duty called *tunira*. The term, of uncertain origin, had come to mean "holy receptacle." Curious about it, Kifo had once done some research. There had been two likely candidates for the basis word: a Southern Tembonese word, "tchondra," which meant "servant," and a Swarussi term, "tundudira," which meant "hole." Either, Kifo supposed, was equally useful.

Two minutes later the door to his cube chimed. He called it open, and the sister, draped in her robes, stepped inside. Her cowl was back and her face was flushed. She was young, one of the newer ones, and Kifo could not recall seeing her in *tunira* before.

"My Unique," she said. Her voice was soft, with a slight quaver.

Kifo found this caused his erection to grow even more.

He smiled at her. Motioned at her clothing.

She slipped the robe off. Stood naked in front of him. Her breasts were heavy, her mons swathed in thick curly

his solar plexus harder than anything had ever done before
stole his wind despite the protective sheathing of his bunched
muscles—

The man dropped the sword and lunged forward, grabbed
at Bork's shoulders; despite all the years of training, the matador's most basic instincts took over—he locked arms with the
attacker. At the bottom of everything he was lay his great
physical strength, that which he had been able to depend upon
longer than any skill he had. It had never failed him.

They stood like two figures in a holographic statue, strain-
ing. Bork, who had never been bested in a contest of strength,
put everything he had into tossing the attacker to the floor—

And the man grunted and threw Bork into the nearest wall.

The surprise was as bad as the impact. Bork's head slammed
against the wall, cracked and starred the heavy plastic. Stunned
him. Now the sumito pattern tried to claim him, now Bork
would have danced aside and used his skill to defeat the
other, but his reactions were crippled, his senses fogged, his
brain bruised. As he shifted to the side, hands coming up, the
lights went out in the control room of Bork's mind. He fell
unconscious.

Five seconds had passed since the alarm started.

Taz heard the interior alarm go off. She snatched her spring
pistol from its holster and ran for the entrance. She could see
vague forms behind the moisture-fogged plastic but couldn't
make them out. She thought she saw Celona Jorine, and two
huge figures wrestling a few meters away. Nobody was supposed to be inside but Saval and the old lady! How could
anybody have gotten in?

She pulled her coded admit card from her pocket as she
reached the door—

Under him, the young woman moaned quietly in time to
Kifo's thrusts. Her breasts bobbed, rippling in waves, and
her face and body were drenched in sweat. Propped on his
hands, arms outstretched fully, resting most of his weight

on his groin, he jammed himself into her, smacking their pubic bones together almost painfully. He didn't care. He was racing to reach his climax and nothing else mattered, nothing in the galaxy. He moved faster and faster, until her moans were almost a continuous drone and he felt the pressure gathering . . . gathering . . . almost there—!

Bork's vision cleared. He was lying on his side, staring at the base of a bush covered with green thorns. The air smelled funny, a sweetish odor. Roses, he realized. He couldn't remember how he had gotten here. He had no idea how long he had been here.

An alarm *chirred,* over and over, and a woman screamed.

Bork shoved himself up. His head nearly exploded, red plashed over his eyes, he throbbed in tune to his heartbeat. What—?

A big robed figure was approaching an old woman. Bork didn't know who they were, but the big one had a sword.

Whose side was he on? Bork had time to wonder.

The woman screamed again.

"Hey!" Bork yelled. That hurt his head. "Hey! Stop!"

The big robed figure turned. Bork pointed his hands at the guy, both spetsdöds centered on the guy's chest. "Put down the sword!"

The man had something wrong with his face.

A flash of memory hit Bork like a strobe. Being tossed through the air like a child. Bork blinked, shook his head. No. Couldn't be.

The swordsman was five meters away; he could reach Bork in a second, he hurried. "Put it down!"

What was that on the front of his robe? Looked like flies stuck there; no, those were darts. What did that mean?

Armorweave, that's what.

The blackness swam up from some hidden depth and tried to claim him. Bork could feel himself losing it. He staggered, fell to one knee. Fought the thing trying to drag him under. Wished he knew what was going on.

The robed man looked back at the old woman, who w
making a pretty good speed for parts elsewhere. Glanced ba
at Bork. Turned to follow the woman.

"No!" As the darkness washed over his sight, Bork remem
bered that his left spetsdöd carried special loads. He point
the weapon and triggered it. It coughed five times. Only fiv
He didn't hear any explosions. Must be armor-piercing,
thought, only had five in the magazine. And explosive roun
would explode, right?

The last thing he saw before he went under the black v
again was the robed figure grabbing at one shoulder a
staggering. Gotcha, he thought.

Gone.

Bork awoke in a medical box, a minimum Healy un
looked like. Didn't even have the lid down. Taz and somebo
he didn't know stood next to him.

Some of it came back immediately. The client!

"The old lady?"

"Okay," Taz said. "She, uh, got hit on the buttock by one
your darts. Punched right through, didn't do any real damag
She's awake now and pissed off."

"What about the big guy in the robe?"

Taz shook her head. "No sign of him."

That surprised him. "I hit him with an AP dart. He shou
have gone down. How long?"

"You've been out for three hours. The labbos dug arou
outside and found four darts, counting the one that poked
hole in M. Jorine. They say that's all there is."

"I shot all five."

"Then the assassin must have taken it with him."

Bork tried to shake his head. Ouch. "I don't see how. I
took a solid hit. He should have been out."

"Well, maybe he is, but he managed to hide himself real goo
According to the computer, nobody came or went through a
door. Into the atmosphere, poof."

"He wasn't a ghost. Big guy in a dark robe, skinmask. Had sword."

"That's what M. Jorine said. Incidentally, she's decided she as business offworld after all. Going to the Faust System to isit an old friend on Bocca."

Bork thought about that. Then: "How did he get in?"

"I don't know, Saval. We thought you could tell us."

"No. When the alarm went off he was right behind me, not wo meters. Almost took my head off with that sword; would ave, I hadn't moved."

Taz nodded, didn't speak.

The rest of it began to filter in. Some of it was garbled, had o be. There was that part about being thrown into the wall as he were nothing. That had to be wrong.

"You have a concussion, but no major bleeding or brain amage," Taz said. "According to the medics, it's a miracle ou could stand up or move at all after smashing your head gainst the wall like that. The plastic is supposed to be shatter-roof and you cracked it like an eggshell. I told them the Borks ere hard-headed."

Bork blinked. So. That part was right. Whoever the guy as, he was stronger than Bork. A lot stronger. That didn't o down too well. It lay bitter and heavy in Bork's stomach.

was one thing to suspect you weren't the strongest man in e galaxy, another thing to have it graphically demonstrated. Vorse than an invisible assassin, that, which was bad enough. Ie'd relied on his strength instead of his fighting skills and at great power had, for the first time ever, been inadequate or the task.

Bork didn't like that at all. It surprised him, disappointed im, and worst of all, it made him afraid.

SIXTEEN _____

THE UNIQUE OF the Few was disturbed. He had slaked his
sexual thirst and had been quite relaxed—until the news about
Mkono reached him. The biggest and most powerful of the
Few was in the Temple's medical unit, recovering from a
chemical dart fired into him by a projectile weapon.

As he hurried to the unit to see Brother Mkono, Kifo felt a
small worry gnaw at him. True, he had told the Hand that the
road would be thick with danger but he hadn't really believed
it himself. For things to go bad so quickly . . . well, he hadn't
thought it would actually happen.

The worry bit deeper. Chuckled through bloody pointed
little teeth at his discomfort.

"Where is Brother Mkono?"

"This way, Unique."

The big man lay naked on a stasis board, bathed in UV and
assorted healing sonics. Supposedly the human ear could not
perceive these sounds but Kifo always imagined he could hear
a shrill whine dancing through his head when he was near the
medical generators.

"Brother Hand."

Thick muscles bunched in the man's chest. "Brother Death.
I—I am filled with shame. I have failed."

"That is not for you to decide," Kifo said. "Speak to me of
your efforts."

Mkono told the story. He had surprised the matador, had made to cut him down but somehow the other had detected him and avoided the beheading stroke. They had struggled and he had beaten the infidel, but only just barely.

This was in itself fairly amazing to Kifo. The matador must be a formidable foe.

He, Mkono continued, had thought the other too badly injured to continue resistance and had made to slay the target. But the guard had somehow recovered and had shot him with a weapon that defeated the power of the armorweave robe. He had been struck by a chemical dart. It had nearly brought him low, but he had called upon the gods and withstood the poison that called him to sleep. Escaped. Made his way to the rendezvous where the others waited. Been brought back here.

"I tender my position as Hand immediately," he finished.

Kifo blinked. Considered it for maybe a second. "No," he said. "You will continue as Hand, brother. Know that this was only a test and that you have passed it."

The big man frowned. "I do not understand, my Unique."

"In your duties as Hand, have you ever faltered before?"

"No."

"Have any been able to resist and prevail against you?"

"Not until now."

"The gods wished for you to understand that no man is unbeatable, no man can take for granted his own power when compared to the gods."

Mkono's frown deepened. "I still do not see."

"It is the gods who did this to you, brother. You have grown too confident in your skills. They would have you see that you must always be humble, you must never take for granted any victory. Tell me, did you fear you would fail when you began this mission? Had you any doubt at all?"

"In truth, no."

"Ah, but you should have had some thought that failure might happen. A man who knows it is possible will take care to be certain of every move, is this not so?"

"I—yes, I can see that. Then the gods must be displeased with me for my pride."

"Only a little, brother. For did they not allow you to overcome your wound and return here, to recover and return to their service?"

Mkono's knotted brow relaxed somewhat. "Yes. That is true."

"Then consider this a lesson well and cheaply learned, and rededicate yourself to serve."

"I shall, Brother Death."

Kifo clapped Mkono on his uninjured shoulder. It was like slapping a cloth-covered stone.

But as Kifo returned to his own cube, he was still disturbed. It was easy enough to set Mkono's worries to rest; the tiny but worrisome beast chewing at his entrails was not so easily placated. When one such as massive and dedicated Mkono was thwarted, then the man who did such a thing should not be taken too lightly a second time.

In the client's house control room, Bork reviewed the recordings taken by the security cameras. The photomutable gel eyes were set to cover ways in and out of the greenhouse. One of them had a blurry image of the attacker's back, his face not visible, as he moved toward the client. Even with full augmentation, the computer couldn't give them anything more than an estimate as to height and weight, no facial features or even racial characteristics. Guy wasn't basic human, Bork would damnsure bet on that. Some kind of HG mue, maybe even Bork's own stock. And stronger, too.

Why hadn't the cams seen him come in? Or leave? The doors were all clean, nobody in but Taz. Did he have some kind of electronic confounder, something new that could rascal the comp? Bork hadn't heard about anything that could defeat the system he'd installed, but that didn't mean it wasn't possible. He'd got in somehow, and must have left the same way. Even if he were invisible, had a shiftsuit that would put any Bork knew about to shame, the doors would have recorded any openings. And there weren't any holes big enough for a fly to squeeze through. Damn.

Taz entered the room. "She's away," she said. "Police box-car to a star hopper, a quad of ours and ten of her guards along for the ride. She'll be out of the system in a few hours."

"They followed you to Muto Kato," he said.

"I didn't make any effort to hide that I was going. M. Jorine is under wraps tight enough to make her eyes bulge. I don't know the name of the ship she's taking. Or where she's going. At your suggestion, she decided to pick a different destination from where her relatives are. And nobody can follow a star ship in Bender space."

He shook his head. "The guy beat me. And almost took her out."

"But he didn't. You kept her alive."

"Barely."

" 'Barely' is a lot better than the whole force did before."

It didn't make Bork feel any better. He wasn't invincible. He had known that intellectually, but on some level way down past where the mind chugged away, he hadn't really believed it. Beat me? Come on. He knew there were people who could shoot better, some who were faster, some smarter. Not many. Now he knew there was at least one who was stronger. He hadn't really known that before. He didn't think there was anybody who was *all* those things, but now he wasn't sure.

And while he'd been lying in the Healy, he'd thought a lot about Veate and the baby. What would have happened to them if he had gotten killed? Sure, there'd been a lot of danger in his life but he'd never really worried about it before. Because he hadn't really faced the idea that he was ever gonna *lose*. Nothing like getting tossed on your ass to bring that possibility right into the fore, was there? Emile and Juete would be there for their grandchild, Bork didn't doubt that, they had extended family in the form of Sleel and Kee and Dirisha and Geneva, too, but—

But worrying about your spouse and child tended to dull your edge. And you couldn't afford to leap into a knife fight unless you were sharp; that *would* get you sliced up real quick. Especially if you were going up against somebody like the big man in the robes, a man who could throw you into a wall as if you were nothing.

Saval was lost in thought, and Taz moved quietly from the room and left him to it. She had mixed feelings about the episode with the assassin. On the one hand, she wished they could have stapled the guy and put a full stop to it. On the other hand, her brother *had* kept one of the Guillotine's intended victims in one piece instead of two. Aside from the life saved, her stock had risen in the department. She'd told them Saval would protect the woman and he'd done it. Not a completely successful operation, but the main objective was accomplished. Maybe they could catch the killer next time. If there were a next time.

Walking through the rows of fragrant flower bushes, Taz absently ran her thumb over the com unit on her belt. Found herself pulling the little plastic chunk free and beginning to make the call.

She stopped herself. Frowned at the com. She didn't want Ruul to hate her. But he hadn't called, not after her little trick with the pheromones. He was ashamed, she knew that. He didn't need to be. She'd almost commed him a dozen times, to tell him what she had done. I cheated, Ruul, she would say. It's not your fault. I'm sorry.

As she had before, she recrowed the com to her belt. Something wouldn't let her do it. Was it some kind of test? Was she trying to see how far she could push him, how long she could keep him dangling? Her motives were unclear and he didn't really know what she wanted from him.

Why the hell couldn't things be easier when it came to this kind of shit? Why couldn't she handle her love life the way she did her job? Put the pieces together in neat patterns and see the whole picture? Take the step she kept avoiding?

As she walked, she came to a strange-looking bush near the end of one of the rows. There were a number of red blossoms, but grafted onto the bush were two flowers that stood out against the darker hue. These were yellow, almost a butter color. One was open fully, the other still tightly closed, past the bud stage but not yet ready to unfurl. Odd, they looked almost like a mother and daughter there, surrounded by all the others.

Mother and daughter.

That opened up the gates in Taz's memory.

She had a name, but Taz at twelve seldom thought about her mother as anything other than "Ma." Just as "Da" was her father. She hadn't ever really related to them as people other than her parents. They must have had lives before she and Saval had been born, before they had met and married, but Ma had never talked about it.

Until the day Taz got her first menstrual flow.

Taz had taken sex edcom, she knew the physical manifestations and what they meant, but the actual event had been a surprise.

It was on Kaplan, in the Beta System, where her da had signed on with an ore extractor in the outback for a six-month job. They lived in one of the prefab everlast cubes the company provided for its workers; there were whole neighborhoods of them, all the same. Square, faded green blocks, evenly spaced along access roads, identically constructed inside and out. Some of the permanent workers had decorated the outsides, splashed them with color or planted fast-growing trees so they'd stand out, but you could still get lost easy unless you knew your row and cube number.

She'd been out playing with some of her friends, two of them were mues, two of them basic stockers, a complicated game that involved touching three people in a changing sequence for each tag. The day was springlike, even though it was still late winter, the sun shining brightly, the sky blue green and cloudless. Taz had made a touch and darted between two cubes and hidden under a mandrill bush. The boy chasing her had run past, missing her.

She'd grinned, but then felt something running down her leg under her skirt. Put her hand down to wipe it away and brought up bloody fingertips.

For a moment she thought she'd cut herself on the bush when she'd dived under it, but a quick examination showed the flow wasn't from a wound.

The cramps she'd put down yesterday to the green plums she'd eaten and the sense of nervousness she'd felt suddenly made a different kind of sense. Her flat breasts had been sore, too. She'd read about the signs of hormonal changes in the sex edcom; she was quick enough to know what had happened. Only last month Shev had started her cycles, and Taz had heard her bragging about it enough. So it wasn't a big deal, but even so, she suddenly found she wasn't interested in the game of digit tag any more. She pulled off her sockshoes, used the top of one to wipe her leg, then tucked it into her underwear to catch the blood.

She headed for home, hearing her friends yelling as they ran chasing each other. She felt . . . different. She had crossed over from being a child into some other realm. She wasn't a woman, not in the sense she thought of adult women, but she wasn't a kid any more, either.

Ma was working on the inside of the cube, stringing a thin and close-mesh net across the main room wall behind the holoproj. The net had moved with them for the last few years and Ma would attach different things to it as decoration in whichever temporary shelter they occupied. There was a holograph of her ma's mother, who had died before Taz was born. An air plant she'd gotten when they'd lived on Farbis. Two streamers of blue silk, ribbons Saval had won in singing contests. A poem Taz had written for Ma's birthday two years ago, so crude as to embarrass Taz whenever she saw it but which Ma refused to let her daughter throw away. Other little things that had some meaning to her.

Ma smiled when she saw Taz come in, then blinked and said, "Tazzi? Are you okay?"

Taz wanted to keep it a secret. But she also wanted to tell somebody who knew what it was like. That urge won out.

"Yeah. I—my cycle started!" She couldn't keep the excitement from her voice, even though she wanted to keep it matter-of-fact no-big-deal in tone.

Ma's smile came back, but with something new in it. Almost sad. "How wonderful," she said. "How wonderful." She came over and hugged Taz, and while that usually bothered Taz when her friends were around these days, right now it felt great.

People sometimes said they looked just alike, Ma and her; but Taz couldn't see it. Sure, Ma had the same dark hair on her head. And the wispy pubic fuzz Taz had recently sprouted was the same color, too, only it couldn't ever possibly get as thick as Ma's. She hoped it wouldn't; when Ma went swimming or lay on the beach, she looked like she had a furry animal curled up on her belly. Da thought it was great, he liked to tease her about it, but people would sometimes walk by and stare at Ma's crotch like it was weird and Taz didn't want that.

Too, Taz was big-boned like both parents, and she had that little cleft in her chin like Ma, but that was about it, as far as she could tell.

Well, until now. Now they had something else in common.

"Come on, I'll make you a fizzie," Ma said.

They went into the tiny kitchen and Ma opened the pantry and produced a cannister of the bubbly drink, shook it and squeezed the cooler ring. In was ready in a few seconds. Taz sipped at the icy fruit taste.

"I remember when I started," her mother said. "I was a year older than you. My ma never talked about it and my sex edcom was kind of spotty, we moved around so much. I thought I was sick, that I was dying."

"Funny," Taz said.

"Yes, it is, isn't it? Right away my breasts ballooned and my hips grew. In six months I had boys and girls calling for all kinds of new games." Ma shook her head. "Such a long time ago. I met your da not a year afterward. We got married in a few months. Saval was born a year later. I was fifteen T.S."

Taz did the math in her head. That would make her ma thirty-one T.S. now. Old. Real old.

"I can't complain. You and Savvie are the lights of my life. And your da, well, he used to be really something before work wore him down so much. Used to laugh a lot, bring me little gifts, take me to concerts and fests."

Da? *Her* da did that?

"I could have had a job, I had the right genetics for it, but my family was old-style, just like Cemer's."

For an instant the name didn't mean anything. Oh, Da, of course.

"You don't see much of that any more, old-style contracts. Not much tradition left today, but our families would have curled up and died if they thought we were going against it. Most contracts today are open-marriage, non-trads, group or limited-term or whatever. Not the Borks and the Takstines, though. We sign on for lifetime contracts. All or nothing, that's us."

Her mother sighed. "You miss a lot that way. But there is a strength there you don't get with a renewable or communal. It's hard, but . . ." she trailed off.

Taz felt a great sadness welling from her mother, a deep and painful flow that washed over her. She didn't fully understand it, but later she would determine that the single word which described it best was . . . regret.

"But it has been worth it," her mother said. "Really."

The hormones surging through her system must have been affecting Taz, she knew that later, too, but in that moment, what she felt from her mother was that her marriage to Taz's father had been anything but worth it.

"Someday you'll see," Ma said. Then, "Come on, we need to get you some insert buttons until we can get your implant and suppressor. Back when I was a girl, we had to go through this bleeding every month."

That seemed pretty unreal to Taz. Everybody just got a suppressor and that stopped it, unless you were allergic or something. How messy it would be otherwise, having to put in buttons and change them when they got soaked. Yuk.

And the conversation about her mother's youth and marriage was overshadowed by the importance of what was happening to her. She didn't think about it until years later. And by then, it didn't really matter any more.

Looking at the rosebush, Taz shook her head. No. She wouldn't call Ruul. Damned if she would. She had a murderer to catch, a life of her own. If Ruul wanted to sulk and feel bad, that was his problem. Not hers.

Really. It wasn't.

SEVENTEEN _____

IT CAME TO Kifo as he sat meditating that the war against the unbelievers needed to escalate. Thus far he had merely been picking the worst offenders off one by one. Most probably had not known what they had done, or to whom they had done it, and that was part of the original strategy. First he had to create a fear so deep that when he finally did reveal to the next victims what he wished and why he wished it so, they would be terrified enough not to spill the information to the authorities. It would not do that the police realized too much too soon. Not until the gods were ready to assume their places.

Now, however, he could see that his chosen path was too narrow. It must be widened, turned into a twelve-lane travelway, and that meant removing a great number of obstacles in a hurry. It was time to move, and if that required hundreds or thousands or even millions of people had to be crushed under the machineries, then so be it. Nothing could be allowed to thwart the will of the gods, no heart among the Few allowed to be faint, regardless of the cost. Still, he could hardly hope to be so ambitious with only one Hand at his disposal. One could only do what one could.

Kifo smiled. The price for becoming a god might be high but certainly he was willing to pay whatever it took. A pity he did not have godlike resources at his beck. To wave his hand and remove hordes would be fine indeed.

• • •

Bork was in Taz's gym, but he couldn't seem to get his workout going. The weights seemed heavier than usual; the kiloage he normally handled with ease he could barely move today. He kept thinking about his failure.

"Saval?" came the voice over the house intercom.

"Yeah?"

"The computer has got something for us."

"On my way." He was glad for an excuse to shortstop his session. Had the decay of age he sometimes worried about set in? Was it the depression from his encounter with the hooded giant? Or something as simple as the crack on the head? It didn't matter. He had something to do and that was his main focus now, finding the assassin.

Because when he found him, Bork would get a chance to even the score.

Taz voiceaxed the computer and called up the stats. Graphs and charts and lines of data lit the air over the console. Next to her, Saval scanned the material while she talked.

"The cruncher came up with this," she said, waving at the holoproj. "Nine of the thirteen victims, plus Celona Jorine, all gave money to the Center for Tolerance and Reason."

"Which is . . . ?"

"A kind of unitarian thinktank HQed on Simba(.)Numa. They espouse some encompassing faith, all people are brothers and sisters, all religions are paths up the mountain and equally valid, like that."

Saval nodded. "Okay. So ten of fourteen gave these people money?"

"According to the records uncovered so far. Now that we know what to look for, the computer is trying to find if the others might have contributed. Could have done it anonymously, maybe."

"It must mean something," Saval said. "But what? Who would be pissed off enough at them for doing this to kill them? If this is the real reason?"

"I dunno. Let's talk to somebody there and see can we find out."

A few minutes later they had a line to the Information Chief of the CTR on the next-door-neighbor planet. The chief was a florid-faced, heavyset woman of sixty, hair worn long and in a swept-forward breaker-style that threw a shadow over her forehead and nose. Because it was close insofar as White Radio distances went, there was almost a ten-second time lag in transmission.

"Who," Taz asked, "would dislike your patrons enough to consider killing them?"

After the back-and-forth delay, the woman said, "Militant factions in any one of thirty or forty religious denominations I can think of might go that far. We preach tolerance here, and universality. Those who consider themselves upon the only true path can be threatened by the idea they are only one of many."

"Hard to believe," Saval said.

"M. Bork, throughout history the bloodiest wars have always been religious ones. Holy men who would turn the other cheek over property or national boundaries, who would not lift a hand to protect the life of a brother, will sometimes cheerfully slaughter a room full of newborn babies in the name of their god. If you *know* you will go straight to your version of paradise to sit at the hand of your deity when you die, you might happily charge barehanded and naked an army—you have everything to gain if your faith is strong enough."

"Yeah, I guess I knew that."

"We preach a kind of unconditional love. Most religions attach a lot of strings to their rewards. You toe the line or you lose the prize. We tell people they don't have to do it. Those who preach otherwise think we're calling them liars, or worse, that their gods are false ones. We don't, but they sometimes choose to see it that way."

After the connection was sundered, Saval and Taz looked at each other. "It's a break," she said. "I'll have comp central pull a list of all the established religions on Tembo. We can eliminate the mild ones right off—I don't see the Buddhists or the Trimenagists or the Jains lopping off the heads of their enemies. We should be able to find this kind of fanatical organization pretty quick."

"It could be just one twisted arrow," he said. "Might not be official church policy."

She shrugged. "Better than what we had before. It's something to run down."

"Yeah, you right about that."

While they waited for the download from comp central, Bork sat staring at the wall. Even if the assassin was a religious fanatic of some kind, that didn't explain *how* he had gotten into the locked and guarded rooms. Teleportation wasn't possible, unless somebody had made a breakthrough in physics and kept it to themselves. Somehow, however, somebody had defeated all the state-of-the-art sensors Bork had set up, bypassed the wards and gotten in—unless they had already been there. That seemed as impossible as materializing out of the air, given the scans and direct searching Bork had done. Teleportation *and* time travel, maybe.

Yeah. Right. That didn't seem real likely.

But they *had* gotten in, so it was possible; start from there. But—*how*?

Before the information she'd requested was finished loading into her portable flatscreen, Taz got a call from the early-shift WC.

"Your friend the Guillotine sent in more threats," the WC said.

"More, plural?"

"Yeah. Fifty of 'em so far. The calls are still coming in."

"Jesu Damn."

"Yeah, well, it's worse. One of 'em is already past tense. And your friend has stopped messing around with swords."

"What does that mean?"

"It means somebody tucked a military-grade implosion bomb into the victim's cube. He's inside a supercompacted ball along with his mistress, two dogs and some expensive artwork and bedding, all squashed flatter than a wirehead's dick. The labbos are running around like ants on a hot plate."

"Oh, fuck!"

"You better get your butt in Bender and shift to hyper, Chief. The media are pounding on the doors and screaming for blood and the Supe will have to throw them somebody to keep it from being his."

Before the WC had faded from the air, another incoming call lit the com. "Who the fuck is it?"

"Ruul Oro," the computer informed her.

Ah, shit. Not now. She didn't need this *now*!

Taz swallowed. "Put it through."

Ruul's golden visage shined from the proj.

"Hello, Taz."

"Ruul, look, I know I owe you an apology and an explanation, I really shouldn't have done what I did, I'm sorry, but I'm really jammed here now—"

"This is professional, Taz, not personal."

"Huh?"

"You know that assassin thing you're working on?"

"I'm up to my eyebrows in it," she said.

"Well, I must have offended somebody."

Her heart froze; her body felt as if it had been shoved into a deep pool of liquid oxy. No. Don't say it, please let it be something else! "Ruul—?"

"Yep, it seems I've made it onto the killer's short list, Tazzi."

For a wild moment, she thought she could hear whichever god she'd offended laughing maniacally in the distance.

When Taz came into the room, she was pale and shaking. Bork came up from the couch. "Taz?"

"The killer has made more threats," she said. Her voice was calm, almost matter-of-fact. "He's gotten expansive. More

than fifty people threatened so far. And one of them has
already been murdered—with an implosion bomb."

"And—?"

"And one of the new would-be victims is Ruul Oro."

"You better sit down and tell me about it," he said.

She nodded. Moved to the couch. Sat.

"I told you we were lovers," she said. "But it was—is—
more than that. There's is a . . . depth there, Saval. I think
about him all the time. I want to be with him, to make love
to him, to run around and cook and clean for him, to make
sure he's dressed right, his hair is styled, to hear him laugh,
just to sit and watch him sleep."

Bork shrugged. "You love him."

"Yes."

"And he doesn't love you?"

"Worse. He *does.*"

He frowned. "I'm missing something here. You love him,
he loves you. What's the problem?"

"He wants to marry me. Lifetime contract. Oh, he's not like
Da, I can work if I want, we can have children or not, I won't
have to sit at his house while he's out in the world with nothing
to do, he wants me to do whatever I want."

"But you don't want to marry him."

"I *can't.* You know how it was with Ma. I won't be enslaved
like she was, trapped in something she couldn't leave! I saw
what happened to Ma. She lived and breathed on Da's whim.
Half her life was spent waiting for him to come home. When
he died, she died. She still breathes, but she's gone. He was
everything to her."

"Taz, it's not the same. You're not our mother. You have a
job, you already have a life."

"You don't understand, Saval. I do now. But if I were
around Ruul, I would do whatever he asked me to do. Quit
my job, stay home, anything. I can *feel* it in myself. I want to
please him so bad it feels like a knife in my belly when I do
anything to disappoint him. If he frowns I feel physical pain.
It scares me, it scares the piss out of me. The only way I can

manage it at all is to stay away from him. The last time we were together I knew he wanted me. But he has refused to have sex with me unless I marry him. He is like our parents, he believes in old-style mate contracts. But I knew he wanted me, so I seduced him. Then I felt guilty for making *him* feel guilty!"

Bork slid over and put his arm around his sister.

"And now this. The killer wants him. If Ruul dies, then my problem is solved, right? I'll be free.

"But if he dies, I won't be able to stand it!"

"Have you discussed this with him?"

"A few thousand times. I've told him I can't marry him but he won't listen to it. With him it's all or nothing."

"Sounds like a problem, all right."

"Yeah, well, it's worse. He's coming here."

"Here?"

"Yeah. I can't stop what I'm doing to go and guard him. But I don't trust anybody else to take care of him, either." She looked at him.

"I'll watch him, kid."

"Thank you, Saval."

"Might get uncomfortable for you."

"I don't want anything to happen to him. After this all gets sorted out, then I'll worry about what happens between us."

"No problem."

She looked at him. "No problem? Damn, Saval, it seems like *every*thing is a problem. Why can't things be simple? There are days when I just want to stay in bed and hide under the covers."

"Welcome to the club, kid."

"Come on."

"You think you're the only person to ever get overwhelmed by life? We all feel like that. Everybody else seems to be smiling and happy and in control and you look in the mirror and see the failure of the century. It's the ten thousand all at once."

"Huh?"

"Old quote, mythical swordsman on Earth, eight hundred or a thousand years back. When faced with ten thousand opponents, fight one at a time. First one, then the second, the third and so on until you get through 'em. Don't try to fight 'em all at once, you'll be defeated by the odds before you start. One at a time makes it a lot easier."

"Even so, you'll have to move like you have a Bender drive in your ass or you'll get chopped into soypro," she said.

"Well, yeah, there's that. But you know what I mean."

She nodded. "Yeah. I think so. The journey of a thousand klicks begins with one step. I lose sight of that sometimes."

"We all do, kid. So you take a deep breath and start over again. No big deal."

She grinned. "You'd really bite him for me?"

"You know it."

"Thanks, Saval."

"No problem."

EIGHTEEN

RUUL ARRIVED IN a police traffic flitter and was tendered by his escorts to Taz and Bork.

Bork watched the meeting between his sister and her lover. The space between them was so full of energy you could almost hear it crackle. They both tried to pretend it wasn't there, but to walk between them would be to risk being knocked flat by the flow. Whatever else was going on, this was going to be interesting.

"Come on," Taz said. "We've got to get moving. Two more bombs have gone off. We have people gearing up for a full-blown panic."

Bork admired his sister's attempt at professionalism. He didn't think it was fooling anybody, but she got points for trying.

The three of them left in her flitter.

Taz found she was breathing too fast and forced herself to slow her respiration. Damn, she didn't need this. Whoever was responsible for this shit was really in trouble now, forcing her into this situation. No, she didn't *have* to watch over Ruul personally. Then again, if anything happened to him and she hadn't done everything she could to keep it from happening, she wouldn't be able to look at herself in a mirror ever again. Dammit!

"Where," Saval said, "are we going?"

"Next guy on the list is only a few klicks from here. We want to get there before the killer does."

Saval glanced at Ruul, then back at her.

"Yeah, yeah, I know," she said. "Still, better with us than not."

Ruul grinned. Taz knew he understood the semi-fugue she and Saval had just played. They were taking him into the jaws of the beast. And Saval's lips twitched with a little grin of his own as he saw Ruul get it.

God, she *hated* this!

As they approached the neighborhood where one of the would-be victims lived, they were overtaken and nearly run off the road by a hovertruck.

"Man in a big hurry," Ruul observed.

Taz watched the truck speed away ahead of them. Thing was pumping a lot of air through its fans and, even so, was still riding awful low. Must be hauling something real heavy.

Yeah, so? That's what trucks do, haul things. Big deal.

There wasn't anything she could put a precise name to, but the truck bothered her. Her car wore a PO designation, flasher and glowbars. For a driver to go whipping around a cool's flitter like that was not real bright. Why was the guy willing to risk a traffic infraction that way? What was so important?

She reached for her com space, double-waved it on. "This is Assistant Chief Bork," she said. "I had a roegg just blast past in an MT van that's dusting the surface with its skirts. He's heading north on Silhouette Lane, cross street Sheen. Somebody pull him over and find out where the fire is."

A TC unit three blocks ahead acknowledged her call. "Copy, Chief. I got 'im."

"People getting blown in and you're worried about a speeding truck?" Ruul said. "Ah, you cools."

"I don't tell you how to deliver jokes, you don't tell me how to deliver the peace." There was a sharp edge in her voice.

"Ouch," Ruul said. "Excuse the blood here."

Don't do this, Ruul—

"We got a runner here," came a bored and cynical voice over the com. "The Chief's truck is ignoring my flashers and blowing faster." Then the voice changed: "Fuck! He's shooting at me! This is TC nine-three, I'm calling a code four-one-six. I got me a shooter here, looks like an automatic shotgun, shit—!"

Taz didn't believe in coincidences when they involved guns. This truck was connected to the assassinations. "Nine-three, stay with him. I'm right behind you."

Two other TC units added their voices to the com, then cleared the opchan. Nine-three started a running monologue.

"—there is a passenger, he's doing the gunwork. Looks like two of 'em, don't see any more. We're turning onto Bracken Avenue, moving west. I'm casting police override now . . . Nope, no good, he'd not slowing, must be running with an illegal coil—damn! My windshield just took a load of shot, looks like number four buck. Low-powered, bet it's air, didn't penetrate more than a millimeter or so. Look out! Stupid son-of-a-shit just wiped out a parked flitter, man, just ate the goddamned side right off it . . ."

Taz rounded the corner, saw the TC unit's glowbar and flashers a block ahead. She opened the throttle and her flitter sped up.

"On your tail, Nine-three."

"We got a block set up here," somebody said. "Corner of Bracken and La Kuhara. We've laid goo, Po'children, watch your fans."

Ruul said, "Goo?"

"Anything using ground effect will be pulling in air for the fans," Taz said. "Goo is a memoryslick plastic fiber. Looks like baby powder when you lay it down. It gets sucked up by the GE intakes, buckyballs right through the particle filters. When the fans chew it, it clumps and reverts to its original casting, which is basically string."

"There he is," somebody said over the com. "Come to daddy, dickhole."

Saval picked it up. "The fans will shut down automatically as the goo jams them. Takes about ten seconds. Even if the guy's got full-flight repellors, he's in a forced-landing situation, and even if he *could* override the safeties, his fans won't give him enough push to maneuver or drive his rollers. End of chase."

"Nice stuff to leave lying on the road for the citizens to fly over," Ruul said.

"That's the beauty of it," Saval said. "Goo biodegrades about twenty minutes after you expose it to the air. Turns into harmless dust."

"Gotcha!" somebody yelled.

Taz throttled her own fans down, dropped the flitter on its rollers, then killed the engine. Her vehicle slowed immediately but still had enough momentum to coast a considerable way. She saw the traffic units ahead of her, saw the hovertruck skid as it fell onto its rollers. The truck slewed, smashed into one of the traffic flitters, eliciting a "Fuck!" from her com. The driver straightened the larger vehicle and continued on for another two hundred meters, slowing to a stop.

Taz rolled through the block and since she wasn't under power, had no problem. The remains of the powdered goo blew up around her flitter in a haze of psychedelic-orange dust. Then they were through and coasting toward the stopped truck. Half a dozen uniforms ran along the road, guns drawn.

The two men in the truck—no, the passenger was a woman—came out shooting. The driver had some kind of carbine, the passenger a shotgun. The driver snapped the carbine up and fired a burst on full auto. The solid slugs hit Taz's windshield, stitched a half dozen dark splotches across it in a descending line from left to right.

"Shit!" Ruul lunged forward and put an arm in front of her.

The windshield was centimeter-thick clear carbonex and it flattened the jacketed metal bullets and stopped them easily.

Taz thought that the weight of Ruul's arm across her chest was quite the nicest thing she had ever felt. He didn't know that her windshield was proof against ordinary gunfire. His first reaction was not to flinch away from the bullets, but to try and protect her. It made her want to cry. Why couldn't he have some goddamn flaws? She made a joke of it: "Damn, I just had the scratches polished out last week."

Ruul apparently realized his arm wasn't going to do her much good and pulled it away. He clamped his hands onto the back of her headrest.

"They don't want us to get the truck," Bork said. "They aren't trying to get away."

Taz braked the still-moving flitter to a stop twenty meters from the shooters. Bullets spanged off her flitter's front armor. "I'll give 'em something else to worry about," she said. With that, she dialed the warblers and flashers up to full. The noise dampers in the flitter cut the roar of sound, but the vibrations of it still came through, thrumming deep in her chest. The flashing lights strobed the two gunplayers with eye-smiting beams. They apparently weren't wearing polarizing droptacs, for both tried to block the flashing lights with upraised hands.

"Stay here, Ruul," Taz said. She glanced at Bork. "Go!"

Taz shoved her door open and rolled out onto the road. The cacophony from the warblers thumped her ears. She came up in a kneeling stance, her spring pistol in both hands. She was distantly aware of Saval moving to her right, more dimly aware that the nearest khaki uniforms were still thirty meters behind them.

She heard Saval's spetsdöd go off and she squeezed the trigger on her own weapon. The driver was about eighteen meters away; she held on his chest.

He fired the carbine, one-handed, but his aim was bad and he dug small craters in the roadway to her left.

Her dart took him and he spun away, trying to run.

The woman was already crumpling as Taz swung her pistol over to shoot.

The man slapped at the middle of his back with one hand as he fell and hit on his knees, then toppled forward face down.

Taz shot the woman, but she was almost prone by then and she guessed her dart missed. Didn't matter. They were both down.

Saval moved right, circling the truck.

Taz got up, crouched and edged left, gun covering the truck. Nobody else got out.

The uniforms started arriving. A loudcast voice boomed out: "YOU IN THE TRUCK, DROP YOUR WEAPONS AND COME OUT!"

Nobody did.

Taz moved so that she could see the open cab was empty.

Somebody shut off the warblers in her flitter. It got real quiet.

One of the uniforms accessed the loading ramp. The door slid up, the ramp extruded.

Except for a thick slab of gunmetal-blue about two meters tall, the cargo area was also empty.

Taz raised from her combat crouch. Holstered her pistol. Looked at the block in the truck. She'd seen something like this before. Where . . . ?

Ah. At the Zonn Ruins. This was a piece of a wall.

Damn. She thought they'd had the assassins. Instead, it looked like all they'd done was collect a couple of antiquity thieves. Damn.

Bork hung back while Taz went to talk to her fellow cools. Ruul moved up to stand next to him.

"I hate this," Ruul said. He nodded at Taz. "She could have been shot. Hurt or killed."

"She's a very good cool," Bork said.

"Yeah, I know. Doesn't make it any easier." He looked up at Bork. "I love her, you know."

"I know."

"She tell you what our problem is?"

"She might have mentioned something about it."

Ruul shook his head. "I don't understand women. I love her. She says she loves me. All I want to do is have her around, all the time. I want to *do* things for her, take care of her. Cook her meals. Sleep with her. I want her to live with me for the rest of our lives. She doesn't want that."

Bork said nothing. Funny. That's exactly what she does want.

"I don't understand. You married?"

"Yeah. Got a baby son."

"Ah."

Bork said. "Being contracted doesn't help. I don't understand women either. Seems like the older I get, the less I know."

"Fuck if that ain't right," Ruul said.

It wasn't really his place, but Bork felt for Ruul. He liked the guy. "It'll work out," he said.

"You think so?"

"Well. No guarantees. Taz has got some old recordings to deal with, it might take some time. Family stuff."

Ruul sighed. "I'll wait as long as it takes."

Bork nodded, didn't speak. He thought maybe Ruul just might. The two of them watched Taz direct the uniformed officers.

NINETEEN _____

A TRAUMA TEAM hauled the two unconscious prisoners to the medical unit. The thieves should be fine once they recovered from the effects of Taz and Saval's darts.

But as Taz stood watching the lab workers go over the truck, several things didn't make sense. Most heisters didn't fool around with guns, so potting at the traffic cool was unusual enough. Could be they were repeaters and a fall for this would be a hard one; still, it felt wrong.

Then there was the hunk of Zonn wall in the cargo area. The closest place they could have gotten it was way the hell and gone out the Snake Road—there weren't any ports in this direction, space or sea, no mag-rails, nothing. Where were they going with it? Planning on driving into the interior on a main flatway? That was pretty stupid; they had to know even a routine stop-and-look would trip them up. Okay, maybe they had a private boxcar stashed in the woods somewhere, but Orbital Control would spot it soon as it hit the grid and the Coast Guard would go calling. Lot of risk for an antique with no value except to a collector.

Plus there was the fact that nothing had been reported stolen from the ruins. There were full-time guards there; it wasn't a matter of sticking the thing in a back pocket and strolling off with it: this artifact had to weigh twelve, maybe fifteen hundred kilos. That meant machinery to lift and transport it to

the truck. And a call to the guards had come up blank. Either
they were asleep out there or the slab came from somewhere
else. And if that were the case, where *had* it come from?

Yeah, something was off here.

"Anything on the victim we were going to see?" Saval
asked.

"No. It's quiet there."

They both looked at the truck. "I think maybe these two
might be involved," Taz said. "I thought so at first, changed
my mind when I saw they'd swiped that"—she pointed at the
chunk of Zonn material—"but now I think maybe my first hit
was on the mark."

Ruul said, "Why? Were they going to drop it on somebody?
Seems like a pretty inefficient killing device, you ask me."

Taz started to snap at him—Nobody *asked* you, Ruul—but
he had a point. There wasn't anything logical about it, it was
just a feeling.

Saval said, "I hear you, Taz. It could be just a coincidence.
But maybe not."

"Chief?" came a voice from her com.

"Go."

"This is Biltless, in the wagon. The IDs on the two perps
are phony."

"What a surprise," she said.

"We're running retinal scans. Should have something in a
minute . . . uh-oh."

"What?" Taz said.

There came background shouts, medical types spouting
jargon:

"—class four convulsions, watch his hand—!"

"—Christo, she's arresting—!"

"—What the hell is going on—?"

"Biltless!"

"Chief, the perps are going bugfuck here!"

More background walla:

"—damn, damn, he's shut down, no pulse here!"

"—she's puking and aspirating the vomitus—!"

There was a long pause after that. Taz called Biltless, got no answer.

Then: "Chief, Biltless."

"What's going on?"

"The perps, ah, they're dead, Chief."

"Dead?"

"Yeah. Some kind of reaction to the stingers or the 'död darts the medics think, maybe."

Taz and Saval exchanged glances. Saval shook his head.

"What?" Ruul said. "What?"

"Just like on Muto Kato," Taz said. "The guy who shot at me there, he died when they tried to question him. Some kind of mental *tsunami,* a block. These guys are connected to it."

"*Were* connected," Saval said.

"Damn," Taz said.

"Now what?" Ruul said.

"We got two bodies, a truck and a stolen artifact," Taz said. "That's more than we had an hour ago. We start to run them all down. Records will find out everything we know about the truck. We've tapped into the GALAX crime net for reports on missing Zonn stuff. If the two dead guys have ever been eyeprinted in this system, we'll get some kind of ID on them. Then we put it all together."

"How long will it take?"

"However long it takes," Taz said. "Meanwhile, it seems as if the assassinations have stopped. We still have to eat. Let's drop by the Owl and see what looks good."

"You are so damned calm about all this," Ruul said. "I don't understand how you can do that."

"Part of the job, right, Saval?"

"Right," Bork said.

At the Owl they managed to get all the way to a table before Pickle showed up. "Ah," the woman said, "I see you two are keeping company again."

"In a manner of speaking," Taz said. "Everything okay here?"

Pickle made a rude sound. "All this killing business is so awful. What stupid people they must be. Irritating in the extreme."

Ruul said, "You sound upset. You didn't get threatened, did you?"

Before Pickle could speak, Taz cut in. "No. And that's why she's upset, isn't it, sweetie? Didn't make somebody's list?"

You could have slain a room full of diabetics with Pickle's smile. "You know, for a fat and torpid cool you do manage a lucky shot now and then, Tazzi. Dear."

Pickle turned away and stopped a waiter with her icy stare. "This table eats for free tonight," she said. "Later, loves." She spotted somebody near the door. "Oh, Temano! How good to see you again!" She hurried away.

"You got her, but you'll be sorry," Ruul said.

"I know. Her claws will be so sharp next time I won't even notice I'm cut until I see the blood."

Saval shook his head.

They were halfway through the meal, which was an excellent mélange of game hen, fingerling crab and deepwater seaweed all cooked in sweet and hot sauce, when Taz's com came to life.

"Yes?"

"Chief, we got an ID on one of the dead guys in the truck. The woman. Work name was Refu koo Mkunga. Local girl, grew up down in Kiyoga. She lists as a licensed trull, but her last renewal and medical was almost five years ago, nothing on her since. We got primary ed records, address of a biological sister, goes by Mgongo tundu Ndizi, lives in the roach's belly, also an LT. Um, that's about it, Chief. No criminal record."

Taz shook her head. "Jesu. Okay, upload the sister's address, I'll check it out. Any more activity on the assassin?"

"Negative."

"Keep me current. Discom."

Taz looked at her food. She wasn't hungry any more. This could be a good lead.

Saval raised an eyebrow.

She said, "The dead woman was a whore, but dropped off the rolls a few years ago. Maybe her sister can tell us something. She works in Mende." She shook her head again.

Ruul chuckled.

"Something funny?"

She looked at Ruul.

He turned to her brother. "The names. Roach Town whores are not the most subtle of creatures. The dead one's name means, more or less, 'Deep throats your eel.' The sister's working name translates as, ah, 'Banana in the back hole.' A banana is a yellow tropical fruit, it's shaped rather like, ah, a large—"

"I know what a banana is," Saval said.

"Well, finish your food," Taz said. "And let's go see if M. Ndizi can tell us anything more than how she got her colorful professional name."

Bork had seen worse places, but not all that many. Mende Town was one of those old inner-city capsules you could find on a lot of frontier worlds. Built when land was cheap and regulations were lax, such neighborhoods tended to blossom haphazardly in all directions, outward and upward, and there was seldom any kind of uniformity as to construction methods or materials. Housing sat next to industrial areas, streets were crooked and narrow, little more than alleys in many places, and topography tended to dictate the shape of civilization. If there were rivers, streets ran next to them and followed the meander. Mountains and lakes or swamps usually ended the sprawl, until it became cost effective to blast or build over them. Generally by the time that happened, the early buildings would be falling into disrepair, a hard-core urban complex that people left for newer pastures as soon as they could afford the move. It was a cycle repeated over and over on new planets where men and mues had gone to escape the more regimented worlds of straight roads and communities planned down to the specific kinds of grass allowed for ornamental lawns.

And as the old urban sprawl decayed, those left behind were usually the ones too poor to leave, too set in their ways, or too venal. Hard pubs sold the legal drugs and then some; sex and gambling and other pleasures frowned upon in more polite and upscale areas would always find takers in Mende Town. Like the roach it was named for, somehow a place like this always managed to find a way to survive.

They passed a ruined groundcar parked on the side of the road. The car's wheels had been stolen, the windows smashed or pried out, the interior stripped of seats and servos and controls. The heavy plastic body had been chipped and cracked, graffiti sprayed or burned into it. Apparently the car had become home to a nest of small animals. Something that looked like a cross between a donkey and a squirrel and about the size of a tabby perched on the rear deck, and another smaller version of it peered through the side window at them when they fanned by.

"Punda dogs," Taz said. "They eat rats, so nobody bothers 'em."

Taz dropped the flitter to its rollers and slowed the vehicle considerably. "Gets a little tight in here," she said. "No point in banging it up any more than it already is."

Bork nodded. The carbonex windshield still held the slugs the truck driver had fired at them, coppery-gray blobs that seemed to float in the air in front of the flitter.

The street narrowed. Here and there people stood or leaned against dirty everlast walls, sometimes in pairs, now and then in small groups, never more than four or five. They watched the flitter go past, and Bork was reminded of a zoo he'd been in once, when the keepers had come to feed the predators. The keepers had been armed with shockstiks, and the animals had kept their distance; the lupes, vulps, big cats and even the snow lizards had learned to stay clear of those nasty and painful electrical rods. That's how the people here looked: ready to leap upon them, but made wary by the police insignia on the flitter.

Ahead, a rat ran across the road. Right behind it, one of the things like those Bork had seen nested in the trashed car. The rat was fast, but the punda dog was faster. It leaped, came down in front of the rat, rocked up on its forelegs and kicked with both hind legs. The back feet snapped out so fast and hard Bork didn't actually see them hit, but the rat snapped into the air like an acrobat and did most of a back flip, landing on its head. It quivered, but didn't move otherwise. The punda dog came down, turned, picked the dying rat up with its teeth, and padded away, managing to hold its prey up high enough to keep it from dragging on the dirty plastcrete. By the time the flitter came level with it, the punda dog had already ducked into a dark and narrow alley behind a large barrel-shaped dump cannister.

"See?" Taz said.

They made several more turns, moving deeper into the heart of Mende Town. Bork tried to keep the twists straight in his mind. He had a pretty good sense of direction, but this was starting to look like a maze.

"Just ahead," Taz said. "We're going to a pub and sleepshop called The Hollow Victory."

"Interesting name," Ruul said. "I don't believe I've ever been there."

"It's not on the slumming circuit. Guy who owns it was a trooper during the revolution, in the ten-kay stationed in the Kar System. Part of his unit decided to switch to the winning side early and wound up fighting against those who didn't. The story is, he killed his own twin brother."

"Terrible," Ruul said.

"Worse than that. The fight took place two hours after the surrender. They were out of contact with their commanders, didn't know the revolution was over. There it is, just ahead to the left."

The buildings all looked gray in the dwindling sunlight, some darker, some lighter, but lacking any brightness due to the cheap but durable plastic from which they'd been built.

"I don't see a sign," Ruul said.

"Isn't any. If you don't know where it is, they don't want you wandering in accidentally. This is where Madam Banana has her office. And don't say it, Ruul."

He laughed. "I must need to get some new material. You know me too well."

To Bork, Taz said, "He can be pretty funny when he wants, but he never passes up a cheap shot. He would have said, 'You mean her orfice.' "

Ruul laughed again. But in it, Bork heard a slightly strained tone. The laugh was like the place they were approaching. Hollow.

Taz pulled the flitter off the road until it was nearly touching the blank wall. She set the intrusion alarms, power kill code, and, Bork noted, a hands-off van de graaffer. Those weren't exactly legal most places, Bork knew. Anybody who laid bare hands on the flitter would get zapped enough to knock them sprawling, as well as triggering the other alarms. None of which would stop a skilled and determined thief, of course. Then again, few thieves good enough to bypass a full-rout flitter system would bother to do so just to steal a mid-range police unit; it wasn't worth the effort.

Bork slid out on Taz's side of the flitter. Looked around. The alley seemed quiet, but that didn't always mean anything. He saw Taz scan their surroundings, decide they were safe enough. He smiled a little. She was pretty good, for somebody who wasn't a matador.

"Let's go see what we can see," she said.

With Ruul between them, Bork followed her to the door.

Things were not going well, Kifo knew.

He sat in his office, a smallish place he seldom used, staring at the Sacred Glyph. The talisman sat upon its plush cushion in the middle of the desk, waiting for his pleasure. Not that he could call what he felt pleasure, not by any means. The loss of two of the Few was regrettable but hardly a telling blow. The loss of one of the Zonn fragments was ever so much more painful. It had been so unexpected. Some kind of fluke, a freak accident, but still, chance had favored the enemies of the gods, and Kifo worried over this as a man might a jagged tooth. His tongue kept going to the rough spot, discovering it anew each time.

He had, he had to admit, panicked when he heard the news. He had shut down all operations immediately to give himself time to think. Now that he had the time, he realized that the loss of the fragment was not the end of the world; still, it might hurry the timetable somewhat. The links were tenuous, probably too thin to support even the weight of a few questions, but given how lucky his opponents had been thus far, one could not be too sure. Best he eliminate any lines that might lead to the wrong places, at least until he was further along in his endeavors. Past a certain point it would not matter, but until then he should not let things get out of hand. The gods hated hubris in their subjects. Mkono had demonstrated that, had he not?

Kifo nodded. Yes. The two who had failed were dead, and rightly so. Anyone who might connect them to the Few had to lose that ability quickly. And the dead do not tattle. He reached for his com.

TWENTY

THE HOLLOW VICTORY surprised Ruul, Taz could see that. She didn't know what he expected, but what he saw was a neat, clean, small pub. There were a dozen tables that would seat as many as four each, a long bar with a footrest that ran the length of the main room, backed by a mirror that made the place look larger than it was. Twenty-five or thirty customers sat at the tables or leaned against the bar when the three of them entered. Flickstick smoke purpled the air, plastic steins clinked, people conversed. The talking continued, there wasn't a hush or anything, but within a few seconds everybody in the place knew they had official company. You could see it in small gestures and quick glances, nothing overtly obvious. Many of these people made their living on the edge, and a slip usually meant blood. They paid attention to what went on around them. Some of them had seen her before, some of them might recognize Ruul from the entcom, but they didn't know Saval. The matador uniform and back-of-the-hand guns would probably get him a clear passage even if he were no larger than a small child; big as he was, he merited a second look.

"One other thing I probably should mention," Taz said. "Guy who runs this place, name is Rugi. He was on the Confed side during the fight that killed his brother. Just so you know."

They approached the bar. "Hello, Rugi."

"Chief. What's your chem?"

"Splash is fine."

The man was tall, lean to the point of being skinny, dark, with light brown curly hair. He wore a sculpted hand wand in a clear plastic appendix holster. The stunner had been molded to look like a stylized lightning bolt, colored a brilliant yellow. Was probably boosted to illegal standards, too, not that Taz cared about that. What he did in his own place was his business.

Rugi set up three steins of the mild liquor. Nodded at Ruul. "I like your stuff," he said.

"Thanks."

He looked at Saval. "This must be your brother."

"Word gets around," Taz said, sipping her splash. "Saval Bork, this is Rugi."

Saval nodded. "Pleasure."

Rugi returned the nod. "I like your work, too. Would have liked it better you'd been on our side." He paused, looked back at Taz. "What can I do for you, Chief?"

"You got a trull who idles here, named Ndizi. We need to talk to her. No trouble, just information."

He nodded. "Southeast corner table, she's the one with shocked green hair."

"Thanks, Rugi." She reached for her credit cube.

"Your stads don't work in here," he said.

Taz nodded, accepted the free drink for what it was worth, a small courtesy.

The woman who specialized in anal pleasures was something of a surprise. Her hair was in an electrostatic swirl, dyed a brilliant green, her clothes either expensive designer silks or a pretty good knock-off in a complementary shade of green, and her face could have been the model for the classic angel. Even features, clean lines, perfect teeth, eyes so clear a dark blue they were probably natural and not lenses. She was petite, wouldn't go more than fifty kilos, and the thin silks did little to hide a very good body. If Taz hadn't read her ID she would have missed her age by ten years. M. Ndizi looked a shining twenty T.S. and she was actually almost thirty-two. She obviously had spent some time under a cosmetic laser lit by somebody who knew how to use it.

She didn't know Taz personally but she knew what she was. "Good evening, Po. You and your friends looking for a party?" She smiled at Saval and Ruul. "Three happens to be my limit at the same time—if two of them aren't overly large, that is."

Funny. She was legal, her license in order, but she was playing with them.

"Mind if we sit?"

"Do."

"It's about your sister."

"I didn't kill her. In fact, I heard it was some cool and her giant brother who did it." She looked at Saval. "You are big, aren't you?"

"You don't seem overwhelmed with grief."

She turned back to Taz. "I haven't seen Koo in a long time, Po. Years. And we didn't get along all that well before she ran off and joined that cult. She changed her name, called herself 'Sister Misery' or some scat, threw away all her past. She died then, far as I'm concerned."

"Tell us about the cult."

The green-haired woman shrugged. "Nothing to tell. I don't know scat about them. I got a com from her when she signed on. Short and not-so-sweet. She was 'renouncing the world,' she said. I never heard from her again." She glanced at the bar, saw something that made her smile.

"What—?" Taz began.

"Hold up, Po," she said. "My sixteen hundred is here. He's a new client, I don't want to keep him waiting." She stood.

"M. Ndizi—"

"Ten minutes, Po. That's all he's paid for. Time you've finished your splash, he'll be happy and I'll be able to pay my rent." She walked away. She had a very tight and well-shaped rear end, Taz saw, obvious the way the silks clung to it.

Taz sipped her splash, looked at the man who leaned against the bar watching Ndizi walk toward him. He was nothing special, average, dressed in freight handler's coveralls, a new set without lube or dirt staining them. Must have gotten all dressed up for his little party. Sad.

She turned and saw Ruul watching the play of buttock muscle as Ndizi walked. Smiled. "Interested?"

He blinked, jerked his gaze away and tried to cover his flushed face with his splash. "Not my type," he said.

There was a door near one end of the bar, and the freight handler and Ndizi moved toward it. She had taken his arm in hers and was smiling at him as they walked.

"He's carrying weapons," Saval said.

Taz didn't get it for a second. "Who is?"

"The guy in handler's clothes. Handgun in a small-of-the-back rig, a knife or short club in his right boot."

Taz looked at the pair moving toward the door. Yeah, now that he mentioned, she could see a bulge under the breakaway cro-tab over the man's spine. She didn't see the boot knife, but if Saval said it was there, she believed it.

"It's a rough neighborhood," she said. "Probably most of the patrons are carrying something or the other."

"The coveralls are brand new and his hands are clean, no stain," Saval said. He came to his feet.

"What are you saying?" Ruul put in.

"Something's wrong here," Saval said.

Taz trusted that instinct, too. She stood. "Go."

The trull and her customer had reached the door. She was opening it with a card she carried. It would register her visit and debit her account for one of the rooms Rugi kept beyond for such transactions as hers.

"Hey," Taz called. "Ndizi! Wait up!"

The woman turned to see who had called her.

The man in coveralls shoved her through the opening.

"Shit!" Taz said, sprinting for the door.

She was fast, always had been pretty good for short distances. Saval was ahead of her, though, and gaining.

The door snicked shut behind the couple, locking automatically. Saval turned and put his right shoulder down, pulled his head back slightly. Hit the door solidly.

It was a good door, heavy cast plastic, designed to keep anybody without a card from passing through. The door held. The frame around the door did not. It shattered under the impact, hinges and lock pulling from splintered wood and screaming metallically at the sudden assault. The door flew inward.

By the time she got to it, her gun out, Saval's spetsdöds had already coughed twice.

Inside the gaping hole Saval had made, Taz got a flash picture of what was going on in that stepped-on slow time that often happened when the guns came out:

The freight handler was falling, one hand wrapped around his throat, the other holding a small pistol pointing at the floor.

On the floor under his gun was Ndizi, face down. The back of her green hair was blotched with bright blood. The long swirl of green silks had risen to reveal her body to the waist. She'd had good legs to match the ass, Taz noted. And "had" was the key word.

Saval reached Ndizi first, squatted, turned her over. Felt for a carotid but was wasting his time. The exit wounds in the dead trull's forehead gaped large enough to admit Taz's thumb and oozed red and pink and gray matter. Three holes, two above the right eye, one below the left that had taken part of the nose with it. Explosive rounds. The best medic in the galaxy wasn't going to be able to bring her back from that. They might keep the body alive, but Ndizi the personality had moved on.

"Shit," Taz said, lowering her pistol.

Rugi ran into the room, his hand wand held out. Taz thought in that moment that he looked like some comic parody of an avenging god, tiny bolt of lightning held in his hand. Other curious patrons moved just outside the opening, but hesitant to enter.

Taz pulled her com. "This is Bork, at Rugi's pub in Roach Town," she said. "Get a clean-up team over here and a body wagon. And if if you can find a medic who can short-circuit a brainblock, we got another one like the two who died in that truck shootout. Hurry."

"They're worried," Saval said as Taz moved to stand next to him. "She knew something they didn't want us to find out."

Taz bent and pulled the dead woman's com from her shoulder bag. "This is Tazzimi Bork with the Leijona Police," she said. "I want a record of all calls to and from this code uploaded into my flatscreen immediately." She looked at her brother. "If the killer did call her to set this up, maybe we'll get lucky."

"They've been pretty careful so far."

"If we'd been thirty seconds faster she'd have given us the name of the cult her sister joined," Taz said. "That sounds like they're maybe not as careful as they think."

She turned to Rugi. "Keep everybody out of here until the clean-up team gets here, Rugi. You know this guy?"

"He hasn't been in before, Chief."

"Okay. If there's anybody out front who doesn't want to be intimate with our people, tell them to take off—but I want their names and where to reach them later. Just me."

"Thanks, Chief. We know who our friends are."

"Good."

This was bad, Taz knew. To lose a witness with a matador and an Assistant Chief of Police looking right at her when it happened. But when they walked back into the main room of the pub, it got worse.

Ruul was gone.

TWENTY-ONE

TAZ FOUGHT A losing battle against panic. Her belly twisted, her bowels went cold, and she had trouble catching her breath. If somebody had come through the pub's door carrying a big stick, they could have walked up and swatted her with it, she'd have just stood there staring at them.

Saval took over.

"Taz, look in the fresher. Go and see if he is in there. Go."

Sudden hope lit up in her. The fresher. Of course, how stupid. She herself had to pee, and Ruul had never been able to drink and travel for more than a few minutes before he had to stop, she remembered that. The fresher—

But, no. Nobody was in the fresher. The private stalls were all empty; she checked.

When she returned to the pub's main room, Saval wasn't in sight. Rugi waved her over. "He went out to check the street," Rugi said.

"Did anybody see Oro leave?"

Rugi shrugged.

Taz turned to the other patrons, the ones who hadn't run when the shooting started. "Did anybody see the man we came in with leave?" Her voice was loud enough to carry throughout the room.

A short but heavy man close to her sneered. "What, do we look like the lost and found?"

Ordinarily Taz was a good cool, able to keep her emotions controlled on the job after all the years on the streets. In any one of a hundred situations the big man could have mouthed off and she would have let it pass. Not now.

Taz took two steps, grabbed his shirt front, bunched it in her fists and lifted him. The material of his shirt was good, it held, and while his toes stayed in contact with the floor, there was very little weight on them.

"What did you say?"

From behind her Saval said, "Taz."

Her rage was hot enough so she considered seeing how far she could throw the guy. He tried to speak but nothing came.

"Taz."

Her vision cleared, the red haze faded. She put the man back onto his feet. His eyes were considerably wider than they had been, and if he had anything else clever to offer, he must have misplaced it while he was up in the air.

A smallish woman broke the tension. "Two guys in new coveralls walked him out," she said.

Taz turned away from the frightened man. "And nobody objected," she said.

The little woman shrugged. Wasn't her biz. People around here didn't poke at stuff that didn't concern them; that was a good way to get your face blown off.

Taz knew this, but the fear lying in her belly like some malevolent beast threatened to consume her from within and she had to do something—

Saval said, "He wouldn't have wandered off on his own?"

"No."

"Okay. They've gotten clear. I figure he must have been a target of opportunity. The two were probably backup to the one who shot Ndizi. They saw us go after her, decided we were more than they could handle, took Ruul instead."

"I can't believe I left him there alone," she said.

"*We* left him alone, Taz."

"You could have handled the one guy. I should have stayed with Ruul."

"This doesn't help. Beat up on yourself later when you have the luxury of time. Now you can't afford it."

She gave him a choppy nod. He was right. Where were her brains? There was a procedure for kidnapping. She pulled her com to report it, to set the machine in motion. They had one of them, still alive, they might be able to keep him that way. They had a little information—Ndizi had told them her sib used the name "Sister Misery." The computer could scan religious groups for similar cult noms. She had the police resources of an entire planet at her disposal, plus she had Saval. They'd find him.

She turned back to the man she'd grabbed. "I was out of line, citizen. If you want to file a complaint—"

"N-No," he said quickly. "N-No problem."

Taz turned away, the man fading from her thoughts. Ruul. They'd find him.

And if somebody had hurt him, they would be sorry they'd ever been born. She would see to it personally.

Bork watched his sister, saw her settle down and begin to do her work, and felt a little better. Not much. He had broken the first rule of a bodyguard by leaving his client unprotected. He had told Taz he would take care of her lover and he had failed to do it. That, coupled with his defeat by the assassin, rocked Bork pretty hard. The years of living easy after the revolution had dulled him, he had lost his edge, and it didn't feel good to know it. He was a half step slow here and if he didn't do something about it, he or Taz might wind up dead. It was not something he'd ever worried about before, but it worried him now. It was not so much the going that frightened him, but what he would leave behind. Little Saval would grow up not knowing his father. Veate would find another lover—being an Albino, she couldn't *not*—and somebody else might be hoisting her son onto his shoulder, doing all the things Bork should have done. If he died, it would be as if *they* had died, the effect would be the same, they would be lost to him.

Everybody went over. It wasn't something Bork had ever

thought much about. With drugs and diet and exercise, a careful man or mue could extend his lifespan to a hundred and fifty or sixty years. If what Sleel had told him about the plants they were growing in The Brambles was true, that span might be extended to eight or nine hundred years. It would be tragic to die when that kind of breakthrough was just around the corner. Eight hundred years with Veate wouldn't be too long. To live to see your great-times-a-dozen grandchildren; there was a miracle men had dreamed about ever since they first learned what death was. To lose that would be a bigger loss than what your own great-grandfather had stood to lose in his time. Dying of a fatal disease when the cure was almost ready was worse than if no cure were possible.

No, death hadn't seemed real to him before; he was too vital, too strong. He had walked through a revolution, a big target, and death had missed him every time. Not even a serious injury had ever slowed him down; a few strains, that was it. His genetically improved constitution kept him from falling sick with most of the common illnesses they hadn't yet found preventions for, and when he was cut or bruised, he healed faster than did ordinary men. He had been designed for planets with heavy gravity, his body made to withstand more than basic stockers and until he had clinched with the assassin, his body had never really failed him. But it only takes one loss to make you realize you *can* lose, Bork had learned. And that knowledge is a fertile breeding ground for fear and doubt, both of which could grow up to kill you. Excessive caution can slap you just as dead; he'd learned that at the Villa. Hesitate at the wrong second, and you will be lost just as surely as if you leap too quickly.

Bork had never really appreciated how thin a line you had to walk to survive in the galaxy. And that appreciation, he found, didn't help things at all; it only made them worse.

Kifo looked upon the two brothers with a certain kind of wonder. Perhaps stupidity was contagious? Perhaps one of them had infected the other?

He knew the man they had collected. He was some kind of actor, aside from being loosely associated with the police-woman.

"Your assignment was to back up Brother Agony, was it not? While he slew the whore?"

"Yes, my Unique," they said in perfect chorus.

"Then why this?" He waved at the actor.

The two brothers glanced at each other. The shorter one said, "Well, when Brother Agony was attacked, we thought this one would be a good hostage. To . . . uh, to uh, frighten the woman cool."

Kifo shook his head.

"I see. And did you recognize the big man with the police-woman? The matador?"

The two glanced at each other again. The taller one was slightly quicker with his reply: "Yes, my Unique."

"You know this was the man who fought Brother Hand to a draw." This was not a question and both men knew it.

"Y-Y-Yes."

"And you thought that if he could do that to Brother Mkono then you would certainly be defeated did you face him, did you not?"

The faces of both men were filled with shame. There was no need for them to speak.

Kifo shook his head. "Take him out and kill him," he said. He nodded at the actor.

The three started to leave. "No, wait. As long as we have him, we might as well keep him. If by chance the authorities try to molest us, perhaps he will serve some purpose. Put him in the punishment chamber."

"Nice to meet you, too," the actor said.

Kifo shook his head.

When the trio had departed, Kifo sat and stared at the wall. The gods had given him what seemed a plump and ripe fruit, beautiful to the eyes and pleasing to the nose—and after allowing him one delicious bite, had made it go bitter in his mouth. The Unique of the Few felt sour all over. A simple precaution, to remove a link tenuous at best, had met with unexpected resistance. A small seed that might well have been dismissed as trivial even *had* it been uncovered had suddenly blossomed into an exceedingly ugly weed in his garden. The brain-death command implanted in the Few who were at risk *could* be circumvented by a clever and quick enough neuromedic. Once the block was thus short-circuited, then any whack with a cheap electropophy machine or encephaloscanner could dig out whatever the simadam wanted. The chance that such a thing might happen had existed all along; Kifo had hoped to put it off for a longer time. The unbelievers had collected yet another of his people, and he must assume that they would be expecting the mental shutdown. Whether they had learned anything from the whore whose sister had been one of the Few was pretty much moot.

Kifo looked around at the inside of the meditation chamber. It was only a building, true enough, but he had spent much of his life living and learning within the walls of it. It would be hard to leave without a certain regret.

Then again, a building was as nothing to one who was on the way to becoming a god. He would create finer places with a backhand wave, once he joined the ranks of the Zonn. And were he to join them, it was best that the unbelievers not catch him or his people before it happened.

Kifo keyed into the temple's broadcast system.

"This is your Unique," Kifo said. "The Few are about to depart for Paradise. Ready yourselves."

TWENTY-TWO _____

BACK IN HER office, the practiced motions of her job mostly carried Taz through her worry. After more than half her life as a cool, she had learned that inertia was a potent force. If you picked a direction and just kept moving, sometimes that would be enough. Inertia. She tried not to think about Ruul. Of how she had let him down . . .

"Chief, here's the read on that name," came a voice from one of the computer operators.

Taz punched the code up on her monitor.

"Saval," she called as she read.

He looked up from his work using her flatscreen.

"We have an ID on the group. 'Sister Misery' is crosslinked to something called the Temple of Despair. The Chosen Few. They have a place here in the city."

Saval moved to stand next to her, reading the holoproj over her shoulder.

"Sketchy," he said. "Doesn't say anything about what they believe, just bare bones. Look at the names: Despair, Misery, Angst, Grief, head guy is named 'Death.' Cheery bunch of folks."

Taz glanced at the list. "Says the leader is called The Unique. Damn."

"What?"

"Remember the guy whose brain fried back on Kato? The one thing he said before he checked out?"

Saval nodded, appeared to be scanning his memory. " 'Moja.' "

"Yeah. Well, in Tembonese 'moja' means 'lone' or 'one.' It might also be taken to mean 'unique.' "

"Whoops," Saval said.

"Yeah. It's enough to fan on," she said. Taz tapped in a call code. "This is Assistant Chief Bork," she said. "I want a Tactical Insertion Team ready at the front entrance in five minutes and I want half a dozen tans in riot suits waiting for them when they get there."

"Caught it clear, Chief. On it."

She looked up at her brother. "Let's go talk to these Chosen Few," she said.

The insertion team's van idled outside the building as Taz and Saval exited. Taz spoke to the Team Leader, gave him the address and what information she had. The van fanned away, a blast of warm and gritty wind washing over Taz and Saval. Smelled like lube. Six traffic units followed the van as the siblings moved toward Taz's flitter.

"Tactical Insertion Team?" Saval said.

"An unfortunate choice of names," Taz said. "Somebody wasn't thinking about the acroynm. Want to guess how long it took before somebody started calling them TIT-suckers?"

Saval shook his head.

The team would secure the perimeter of the temple and keep Taz informed via com. If anybody came out with Ruul in tow, Taz could have his captors taken out. A large-caliber metal projectile zipping along at a thousand meters a second would stop a bad guy instantly if it hit him in the head. The TIT snipers had state-of-the-art water-plasma rifles with shock-armored full-holoproj pinprick scopes. The stocks were sculpted carbonex and wedded to the actions by sixty precise and very strong welds. You could drop one of the weapons off a building and it would probably still shoot true, and the men and women doing the shooting were good enough to drill a target through the eye at a hundred meters—and you get to pick which eye.

Even so, Taz hoped it wouldn't come to that. She didn't want to risk Ruul's life.

They were halfway to the temple when the call came back: "We've got the building lugged down, Chief, but it's real quiet in there. The wolf ears can't hear anything, motion detectors and doppler come up clean."

"Shit," Taz said. "Hold your positions."

She glanced over at Saval. "Sounds like they're gone," she said.

"Yeah, it does. We'll see."

The Nine were in the first coach to arrive at the ruins. Kifo would take seven of the Very Few with him, leaving Brother Mkono behind to sow a few dragon's teeth among their enemies. It was heady, the feeling he had, knowing what he knew. Fifty others would also make the crossing. Some of the lesser brothers and sisters would have to be left behind; they were even now scattering themselves from the city, some going into the highlands, others downcountry, a few offworld. Too bad he couldn't take them all, but one could not request too much hospitality from the gods. Among the Few, only three still alive had communed directly with the Zonn and none more than once save himself. It would be an adventure, to take so many into the Realm. He had gone four times before, and he had studied closely the old records, the Book of Rules about what to expect and how to deal with it, compiled by the Uniques before him. Even so, there were dangers waiting to trap those whose faith was less than complete, whose attention wandered in the slightest. Ah, yes. An adventure, indeed.

In the city many of the wheels of Temple business would be rolling to a temporary halt. The authorities would find nothing more than ashes and frustration when they arrived to seek the Few. Kifo was ahead of them, as he had always been ahead of them; whether it was merely one step or five, it mattered not in the end.

The vouch hummed behind him as he alighted. The fresh air and plants smelled glorious this day. The sun had already cooked up a mass of fat purple clouds for the day's lunch of rain and wind. Not that it would matter to Kifo.

There were a few loose ends that needed to be tied off. The hostage taken by the bumblers in Roach Town would have to be eliminated. Certain computer systems destroyed. All bridges were not to be burned because Kifo planned to return to this world of men—the full implementation of his plan—no, of the *gods'* plan—was not quite ready. But one step at a time, one step at a time.

"Brother Mkono."

"Yes, my Unique."

"You have your instructions."

"I do."

"Attend to them."

"I shall."

There was hardly any worry about other tongues wagging, not at this point, but Mkono had leeway to silence any he might find worrisome. In a few minutes, Kifo would be beyond human justice, but did he return—no, *when* he returned—he would prefer it to be a place where the gods' enemies were befuddled. It hardly took much to do that, given their normal states of mind; still, they had managed to stumble into things and upset a few tables and chairs by sheer luck. Sometimes the gods did that, smiled on their enemies. Kifo did not pretend to understand why they did so, but it was enough to realize that they *did*, and therefore he should prepare accordingly.

Perhaps when he got to be a god such things would be made clear to him. Surely they would.

The other coaches began to arrive. The sense of anticipation flowed through him as might a high-voltage electrical current. It was not every day that a man crossed into the land of his gods. He was quite looking forward to it.

• • •

The temple was, as the insertion team had indicated, empty. As Bork and Taz went through the place behind the team wielding its electronic scanners, it was apparent that the inhabitants had left in a hurry and chosen to travel light. There were clothes, personal items, readers, even drying laundry still in evidence.

The building was pretty impressive, fine woods and other materials used in its construction, and it had a pleasant, somewhat spicy odor to it.

"Computers are wiped," one of the men said to Taz.

Bork wandered around, trying to get a feel for the place. He found himself in a fresher. Nothing special about it, a shower, bidet, notions cabinet. He started to leave, then spotted a bit of cloth stuck to the back of the bidet's bowl. The cloth was the size of a thumbnail, torn raggedly around the edges, hard to see unless you were looking for something like it. Blue. He didn't touch the tiny scrap.

"Taz, you want to come in here?"

She arrived a few seconds later.

"Take a look at this." He pointed at the cloth.

She squatted, peered around the back of the bidet. Sucked in a quick breath.

"Yeah, that's what I thought," Bork said. "Could be from the jumpsuit Ruul was wearing."

"It is," she said. "He was here. He left it here for us to find. He knows we'll look for him."

She raised from her crouch, pulled her com. "This is Assistant Chief Bork. Put out a national pickup on any member of the Chosen Few, see the file this op code. They are wanted for the kidnapping of Ruul Oro, see the file for stats and pix; murder, attempted murder and probably a few other things we don't know about yet. They are to be considered armed and dangerous, approach with extreme caution and notify me immediately."

As she and Bork waited for the labbos to come and collect

the spot of cloth, Taz said, "Now, the question is, where did they go? And how did they know it was time to leave?"

"At least we know who they are," Bork said. "That's a good start."

Taz nodded. "But we don't know how they did it."

"We catch them, I bet we can persuade them to tell us."

"Oh, you can bet your ass on that, brother."

TWENTY-THREE

THERE MIGHT BE further clues to be gained from an empty temple, surely the labbos thought so, but there was nothing more useful there for Taz or Bork.

They went back to her office. While Taz was in the lab trying to hustle up the techs, Bork decided to call home and see how things were going. The last time he'd talked to his wife, she'd said her parents were coming back for another visit.

Once again, White Radio did its magic and Bork found himself facing a holographic projection of Veate.

He grinned when he saw her. Little Saval was asleep, she said. The boss and Juete had arrived.

Across the light-years of space, Bork explained his frustration about the problem of opponents who could appear and disappear at will. Her mother and the boss sat in the background, listening. Maybe they could offer something he was missing?

When Bork finished, Juete cleared her throat.

"You say these people are connected somehow to the Zonn Ruins?"

"Yeah, we think. We found a chunk of one of the walls in a truck, dunno what they were doing hauling it around. Taz has a couple of men on their way to the ruins to check it out."

Khadaji looked at his wife. "The Cage?"

She nodded. "Could be."

Bork said, "What, something?"

Juete smiled. "Well, though it's never come up in conversation, you might as well know that your mother-in-law has something of a past. A long, long time ago, I spent some time in prison. In the Omega Cage, actually."

Veate said, "Mother!"

"Oh, yes. There were those who would do anything to own an albino. I . . . killed one of them and wound up the personal property of the Confed warden who ran the Cage. Back then, it was a one-way trip to be sent there."

"Then how did—?" Veate began.

"I escaped. Along with a few others. Very dramatic. In the end most of the escapees died, but three of us got offworld."

"I thought the Cage was supposed to be escapeproof," Bork said.

"So they said. But my lover was something of an expert on such things. And he knew something of the Zonn."

"The Zonn?"

"Yes, Saval. You see, we escaped from the Cage by walking through their walls."

It was raining in the city, a tropical shower replete with high-voltage cracks and ship-lift thunder.

"Anything from the guys you sent to the ruins?"

"Not yet. They should be there by now."

Bork explained it to Taz as she drove them toward her cube. "So Juete's lover, a smuggler named Maro, learned from some scientist or the other that the Zonn walls weren't really material at all, but force fields that were some kind of doorways to another dimension. He found a way to breach the fields and to pass through and into the place beyond."

"Sounds unlikely," she said.

"Yeah, I thought so, too. Then again, it would explain a lot. Clarke's Law."

The flitter zipped past a stalled hovertruck. The driver made an obscene gesture as the backwash spattered him with mud. Clarke's Law said that a highly advanced technology might well appear to be magic to a less advanced society viewing it.

"Maro built something like a Bender drive. With it, they walked through the Zonn dimension until they found a way out of the prison."

Taz shook her head. "Even if that's true, how does it help us? These jobbos are supposedly walking through *normal* walls, not the Zonn stuff."

Bork shrugged. "I dunno. But those chunks of Zonn material in the trucks we found, they might have something to do with it. Maybe the Few have gotten hold of some device that lets them do the same thing to stone or everlast that Juete and the others did to the Zonn walls. We're dealing with technology we don't understand here; a lot might be possible."

"So unreal," Taz said.

"Yeah, but I don't have any better ideas. You?"

"Not at the moment, no."

"Anyway, Juete and Maro split up a long time ago, but the funny thing is, I know the guy."

"*You* do? How?"

"While back the matadors had some trouble with an old enemy. I knew somebody who had an in with Black Sun. Turned out the guy we wound up with was Maro. He runs a big sector of the organization."

"Jesu, Saval, you trust Black Sun?"

"Not particularly, but Maro did us a favor and we returned it. We're even, but he knows he can deal with us."

"I don't like it," Taz said. "You can get burned real crisp playing with a crime syndicate like the Sun."

"Right now I'd talk to the Devil himself to stop these people," Bork said. "And to get Ruul back."

"Yeah."

They got to Taz's place. Saval checked the wards, found them clear, and they went inside. The call came a few minutes later.

The man on the proj was gray-haired and fit-looking, somewhere in his late sixties, Taz guessed. He looked tough, hard.

"M. Bork," he said. "How is it you know Juete?"

"She's the grandmother of my son."

Maro chuckled. "Hard to visualize Juete as a grandmother. I guess time defeats us all in the end. What can my . . . organization do for you?"

"Nothing. But you personally can, M. Maro. We have a problem here with some folks who have apparently gotten some kind of control of the Zonn artifacts."

Maro shook his head. "The Zonn. Jesu, I haven't thought about them in years. The super race who went away."

"M. Maro, I'm Tazzimi Bork. Why is it I've never heard anything about all this voodoo stuff before? There are Zonn ruins all over the galaxy, aren't there?"

"Yes. But after we broke out of the Cage—Juete told you about that, right?—the Confed got nervous and quashed all research on the Zonn. Cleaned every file they could find. I guess they thought it had some military application, probably it does. But before they could do much with it, the revolution came. I suspect it got lost in the shuffle. Lot of records were destroyed rather than allow them to fall into the hands of the rebels."

"Sounds as if you checked this out."

"It's my business to know things. I had a personal interest but it was a while back. Life moves on."

"We think a local group of fanatics have figured out a way to move through walls," Saval said. "You know anything about that?"

Several billion klicks away, Maro nodded. "I had some information I brought with me to the Cage when I knew I was going there, but it was a long time ago. The technical stuff was mostly beyond me. I had a droudman whiz who could get his brain in a lot of files; he did the actual work on the device we used. Maybe he could tell you more. Here."

Maro tapped a keyboard. A long series of numbers lit the air.

"He goes by the name of Scanner," Maro said. "He's on Mtu, or was last time I checked. Tell him I sent you. He'll want something to make sure you aren't lying. Tell him he still owes me my cut for what he got for Karnaaj's ship."

"Thanks," Saval said. "I owe you."

Maro nodded. "Another thing. I don't know where the Zonn went, but they left something behind. Echoes, energy patterns of some kind. Ghosts, maybe."

"Ghosts?"

"There was a torture chamber in the Cage. Prisoners got put into it, they came out damaged mentally, real blitherers. The condition was permanent. The room was enclosed by Zonn walls. Whatever they were, spirits or recordings, they took over anybody who stayed in the place more than a few minutes."

"Sounds like firsthand knowledge."

"Yeah. I went into the Zonn chamber."

"You don't sound insane to me."

"When I was young and stupid, I spent some time in a minor religious cult, the Soul Melders. I learned a pretty fair meditation technique while I was there. Part of it was a mind shield; they had a real paranoia about empaths. It got me through. If you are going to play around in the Zonn space, you'll need to be careful."

He started to discom. Stopped. "You're a lucky man, Bork, if Juete's daughter is half the woman her mother is."

"I am and she is," Saval said.

The air cleared abruptly.

"We might as well call the techie," Taz said.

Saval initiated the com.

Scanner wore an old-style droud, the plug over his ear covered neatly by a remote caster that rainbow-gleamed like oil on water against the man's white hair. He apparently ran some kind of investigative service on Mtu, according to the ID pattern on screen while they were waiting for him to answer the com. Mtu was a fair distance from Tembo; the transmission delay was therefore short. The infamous White Radio Skip—nobody had figured out yet why the delay was shorter the farther away you got between stations.

"M. Scanner, I'm Saval Bork. Dain Maro said you might give us some information."

"*The* Saval Bork? I've certainly heard of you. I don't believe I know a Dain Maro, though."

"He said to tell you you still owe him for Karnaaj's ship."

The old man laughed. "Oh, *that* Maro. Hold a second."

Scanner closed his eyes, opened them almost immediately. "The connector wave is clear. Zap away, citizen."

Bork explained the situation.

"Hmm," the old man said when Bork finished. "I dunno how they manage that. I have the specs for the device we cobbled together in the Cage; I can download those. You got access to a decent E-lab, and a couple techs with good hands, you can build it pretty quick. It should open a hole into the Zonn dimension through their walls. You want to be sure you get everything boarded and harmonized right, though. There's a chance you could blow up half the planet if you do it wrong."

Saval looked at Taz.

"I poked around in it a little since, but I can't say I've added much to what we did back then. I wasn't ever much on theory; I'm a tinkerer."

"We appreciate the help."

"Another thing. I couldn't make complete recordings while we were messing around during our escape, but I remember it okay. The Zonn dimension is spatially weird, really weird. You get in, take five steps and return to normal space, you might be half a klick away from where you started. Or you could move a meter to the left and then back to the same spot and *still* be a long way from your departure point when you step back over. Physics does some fancy shifting in the Zonn space. They breathe the same air, but that's about all. It's like going into an alien nightmare. It's a scary place to visit."

"Doesn't sound like it'll put Vishnu out of business," Taz said.

"Not unless your idea of a pleasure world is insanity," Scanner said. "I'll upload the data. Good luck, citizens. You'll need it. You talk to Maro again, tell him I hardly broke even on that rundown ship we stole."

After Scanner was gone, the two of them sat in Taz's cube, pondering what they had learned.

"This Zonn dimension seems like a place we don't want particularly to go," Saval said. "Assuming we believe any of all this." He waved his hand at the blanked proj space. "But I think we're gonna have to check it out, though."

"Why?"

"The Unique and his followers have vanished. No sign of em anywhere."

"It's a big planet," she said. "Or he could have had offworld transport hidden somewhere."

"Yeah, maybe. But I don't think so. You know what else I think?"

Taz nodded, blew out a puffed-cheek sigh. "Yeah. Kifo and his crew are hiding out in the Zonn dimension."

"We have a religious fanatic here. If he thinks his gods live here, where else would be safer?"

"Oh, man."

"Yeah," Bork said.

TWENTY-FOUR

MISSEL SCANNED THE data on his monitor. The info crawl was beyond Bork's understanding, but he watched the man nod as he read the material. The interior of the lab was ahum and aglow from computer screens and assorted forensic machineries. Taz paced behind the lab tech, glancing at him and the holoproj now and then, but unable to stand still.

"This is great stuff," Missel said. "Look at that power curve!"

"Can you build it?" Taz asked.

He blinked, said, "Pause," to his computer. Looked at Taz. "Oh, sure. The schematics are simple enough, nothing we can't lay our hands on. Must have been interesting trying to cobble it together inside a prison, though."

"How long will it take?"

Missel blinked again. "How long? Well, if you can approve the parts—I'll need a purchase order—not all that long."

"Can you be more precise?"

"What time is it now? Tomorrow morning, if I start in the next hour or two."

"I'll get your purchase order number."

Bork said, "We were warned that this could be dangerous."

Missel looked at the frozen holoproj, then back at Bork. "Nah. I can wire a fail-safe circuit into the system, one of

the new Graham-Lachmans. Wouldn't be any more risky than
a standard jump into Bender space. Christo, half the boards
in this design are fifty years out of date. Look at that, the
interlock is visual purple bacteria complex, nobody has fooled
with VPBC for anything but lume controls and household
appliances for at least two decades. I'm surprised there isn't
copper wire and vacuum tubes in here. This is the future, man,
we don't use stone knives any more."

"Get moving," Taz said.

Kifo gathered his flock and explained briefly what was
about to happen. The Very Few were unperturbed; some of
them had made the crossing, and the ones who had not looked
forward to it. The rest of the Few were, to varying degrees,
eager or fearful. None wished to stay behind, however. This
was the penultimate moment in their lives.

When Mkono finished his business in the mundane world,
he would return here. Brother Hand was the only member of
the Few beside himself who knew the Walk Through the Wall
meditation well enough to make the crossing alone. A portion
of the wall would be softened enough to admit the giant brother
when he arrived; Kifo could do that from the other side.

The entertainer who had been taken from the public room
stood outside the chamber, held by a pair of the stouter brothers. Mkono would kill him and return to the city.

Kifo smiled. While he bore the kidnapped man no particular
malice save his association with the policewoman, he felt a
perverse thought grip him as he watched the captive watching
the Few. Should he not allow this doomed soul to see what
he was missing before his death? To witness the Few as they
crossed into the Realm of the Gods by walking through what
appeared to be a solid wall, and more, a wall of the hardest
substance known to man? True, no outsider had ever seen such
a thing; then again, he would not be telling tales afterward.

Kifo nodded to himself. Perhaps the poor soul could even
take some comfort from it. To see a miracle and then die
might enforce some mistaken belief and allow the fellow a

moment of peace. In a universe where men could do such things, surely redemption had to exist?

Kifo said to one of the women, "Go and tell Mkono to wait for my signal before he eliminates the captive."

The woman hurried off. Kifo watched her approach Brother Hand, saw him nod and glance at his Unique.

Kifo turned to his flock. "We begin," he said. "Still your minds and allow your faith to fill you."

The Chamber grew quiet; no manmade sound disturbed the air within the three Zonn walls. Kifo fingered the Sacred Glyph in his robe's pocket, slid his fingers over it, feeling the coldness of the holy relic. He became aware of the wall in front of him changing, of a swirling in the material. It was like smoke in a scanning laser, bound by the wall's shape but boiling inside the confines of the planes. It needed the Glyph and a proper mindset to accomplish, but the Few had spent years preparing for this.

Kifo said, "Brother Angst, you may cross first."

"I am honored, my Unique!"

The man was thirty years older than Kifo, had been instrumental in teaching him the ways of the faith, and it seemed only proper to allow him this small favor. Once in Paradise, what did it matter who arrived first or last?

Brother Angst stepped toward the wall, hesitated not even an eyeblink, and vanished in the steely murk. An involuntary gasp escaped from those who had never seen the phenomenon before. Even the Unique still felt a sense of amazement after having witnessed and done it himself a number of times.

"Sister Weary?"

The second member of the Very Few squared her shoulders and strode forward, vanished from the world.

Kifo turned to look at the prisoner. Mkono held the man by the shoulders. He was staring, all right. His mouth hadn't gaped, but his amazement was plain to see. It made Kifo feel a certain sense of power. Perhaps he should not have reacted so hastily in having the two cools who had come snooping killed. It would have increased his pleasure to see their wonder before they died. Ah, well. Even a candidate for godhood could not think of everything. Perhaps he would revive them once he became a god and allow them to see it then. He laughed at the thought. Ah, the power of a god!

The passage continued, each of the Few in turn stepping up to the wall and vanishing into it. They knew to cross over and wait until he arrived to lead them. The Zonn realm was not a place in which to wander around unguided.

When all in the chamber had crossed save himself, Kifo turned and waved at Mkono. The big mue nodded, slid his hands up and around the prisoner's head, twisted sharply, and broke his neck. The man fell in an untidy heap. Mkono waved once, then turned and walked away. He did not look back.

Kifo nodded. So much for that little problem. He stepped up to the swirling wall and into it. He felt the bone-freezing blast of cold that always came with the crossing. As he took the step that would end in another world, another universe, he heard a small humming behind him. Ah. The vouch. He had forgotten to shut it off. He wondered idly how long it would wait here for him. Given the life of the power system, it could be years.

Well. No matter. It was only a machine, loyal, but of no importance. Not to one who was going to be crowned a god. He would hardly need it when he returned.

Taz attacked the weights in her gym, slamming them back and forth, doing too many sets and reps, trying to blunt her anxiety. She tired herself but did not quell the worry.

If Ruul were here now, she would marry him in a second. All it took was the knowledge that he might not be around to make Taz realize how much she really loved him. She hoped it wasn't too late.

She had no patience with the workout machines. She loaded plates onto the bar, squatted with more than she could safely handle, managed to keep from falling and being crushed. The dumbbells she bench pressed were five kilos past her usual maximum and she did too many sets.

After an hour she couldn't move any more weight. Her muscles were pumped so full that she could barely bend any joint; it was as if she had balloons under her skin, skin stretched so tight it felt as if she moved suddenly it would tear, spilling her muscles, her guts, her bones onto the gym floor.

She went to the shower, dialed the spray to its hardest and as hot as she could stand it. Vapor fogged the room, coated the mirrors, condensed and ran down the walls.

The two POs sent to check out the Zonn Ruins had not reported in. Two more units were sent to find out why. It was dark and they had found the flitter but no sign of the missing officers yet. Taz didn't doubt that the pair had met resistance of some kind and might be fertilizing plant roots somewhere. She hoped Ruul wasn't with them.

When her fingers started to pucker she shut the water off. Stood under the dryer until she was parched. Went to her bedroom and sat naked on the bed. Stared at the wall.

She should try to get some sleep; but no, she knew it would be a wasted effort. Despite the grueling workout, despite the long shower, she was still wired. And she didn't want to take any chem that might make her dull and stupid if a call came in the middle of the night. Better to find something useful to do, she had to be awake—

The com chimed. She swatted it to life before the first cycle ended. "Yes?"

"Chief, this is Thumal."

The WC for the corpse-stealer's shift. "Go."

"We, ah, found Nestom and Parleel. At the Zonn Ruins. Dead. Broken necks."

"Jesu Damn."

"Yeah. And we found Oro, too. Also a broken neck."

Taz's heart froze, her body turned to steel. "Oh, God." Time stopped, the universe burned, she with it. The final death-rattle of her words grated from her as stone slammed into diamond: "Oh, God!"

Ruul was dead. All was bleak beyond words.

"He's lucky," the WC said.

For a beat it didn't make sense. She blinked. Found she had one final word in her: "Lucky?"

"It's a fucking miracle, that's what it is."

"What are you talking about?"

"Him surviving like that."

Taz was born again; Atlas returned, took the weight of the planet from her shoulders. Allowed her to go free.

Ruul was alive?

Alive!

"He's in pretty bad shape," the WC said. "Gonna be in spinal rehab for a couple months. He'd have been as dead as the others, except when the boys found him, there was a goddamn vouch plugged into him, pumping myelostat and antiplaz and Buddha knows what-all into him. Weirdest fucking thing, a vouch out in the middle of nowhere like that."

Taz was already up and moving, jerking clothes on, heedless of her hair, her face. He was *alive*! She had to get to him.

"He's at the Southside Mediplex. I thought you might have some questions for him so they're keeping him awake until you get there—"

That was the last she heard of that particular call. She was out the bedroom door and yelling.

"Saval! He's alive, goddammit, he's alive! Saval! Get dressed!"

She'd never been so happy in all her life. Never.

TWENTY-FIVE

RUUL DIDN'T LOOK so hot but he was more than a little lucky to be alive. Bork watched his sister beam at the injured man where he stretched out inside his Healy unit, and if love were sunshine the room would look like the heart of a nova. Ruul wasn't going to be feeling much from the neck down for a couple of months, until his spinal cord underwent reversion and repair, but he could still smile.

"You stupid bastard," Taz said. "Why didn't you yell or something?"

His voice was weak when he spoke but didn't quaver. "The two buffoons had a gun jammed into my ribs. Noise would have gotten me pierced. I decided I'd rather put that off as long as I could. Besides, if you and the gray giant had come rumbling back into the bar, they might have gotten you, too."

"I'm a trained cool," she said. "I'd have shot the guns out of their hands."

"Right."

The medic standing next to the Healy adjusting the monitor panel shook his head. "You must have a patron god concerned about you, M. Oro. Not everybody who gets his neck broken has a top-of-the-line vouch idling nearby looking for somebody to latch on to."

Bork raised an eyebrow at the medic. "Just how did that happen?"

"The EEG and MEG pattern locked into the unit's primary care mode belongs to this fellow you're looking for, according to the printout. Apparently something fairly major must have happened to him."

"How you figure?" Bork asked. Taz, focused on Ruul, didn't seem to be paying much attention here.

"Well, the PC mode is what runs these things. Once you are entered into the machine's operating system, you are who it takes care of. It won't leave to help somebody two meters away if they slip and break a leg or something; it is yours. If you die, then the basic first aid mode kicks in and the thing is available to offer whatever it can to anybody who is ill or injured within its range. System default, built into all the top models. The manufacturer makes a big deal out of it but it's basically to cover lawsuits. Wouldn't look too good to have a life-saving vouch idling its motors while people were dropping like flies all around it; that doesn't generate a lot of sympathy for medcoes on the planets where they still use human juries. According to the records, your priest or whoever stopped transmitting his EEG and MEG patterns all of a sudden. With its primary program cancelled, the vouch zeroed in on the nearest human, in this case M. Oro, and when it turned out he was in need of help, as evidenced from his disturbed vital functions, it rolled over and plugged itself into him. The newer models can do that without being specifically instructed to do so; they have some leeway."

"Lucky for Ruul," Bork observed.

"A miracle. The vouch must have gotten to him within sixty seconds of his injury. Another thirty or forty seconds and it would have probably been too late."

"I want it," Ruul said. "The vouch. I'm going to give it an electrical plug of its own and let it graze for the rest of its life. Maybe bring it a mate and breed little vouches."

Taz smiled, something she'd been doing a lot of in the last few minutes. She glanced up at Bork. He knew what she wanted.

"What say we step out into the corridor for a few minutes?" Bork said to the medic.

"Huh? Why?"

"I think Chief Bork there has something she wants to say to M. Oro in private."

"Oh. Oh, sure."

Taz pressed her hand against the thick clear plastic as if the gesture might be able to transfer some of what she felt to the injured man.

"Listen," she said, "I need to tell you something."

"I'm not going anywere. Fire away."

"You still want to marry me? Exclusive contract?"

"Well, I don't know. I'm not really up for it at the moment."

"Ruul . . ."

"Don't get all weepy on me, Tazzi. It's a stupid question; we Oros don't change our minds about such things. I'd marry you in a San Yubi second and you know it."

"Okay."

" 'Okay'? Just like that? 'Okay'? "

"Soon as you get well."

He grinned, tried to move, she could see it on his face.

"What are you doing?"

"Trying to get up and out of this thing. Open the lid. Get me an exoframe."

"I can't. You know better than that."

"Then I am going to get well faster than anybody in history ever has. Why, parts of me are healing even as we speak. I can't feel them but I'm sure they are."

She laughed. "I love you," she said.

"I know. Me, too, you."

Taz laughed again. Why, it hadn't hurt a bit to say that. In fact, it felt quite wonderful.

"Those people are going to be sorry they hurt you."

"Whoa, hold up. You aren't going after them? Not after what I told you? They walked into the fucking wall and fucking disappeared."

"We know. Missel is working on a device that will let us follow them."

"Tazzi . . ."

"Hey, I'm a cool, remember? You said I could work after we were married; it wouldn't bother you any."

"Yeah, well, if I weren't lying here like a sack of soypro maybe it wouldn't bother me."

"Are you going to give me trouble about this?"

He managed a dry chuckle. "Not much. If I were up and myself, I would."

"If you were up and yourself, we'd be destroying the room with our naked bodies and chasing bad guys would be the last thing on my mind. That make you feel better?"

"Well. Maybe a little. Tazzi, be careful. These are sick people, they're dangerous."

"I know. And what they don't know is who they are fooling with. We Borks take care of our families. Always. Saval and I both have scores to settle. The fanatics are the ones you should be worried about."

He essayed a nod. "I think maybe you're right. But now that I've got you where I want you, more or less, I don't want to risk losing you."

"Lighten up, crip. Guys like these we eat for breakfast."

"The man who broke my neck was a giant, Tazzi, bigger than Saval. And he tossed your brother around like a ball, didn't he?"

"He caught him from behind. There isn't a man or mue alive who can come straight at Saval and walk away." It was brave talk. She hoped it were true. But even if it wasn't, she was going after this Kifo Unique. The man had caused a shitload of trouble for a whole lot of people, her included, and one way or another, he was going down. She was going to bring him back and it didn't much matter to her if he were alive or in little pieces when that happened.

Missel shook his head. "Listen, to be sure about this I need a couple of days to run tests."

"No," Taz said. "We can't afford the time. We don't know where the other side of the Zonn trail leads. A couple of days might put them out of reach."

Deep in the bowels of the police electronic lab, Missel shook his head yet again. The device lay on the table, hooked into a test grid. It was no bigger than a package of flicksticks, an innocuous rectangle with a rounded bulge on one end, flat gray spunplast with a couple of buttons and diode-analogs on it. "You're the ones who pointed out it was dangerous."

"Is it dangerous?" Bork asked.

"Well . . ."

"Come on, Missel—"

"Not that we can tell. It's got an overload kickout and a short relay and pin-it. It'll draw power, there's an inducer that will pull more than enough from any place in 'cast radius, plus I've installed a battery that should give you plenty of spare juice, you need it, but . . ."

" 'But' what?" Taz said.

"Look, you have to have a team of scientists on this! I know I'm just a second grade cool-tech, I'm not a theoretical type, but this is *big*! You are talking about a whole new branch of physics here! Interdimensional stuff! There are some guys at the University who would come all over themselves to get their hands on this! We're talking about Helsinki Prize–class stuff here. Listen, I have to pass this on, I can't sit on it. I can't believe nobody ever thought of it before."

"Somebody did," Bork said. He nodded at the device.

"Yeah," Missel said. "That's right, but it got lost. We can't lose it again. I'm sorry, I have to insist on this, this is too valuable—"

"Tell you what," Taz said. "After we collect these geeps, the toy and all the specs are yours, Missel. You can do whatever you want with it. Hell, somebody is gonna win the Helsinki Prize, why shouldn't it be you? You're good enough to work backward and figure out the theory, right?"

The skinny man blinked. Bork almost laughed, held it in but barely. Scientists were a strange breed. It had never occurred to him to try and take credit for this; his face said so as plain as a large-print reader.

"Huh?" he said.

Taz did laugh. "Missel, you don't want to be a labbo all your life. This is your ticket to respectability. Only we get to use it first."

The light of intellectual dawn shined from the man's eyes. The possibilities flooded from him like dance-floor laser beams.

"Oh. Oh, wow."

"Show us how it works," Taz said. "And when we are done, it's all yours. Missel? You there?"

"Huh? Oh, yeah. What?"

This time Bork laughed with his sister.

The slab of material looked as solid as anything Taz had ever seen. She touched it and it sucked heat from her hand— it felt like a chunk of frozen steel. She pushed against the door-sized block and it was heavy enough so it didn't budge.

Missel blinked like someone with dry-eye disease, the device he had produced gripped in a sweaty hand. He had explained the controls to them. They were in a section of the lab that could be closed off, and the three of them were alone. Saval said, "Here, lemme do it."

"Your butt," Taz said. "Me."

He looked at her. "We both go."

She nodded.

Saval took the device. Pointed it at the slab of material. Looked at Taz again, at the tech, then pressed the button.

The gunmetal blue-gray turned to smoke, flowing in wild patterns, but contained by the bounds of the material as a solid.

"It did that before," Missel said. "I tossed a light pen into it and it vanished."

"Well," Bork said, "if we see your pen, we'll get it for you."

Together he and Taz stepped into the wall.

TWENTY-SIX _____

WHEN KIFO STEPPED into the realm of the Zonn, his flock stood bunched and waiting. They were not all afraid, but fear rose from some of them as heat waves do from hot plastcrete. Kifo smiled. The wall behind them towered to infinity, or at least past the height that the eyes of men could see. The ground crawled with a blue fog nearly the color of the wall itself, a sinuous and thick blanket that curled and flowed around the ankles of the few as if it were alive and lapping at their flesh with gaseous tongues. In the distance blue-white lights danced like giant fireflies in the skies above fat hillocks that appeared to move in some kind of repeating S-pattern, each hill moving at a slightly different speed and cycling back to where it began. Visibility was limited to a few kilometers; beyond that a purplish murk occluded the air, giving the already strange scene an even more sinister look. It was slightly cool, though not uncomfortably so. The air had an acrid smell and it tingled against mucous membranes, drying them, making them just a little raw.

Something cried out in the distance, the rattle of a great bird, perhaps, or that which easily mimicked one. A low hum, a drone answered the cry, a sound that resonated deep in the pit of Kifo's belly, as if attuning itself to humans, or perhaps tuning them to it.

An orange light flashed at the edge of his peripheral vision and was gone. When he took a step, red sparks sprayed and showered down, drifting like pollen back into the blue fog. Kifo laughed. He could understand their fear. The landscape was nearly as alien to him as it was to any other among the Few. The wonder of the Zonn realm was that the gods seldom let it stay the same for long. He knew the fog from before, the shifting hills, but the sparks were new to him and the air not quite as he remembered it.

"Come," the Unique said to the Few. "We travel to Sanctuary."

Taz's first impression when she got over the shock of not being in the cool labs was easy: "Jesu Damn," she said. "It looks like a giant warehouse."

There were tall, twisted columns scattered at odd intervals. She couldn't see the tops of them because there was some kind of shimmery yellow fog a dozen meters up that formed a ceiling. It roiled back and forth but seemed to hold its shape pretty much in a flat plane. And it wasn't really as if there were walls to make it a warehouse, but somehow she got an impression of them. When she looked more closely, the walls weren't there. But sort of were . . .

"Here's Missel's pen," Saval said. "I think."

Taz turned to look at her brother. He held something up on the palm of one hand.

A light pen is a fairly simple thing. A tube, maybe fifteen centimeters long, smaller in diameter than a woman's little finger, round on one end, pointed on the other. The outer shell is simple spuncast plastic. Holding it like a wand or pencil activates a small but bright beam, a solid-state bioelectric laser that shines from the pointed end. The device is used to mark on holoprojic or flatscreen monitors. It has a minimal amount of memory, and can be switched from a point to a fan beam. In a pinch it can be used as a light, provided what you wish to illuminate isn't particularly large or far away. You can read a hardcopy note or map in a dim surveillance vehicle, find the key slot to a dark door, find your way to the fresher in a power failure. Not the acme of man's technology, a light pen, but a useful tool.

What Saval held on his palm looked to be a mating between an engineer and a tree. It was almost the right length, but bent and twisted like a boiled noodle. Patches of spunplast appeared as darker spots against a lighter material that looked like bark. Tiny tendrils like rootlets radiated from the diameter in what Taz guessed was a Fibonacci sequence. The entire thing had a glow to it, as if the laser within were lit but diffused through the tendrils.

"Jesu Damn," she said.

"Yeah."

Something growled nearby, and both Taz and Saval spun to face the sound. Whatever it was must be adept at ventriloquism or invisible—there was nothing there.

Saval came up from his shooting crouch. Said, "I want to try something here." He pointed his left spetsdöd and triggered it.

Taz saw the blast of compressed gas erupt from the barrel. Watched the tiny dart fly. She didn't know exactly what normal velocity was for a spetsdöd, probably two hundred, maybe two-fifty meters a second, subsonic, but too fast to dodge, anyway.

The dart that emerged from her brother's weapon did so at perhaps *two* meters a second. If she sprinted, she could catch it.

She started to speak, but Saval waved her silent. "Watch that column," he said. "Eye level, in the middle."

The column was maybe fifteen meters away. Taz lost sight of the spetsdöd's dart halfway there—it was smaller than a housefly, after all—but she saw the little missile when it impacted the column, right where Saval indicated. The action was much like a pebble thrown into a pond. There came a small impact crater, then concentric ripples.

Taz turned away from the column and looked at Saval. "Man."

"Yeah. It hit just as hard, but it took seven and a half seconds to get there. Never seen anything like it."

For a moment neither of them said anything. Then Bork said, "Try your com."

Taz nodded. Good thought.

The com was dead, at least on the receiving end. Maybe somebody could hear her but somehow she doubted it.

Saval waved the little device Missel had built them. "Good thing this has got its own power," he said. "I don't think we're drawing any from the 'cast in here."

"Something else," Taz said. "Given the light pen, I don't think we should stay here a real long time."

"I second that. What say we go back now?"

"Yeah."

Saval turned and faced the wall behind them, pointed the device, pushed the button. For a heartbeat nothing happened and Taz felt a surge of panic. Then the wall roiled as it had before, turning fluid. She began breathing again.

"Let's go," Saval said.

"Yeah, let's. I don't think I've ever looked forward to seeing Missel's skinny face so much before."

The two of them moved as one, stepped into the wall.

And out into darkness.

The place that Kifo called Sanctuary was easy enough to find, though he could not have given exact directions on how to arrive there using normal geographical terms. The terrain here was fluid and there didn't seem to be any landmarks to offer as guides. That big M-shaped hill to one's right, say, seemed unique, but after walking for a time one might look up and notice that it was now on one's *left*. How and when such a transition might have taken place was a mystery. Or one might blink and, between the closing of eyelids and the reopening, the hill could vanish entirely. The Zonns' domain was not a place for someone with an inflexible mindset.

So, one had to ignore such things as shifting mountains and glowing fogs and proceed with determination to reach Sanctuary. Kifo had happened on it accidentally during his second crossing into the gods' land. His next visit had shown him that he could find it again. The method was simplicity itself: all roads led to Sanctuary. One merely had to pick a direction and go and eventually one would arrive. What could be easier?

Something gibbered and moaned as it flew past the troop, the sound of its tortured cry dopplering so close and loud that it must be within arm's reach. There was nothing to see, however. The sound of the invisible shrieker faded to silence. Several voices among the Few called upon the gods for protection. Kifo smiled again. Where else would they be more protected than here?

Ahead, a brighter spot gleamed, a patch of whiter blue against the distant dimness. Ah. Sanctuary. If the Few had been impressed after the initial crossing, they were about to be astounded. He laughed yet again, and the sound seemed to reverberate as if they were in a narrow tunnel. It didn't matter. Sanctuary lay just ahead.

Bork felt the fear try to claim him and he fought it down. It was almost as dark as black paint in here, but not quite. The distorted light pen he still held gave off a faint glow through its tendrils. After a second he could see the tritium dial of his chronograph gleaming brightly under the base of his left spetsdöd, and the tiny green diode on the power pack of the electronic device clutched too tightly in his hand. It was dark, but it was a *normal* kind of dark.

"Taz—"

"Right here. Let me get my belt light . . ."

The small flashlight flared on wide beam and the halogen lamp revealed what looked like a wall of pressed fiberboard twelve centimeters from Bork's nose. When he took a quick step back in reaction, he bumped into something real solid and real cold.

"Where the fuck—?" Taz began.

With his back against something that didn't seem like it was going to move, Bork lifted his right leg and put his foot against the fiberboard wall. He had a good angle and when he straightened his leg, the fiberboard split, shattered, and partially fell away. A couple more kicks and there was a hole big enough for Bork to step through.

Beyond the fiberboard wall was a dimly lit room. Bork stepped out into it, Taz right behind him. Before they could do more than look around, people started yelling.

"Don't move!" came a voice. "Police!"

Taz blinked, shook her head. "Damn, Saval, this is the impound room. It's half a klick away from the lab!"

The WC for the impound was more than a little upset. He very much wanted to know how the fuck she and Saval had gotten past a locked door and two guards into the evidence vault without tripping an alarm or being fired on. She didn't tell him. He was an old-timer, had been on the force for thirty-five years, but fortunately Taz outranked him. She gave him a story about some new top-secret penetration gear, a hush-hush variant of Reason's can opener, and promised to let him know what was going on as soon as she could.

When they were outside alone and heading for the lab, Taz said, "What *is* going on, Saval? You have any idea?"

"Well. We came back through one of the other slabs of Zonn wall. I dunno why, or how, but the stuff must be connected in some way."

"But we never moved. I mean, we went into that . . . place, turned around and came straight back through the same spot."

"Maybe we were a centimeter or two off," he said. "Maybe a centimeter in there translates to a kilometer out here. Or maybe it's a function of time and not space. I dunno. That tech, Scanner, he warned us it was a weird place."

"That's the fucking truth."

"I think we're gonna have to be real careful when we go back into the walls."

"The guys who chopped up all those people and broke Ruul's neck are in there. I'm going after them."

"I said, 'when,' Taz, not 'if.' "

"Listen, Saval, you don't have to do this—"

"Shut up, little sister. I have business to finish, too."

She nodded. Managed a grin. "Missel will probably be surprised to see us come through the lab door."

"Wait until he sees his light pen."

She smiled at that, too, but it was a sober smile. The light pen had been in the Zonn place for only a few hours and it had been changed more than a little.

What would happen to a person who wandered around in there for any kind of time? She wanted to catch the killers sure enough, but she didn't really have any desire to grow roots and stay there permanently. No, thank you. Probably be wise to keep moving, get your task done and come home fast. Then again, a wise woman wouldn't be likely to go back to such a crazy place, did she have a choice.

Well, fuck it. She was a mover, not a thinker. Nobody had ever accused her of being too smart, why worry about it now?

TWENTY-SEVEN

LIKE A PEARL lit from within, Sanctuary gleamed ahead, shimmery white and full of promise. Kifo strode through a field of sparks and fog toward the sacred place. And none too soon, either. The edges of his robe had begun to grow a kind of pale orange feathery mildew; his shoes were too hot upon his feet and the air grated metallically in his nose and throat and lungs. He could also feel the fear of the Few lessen as Sanctuary loomed closer. They knew the story, albeit only from dry lessons instilled by rote. Now they saw the reality.

One of the Few screamed.

Kifo turned in time to see a blurry shadow sweep over the rear of the troop, a moving blot of inky red shot through with swirls of blue. The flitter-sized blob engulfed one of the Few—too fast for Kifo to catch even a glimpse of the face—and in a heartbeat spun away and up. The dark splotch vanished into the haze, taking with it the straggler.

Panic blossomed in the ranks of the few. Like mushrooms after a hard rain, the fear returned and the Few were but an instant away from a blind stampede when Kifo bellowed at them. "Hold!"

Years of obedience to their Unique stopped cold the frightened group.

"There is nothing to fear! That one"—he waved at the sky, realized he didn't know whether the person snatched was a man or a woman—"that one's faith slackened, even on the

209

verge of Sanctuary! Thus was paid the price! If your faith is strong, you need not worry!"

There was a rumble among them, a prayer-filled walla. He understood their doubts. Who could know if their faith were strong enough? Would faith protect them? Was it so?

Well, such should be true, Kifo reasoned. It might be so. What was more important than the loss of one of them was that he maintained his control, his appearance of power and knowledge. The truth of it was that while he was certain the gods meant to elevate him into their ranks, he as yet did not know precisely how such a thing was to be done. Everything that took place in the Zonn realm had to be considered important, every act or lack thereof could be part of a test for him. Did he have to lose all of the Few along the path, well, so be it. They were not important, after all, merely part of his own unfolding. But until the moment when the gods saw fit to reveal their plan to him, Kifo felt it necessary to hold the flock in as much order as he could manage. It seemed the right thing to do.

"Follow me to Sanctuary," he commanded. "And know that the gods do not err in their actions!"

He kicked up more sparks as he turned back to face the goal. He was yet unable to see the pavilion clearly, but he had been there before, and such things as the dark splotch that took one of his people were not allowed therein.

Like frightened sheep, the Few followed him.

True, the gods did not err, but men could hardly understand the reasons gods did things, and the Zonn might choose to wipe the Few away as a sweaty man wipes his brow. Who could say? But a dog who kept a keen eye open might avoid an idle slap by a master who couldn't be bothered to stand and chase him.

Thus did Kifo strive to keep his eyes keen.

Missel regarded the thing that had been his light pen. It lay upon a carbonex work table under a denscris safety dome, illuminated by the table's lamps.

"It appears to be moving," Missel said. "Fascinating."

"Maybe it's about to give birth," Taz said. "Missel, about the other thing . . ."

Without taking his gaze from the mutated light pen, Missel waved her question off. "No problem. Everything is in the viral matrix; you'll have the duplicate in another hour and an half. Chee, would you look at that. The plastic is changing color, there, near the end . . ."

Taz couldn't help but wonder if Missel might not say the same thing were it his hand undergoing the metamorphosis. Scientists were strange beings.

She glanced at Saval. He shrugged, gestured toward the lab's door with a sideways nod.

She followed him outside. They stood in front of the thick observation window out of the lab tech's ken. "What?"

"We need to pick up a few things."

"Such as?"

"Well, we didn't have any trouble moving at normal speed inside the wall, but you saw what happened to the spetsdöd dart. Must be some kind of damping field for stuff past a certain velocity, makes projectile weapons useless. The gadget Missel made works, so we can probably use electrical or nervous spectrum weaponry. Shockstiks, hand wands, maybe."

"Unless something in there likes juice." She nodded toward the light pen at which the tech still stared. "Maybe the light pen's power attracted whatever changed it into *that.*"

"Could be. Or maybe it was the plastic," Saval said. "If we take wands and they turn into tree roots, we'll toss them. There are a bunch of them and only two of us. We'll need some kind of edge. Unless you want to bring help."

"No. This is personal."

"What I figured. So, we'll get a couple of wands, knives, maybe staves or spears."

Taz chuckled. "Funny. Here we are at the peak of civilization, able to travel faster than light from world to world, and we're talking about hunting bad guys with knives and spears."

Saval nodded. "The place inside the wall is a new game and we don't know the rules yet. Best we try and cover as many bets as we can."

"Mmm. Let's go see if the police armorer can turn out some sticks for us. You hungry?"

"I could eat."

"We have a while before Missel's folks finish the dupe. What say we grab a quick lunch before we start packing gear?"

"Sounds good."

Pickle was just walking away from their table when the assassin came through the wall.

The human tide in the Owl was at the lowest ebb Bork had seen, though there were still quite a few people inside. Their table was near the south wall and the big man rippled through the west side ten meters away. It was eerie to watch, like an entcom special effect: the guy stepped out of the wall as if it were an upright tank of water; the material seemed to cling to him slightly with surface tension before it let him go. There might have been a soft *pop*! but Bork couldn't be sure given the background noise in the restaurant.

"Holy shit," Pickle said, stopping to stare at the apparition.

Bork couldn't make the shot unless he moved. A waiter and two patrons were partially between him and the hooded and robed figure, plus Pickle herself. Taz, her back to the assassin, saw something on Bork's face, started to turn to see and speak at the same time. "Saval . . . ?"

Bork shoved away from the table, moved to his left, brought his left spetsdöd up. He'd give the guy a spray of AP rounds and see how he liked that. But he had to get a clear field of fire first. Wouldn't do any good to yell 'Down!' You did that in a room full of civilians without training and maybe a couple would flatten. The rest would just turn around and stare at you. Or worse, stand up and further block your field.

Time ran slow like it sometimes did when things got risky, thick as cold lube in a North Katoan winter.

The assassin saw him. Nothing like motion to attract the eye of a predator. Or prey.

Bork's spetsdöd came up. It should be an easy shot, but you had to allow for the adrenaline surge. The Thing in the Cave would rather run than fight, so its gross moves got better when it was startled; good for speedy legs, bad for needlework—or precision shooting. Bork had practiced with the other matadors to compensate for the hormone rushes, but sometimes the epinephrine storms lashed harder than expected.

This man had beaten him before and the Thing in the Cave knew it. It didn't want to fight: *Go, leave, now! Fuck shooting! Run!*

Bork ignored the cry. His spetsdöd came up, but too high. In what seemed a painfully slow motion, he dragged it back down. *No! Not important. Run! Run fast!*

The assassin leaped back into the wall.

A small sphere, about the size of a big man's clenched fist, fell to the floor where the assassin had been.

"Damn!" Bork jumped. Pickle, mired in the thick time, turned in slow motion toward him but she wasn't important. The customers were out of the way. The waiter twisting in the syrupy air . . .

Window. There was a window, to his rear and right side. Glass? Or plastic?

Pickle moved a hair. Into Bork's path. Taz was coming to her feet but he was already past her. The twisting waiter had dropped his tray at the sight of a man disappearing into a wall and the tray hung in the air, settling slowly, leaving two mugs of something hovering just above it as gravity called to them all: Come to the floor—

Bork's attention was on the sphere. It hadn't bounced very high, couple centimeters, meant it was heavy. Stressed plastic or metal shell, didn't matter which if it was what Bork thought it was.

He hardly even noticed Pickle when he ran over her; she vanished from his tunnel vision and if she made a sound it didn't stick, slid off him.

Almost there—

He dove, grabbed the ball, rolled, came up facing back the way he'd come, slammed into a table. Too much momentum carried him and the table another two meters and into the wall. The table shattered but that wasn't important; what was important was the heavy sphere in his hand. He thumped against the wall, managed to bend his neck forward enough so his head didn't connect when his back hit. It was a stunning collision, pieces of the table, plates, eating utensils flew about him in eccentric orbits but he was still up, still conscious, still able to move. He arched his back, hard, flexed his shoulders and scapulae, snapped away from the wall. Took a step, pulled his hand back, threw the heavy ball as hard as he could at the window. Felt the muscles of his belly knot with the effort as his throwing hand nearly touched the floor.

Let it be glass or cheap plastic, he thought. Don't let it be denscris or clearcarb, please—!

The window was a series of panes, three ovals across, three down, set in a larger oval of carved wood. The ball hit the top center pane with enough force to punch a jagged hole through it.

Plastic. Good.

What was outside that wall? An alley he remembered, an underground refuse disposal chute covered by a grate, some crates stacked up—

"Saval—?" Taz yelled. "What—?"

That was as far as she got. The wall surrounding the window grew a circular hollow; Bork felt his ears pop as the air pressure in the room dropped and the wall suddenly vanished in a perfect circle. There was a flash of bluish light dopplering away. With the supports gone, another section of the wall collapsed. Came a terrible noise, a thousand shovels scraping on plastcrete. Dust ballooned into the room, was sucked out of sight as if by a giant vacuum cleaner. People screamed, tumbled to the floor, and Bork felt himself tugged by a giant's hand toward the hole in the wall. But the pull stopped almost immediately.

All over.

A big chunk of the building's wall was gone, absorbed by the implosion device, but nobody inside had died. Through the now-ragged hole, Bork saw the imploded ball of compacted material buried to half its depth in the hard surface of the alley floor. The outside of the ball was a mottled gray.

Close. Real close.

Spring came. Time melted and flowed normally again.

Pickle, her silks torn from one shoulder, one surgically perfect breast exposed, came to stand in front of Bork. She stood on her toes, put her hands on his shoulders, and kissed him full on the mouth. She thrust her tongue through his lips and passion flowed hotly with it for a moment before she pulled back.

"I never saw anybody move like that before," she said. "You saved our lives. I was scared shitless. God, I want to fuck your brains out!"

Bork managed a nervous laugh.

Taz came up. "Another time, Pickle." To Bork she said, "We've got to go, Saval. The Supervisor just called and wants to talk to me. He must know about the toy Missel made for us. We've got to leave before he tells me not to."

Bork nodded. "Okay."

As they started for the door, Taz said, "You moved pretty good back there, brother. Thanks."

"All part of the service, sister."

TWENTY-EIGHT

SANCTUARY.

Once, Kifo went with a rich jane on a vacation. Well, he had been on vacation, he had been working, but the place was a small island out in the middle of the Mafalme Ocean, toward the equator. The air temperature was perfect for running around naked, not too cool, not too hot, and with a little sunblock spray, that's what almost everybody did. Gentle breezes blew most of the time. Semitropical rains washed the place, usually in the evening about dusk, warm patters that nobody minded. Fruit grew naturally on the trees and bushes, there weren't any snakes or particularly nasty bugs or small beasts about, and the most industrious things Kifo had seen the entire trip—aside from other whores working, like himself—had been gecko lizards chasing moths on the thin screens of the hut the client had rented. As the afternoons wound down, Kifo would make fruity alcohol drinks and he and the client would sit and watch the sun sink into the quiet ocean while he slowly pumped her from behind. It was his best memory as a young man. He had thought that isle the perfect place on the entire planet, perhaps in all the galaxy, until he first visited Sanctuary.

Sanctuary made the island paradise seem like hell.

He leaned on his walking stick and grinned at the rapture he could see in his flock. Not only were they safe here, they were probably feeling better than they had ever felt in all their lives.

Once you crossed into Sanctuary, there were fuzzy white walls off in the distance no matter which way you looked. Even right behind you, a step away from where you entered, it seemed that the wall was kilometers away. Did you turn and step back, you would find yourself outside again, without any real sense of having reached the boundary. Leaving the place was thus always quite a jolt—one second you were deep inside, the next instant, you were out. Like birth, perhaps, only faster.

The air in Sanctuary was heady, perfumed by some smoky, musky scent that always reminded Kifo of hot sex. It was as neutral a temperature as the island's had been, but without the worry of ultraviolet rays. The light was soft, indirect, and he had never seen the source. Not, he would have to admit if pressed, that he had ever looked particularly hard. It was bad form to examine too closely a gift from one's gods.

The ground of Sanctuary was a cushion; it gave slightly underfoot but was like a firm mattress when one chose to lie upon it. Seamless, the ground was slightly darker than the distant fuzzy walls, almost a sand color, and had enough texture to feel slightly rough to a bare hand, though not rough enough to scratch naked buttocks. Because it was so benign a place, Kifo almost always stripped away his clothing when he entered, if not immediately then fairly soon thereafter.

Too, there was something in the air that gave one the sense of well-being that certain psychedelic chemicals did. Having experimented with mushroom intoxication as a young man, he knew the sensation, but this, of course, was better. He felt powerful, potent, grinned almost constantly, and sighed a great deal from the pure pleasure of breathing. Did one but concentrate upon the physical sensations, each respiration could seem akin—albeit somewhat distantly—to a sexual orgasm.

When the old books spoke of this place, they had described it but badly. The prophets of those days must have been speaking from other than personal experience, or else been terrible writers indeed.

Members of his flock had begun to discard their clothing. Some of them stood grinning, enjoying the feel of the place; others linked hands or touched each other or themselves and relished those sensations.

Kifo laughed; the sound flowed from him in silvery platinum peals. The body gloried in the joy of Sanctuary but there was much more ahead for him. Let his flock be distracted by cheap ecstacy; he had bigger goals in mind.

And so far, the gods had not chosen to gainsay them.

For now, he could pause and refresh himself. Then it would be time to proceed onward. To the heart of Sanctuary, a place no man had ever gone.

Only now, Kifo had become the Chosen One. Truly the Unique at last. *He* would go there.

Silver and platinum laughter glittered in the air.

Taz felt a little silly, carrying a wooden staff her own height. Crowed to her belt she had a sheathed knife with a fat blade as long as her hand, an eight-charge hand wand and four photon bombs, as well as a duplicate of the electronic device that allowed passage into the Zonn space. Saval had been adamant about that, and would have liked a third one for a spare, had they been able to get the parts in. He wasn't keen on being stuck in the other dimension, wherever it was.

"You ready?" Saval asked. He wore his spetsdöds, even though they wouldn't be of much use if they behaved as before. Plus he had a stick and wand and photo blinders, too, as well as a simple magnetic compass, no electronics, and a line-of-sight marking laser.

"Yeah. Let's do it."

Even though the geometry and maybe the time and space were all screwed up in the land behind the wall—or maybe *within* the wall—they had elected to try and follow the Few directly. To that end, they had flittered to the Zonn Ruins. Saval lifted the flashing police evidence seal tape and Taz ducked under it. He followed her.

They reached the wall quick enough. "Your toy or mine?" Taz said.

He waved at her. "Might as well be sure yours works."

She pointed the device at the gunmetal surface, pressed the control. Once again the material that blunted diamond drills swirled.

Inside, the terrain, if it could be properly called that, looked much the same as before. Sparks showered up when Taz took a step, and she smiled at that. It had a certain beauty to it. She walks in fire . . .

"Look at this," Saval said.

She turned, regarded the compass he held. It was a thin plastic circle, not much thicker than a stad coin, with a clear cover. A slender needle of steel pivoted on a sharp post, able to turn freely. The needle was magnetized, dark on one end, and would turn toward the northern pole of Tembo, the actual geographic point being close enough to the magnetic one to be accurate enough for general direction. Since the dark end of the needle always pointed that way, aligning itself with the planet's magnetic field, a compass was a simple, if crude, method to find one's way around. Not as good as a radio triangulator, which could pinpoint your location to within six meters anywhere on the world, or even to a broadcast field strength meter, which would relate your position to the nearest power beacon within ten meters.

The needle on Saval's compass spun like the blade of a gyrojet copter, so fast it was nothing more than a metallic blur.

"So much for that idea," Saval said. "Magnetism is fucked, let's see how light works." He peeled one of the photon bombs from his belt. This was a sphere about the size of a child's marble, black plastic coating the outside. Saval squeezed the orb, twice, then once again for a longer time. "Close your eyes," he said, "or better if you turn your back. That way."

She nodded as he tossed the little ball. Turned around and looked away. Three seconds later red light flared, barely visible even with her eyes opened. A pale shadow appeared there faded, the dim red dwindling back to the normal—such that passed for normal here—lighting.

"Well, that didn't seem particularly impressive."

Saval said, "The light shifted into the red; it should have been white. So much for light as a weapon."

"You want to shoot me with the hand wand to see if that works?"

He laughed. "Maybe later. I can use this if the need arises." He waved his staff. It was made of some springy dark wood, was as long as he was tall, as big around as her wrist. "Their weapons won't be any better off than ours."

"Unless they know something we don't," she said.

Taz looked around. "I don't see any footprints."

"One direction is as good as another," he said. "Straight ahead until we come to something that suggests otherwise."

They started off.

Bork maintained a steady pace, not his fastest, but one Taz could keep up with easily. This was as weird a place as he had ever been, no doubt about that. Compass spun like a drive rotor, spetsdöd darts moved like snails, no radio or com worked at all, the light bombs changed colors. He got the feeling that if he stood too long in one spot, he might start growing roots like Missel's light pen had. Yeah, it was fascinating and all, but not a place he'd put at the top of his vacation list. He supposed he could understand why the Few might think it connected to some religious purpose. It was unlike any world unmodified men lived on. Wonder what those hills were doing, moving back and forth like that? Or the significance of the sparks that sprayed every step they took? Maybe this Kifo guy had some answers. Bork would ask him, once they caught him. Whatever his explanation, the scientists were gonna have conniptions when they got in here.

"You doing okay?" he asked Taz.

"Fine."

"Ready for a break?"

"Whenever you are."

They stopped. Bork pulled the water bottle from his belt, took a swig. Swished it around in his mouth, didn't like what it did, and spat it out.

"What—?" Taz began.

"Check this out." He poured a little water into his cupped palm. Five or six tadpolelike things swam around in the tiny puddle. Well, swam wasn't exactly right; it was more like they contorted about, snapping open and closed like little springblade knives.

"Uuughh!"

"Yeah." He tossed the polluted handful of water away, bent and set his bottle on the foggy blue ground. The haze washed over the plastic, hiding it. "Things got through a watertight seal easy enough and grew up real fast."

"Going to limit how long we can stay in here," Taz said, as she examined the water from her own bottle. He didn't need to see what poured out because Taz tossed the bottle away in disgust. "Yuk," she said.

Bork nodded, didn't say what else had occurred to him. If some kind of bug could go through watertight plastic to infect the liquid inside, what might be infecting *them*?

There was a pleasant thought.

"Better keep moving," he said.

Five or six of the Few had gathered themselves into a large naked clump and were engaging in assorted manners of sexual congress. Wet noises emerged from the mass as it undulated on the cushy ground as if it were a single being. Contented moans, groans and slurps rose and hung in the air, calling to any others who might wish to join the gestalt.

Kifo had removed his own clothes to better enjoy the air of Sanctuary, but he kept his walking stick, twirling it in his hands like a baton, keeping time to his internal music.

A dark figure loomed in the distance, coming from the nearest wall toward him.

The Unique felt a small something stir in him. A qualm? A bit of worry? Well, no, not really, this was Sanctuary, after all, but perhaps a hair of unease draped itself over him ever so lightly. Just a hair . . .

Mkono. The lumbering giant had come to Sanctuary.

Ah. That was good. He had a chore or two, Kifo recalled, and then he was to come here.

"My Unique," Mkono said. He smiled, something he did very infrequently back in the human world. It did not look especially good on him, the smile, but Kifo appreciated the energy behind it.

"Brother Hand. How goes it?"

"My efforts were of mixed results," he allowed. "The main tower at the religious institute fell to an implosion device as you ordered, as did the office of the Council of Freedom."

"This is good."

"The restaurant with the ungodly owner still stands. The policewoman and that matador were there. They fired upon me. I triggered a bomb and left it, but it must have malfunctioned, for the building still stands."

Kifo was feeling magnanimous. He waved one hand in dismissal of the failure. "It is of no importance. In fact, nothing in the world of men is of any importance any longer. We are in the lap of the gods, are we not? Who can be bothered with the sniffing and howling of jealous dogs?"

The air of Sanctuary must be seeping into the big man, for his smile faltered only slightly before it resumed full shine. "It is as you say, Unique. I would have destroyed the matador, but he is doomed to live out his life without the grace of the gods. Let him do so—a few more days or years mean nothing compared to this." Mkono waved his hand.

"You grow wise, Brother Hand."

"What now, my Unique?"

"For the moment, nothing. Enjoy Sanctuary, brother. You have earned it."

The ugly smile grew brighter still. And, Kifo reflected, perhaps it was not so ugly as all that. Given a little practice, why, it might become quite attractive.

The air of Sanctuary improved all things, after all.

Even his thinking. Before he had been limited to simple lines, causal-style reasoning. But here, his brain was aflame with oblique ways of considering things, lines that turned upon themselves and made loops, circles, side trips into other dimensions. What had been of great import in Tembo seemed trivial here. Who could be bothered by such old business? Passions that had driven him only days or even hours ago seemed now to be a waste of his energy. Yes, the air of Sanctuary improved all things.

And even *that* didn't matter, either.

Kifo laughed, until he found it an effort to breathe.

TWENTY-NINE

SOMETHING FLOATED THROUGH the foggy air about half a meter off the ground toward Taz and Saval. It didn't look like anything Taz had ever seen before. If she had to describe it she would have said it was kind of like a fat, tailless, legless cat. Didn't seem to have any eyes, either. What she thought were ears were pointed and maybe twice as big as any cat's she'd ever seen.

Saval waved at her, indicating they should move to avoid the thing. Good idea.

They walked at right angles to the floating cat.

It changed direction toward them.

The siblings exchanged glances. Walked a little faster and angled away.

The thing altered its course, gained a little altitude so that it was nearly chest level, and kept coming.

Saval twirled the staff, spinning it easily in a hand-over-hand motion. Stopped in port arms, right end high. "Now's the time to see if the hand wand works," he said. "Tickle it and see what it does. It keeps coming, I'll prod it." He waggled the staff.

Taz nodded. She peeled the hand wand from her belt. This particular stunner was a seventeen-centimeter-long cylinder about as big around as a circle made with her thumb and forefinger, a depress-and-slide switch as the single control. It was police-issue, no frills, but hand wands could be made in almost any shape and she'd seen stylized lightning bolts, dragons, even one shaped like a human penis. Wands threw a short-range, cone-shaped pattern of electrosonics that disrupted neural functions. Shoot a man with one at five meters and he went down for a fifteen-minute nap. Hit a smaller mammalian creature and the scrambled synapses might take anywhere from five minutes to five days to recover, or might not come back at all. Maybe the levitating felix over there just wanted to be friends, but in this place they could hardly take that chance. It was a long way home. If the thing had teeth or carried poison, nobody was coming to help them.

When felix was four meters away, Taz pointed the wand at it and fired. There was a slight hum that rose into ultrasonics. The fog on the lower arc of the energy cone danced in intricate geometric patterns for a beat, then went back to its normal chaotic swirl.

If the beam affected felix it wasn't apparent. It—he? she?—kept coming.

Taz said, "Want me to tap it again?"

Saval stepped forward. "No. It might not have a brain, all we know. But it has mass. We'll stay simple."

She put the wand away, lifted her own stick. It had been a while since the pugil training seminar, but she figured she could hit something that big if she had to.

Saval extended his staff as if it were a very long sword. When felix was two meters away, he jabbed at it lightly with the tip of the stick.

There came a bright yellow flash and a sudden stink like burning sulphur.

"Damn!" Saval said.

A quarter of his staff had vanished. The end of the remaining section was charred; smoke curled up from a faint orange glow within the blackened wood. He let the burned staff droop until it was across his thighs.

Felix hung in the air, no longer moving forward.

After a moment felix began to sink a bit. When it got to hip height, it stopped. It moved toward Saval, a little slower than before.

He stepped back and circled the remains of his stick as if to hammer the creature from above.

Taz watched felix. It shifted slightly, then began to rise again. It took her a second to realize what it was doing.

"It's tracking the stick," she said.

"Yeah, well let's see how it likes a hard whack on the head."

"No, wait. I don't think it wants us. I think it wants the stick."

He blinked, considered it. Shifted his grip and extended the staff away from himself in his right hand.

Felix floated over that way.

"Hmm."

"What do you think?" she said.

"I think if it wants the stick, it can have it."

With that he tossed the staff toward felix, but well past it. The purple fog enveloped the damaged weapon as it fell to the ground.

The floating creature turned, big ears toward the wooden rod, then moved toward it.

"I wonder if we should be messing with the diet of the local wildlife?" Taz said.

"I didn't see a 'Don't feed the animals' sign. What say we go before it finishes lunch?"

"Good idea."

"There's something new that way," he said. "A white blotch, there, see?"

"Yeah."

They moved off, leaving the staff to its fate.

The air of Sanctuary was heady, maybe too heady. It made for difficulty concentrating. There was something Kifo had to do, but at the moment he couldn't for the life of him recall what it was. Naked, he walked about, watching the Few cavort or lie stuporously here and there. Truly they seemed to feel as if they had reached the top of their lives. Maybe it was no more than a kennel where the gods allowed their favorite dogs to run, but as kennels went, this one was extraordinary. Even normally dour and sober Brother Mkono had relaxed, shed his clothes and elected to join assorted sexual couplings. Mkono looked as if he'd been carved from some dense wood, so hard was he.

Kifo giggled. Brother Mkono was hard all over, and his male member was in proportion to his other large dimensions. The woman on the receiving end of Mkono's attention was likely unaccustomed to such size, but did not seem to be complaining of it.

Very interesting to watch, but there was something else Kifo was supposed to do, wasn't there? Something important?

He waved his walking stick, became fascinated by the thousands of ghost walking sticks that strobed behind it. Drew interesting patterns in the perfect air, watched them fade slowly. Ah, well. It must not be too important, else he would remember it.

"Looks like a wall of light," Bork said.

Taz nodded. "Can't see anything through it."

Bork moved closer, close enough to touch the wall. Reached out, thought better of it. Given the way things were in this world, maybe putting your hand into strange places like this wasn't a good idea. "Try your staff," he said.

Taz extended the stick. The end of it vanished into the whiteness. "Doesn't feel any different than the air," she said. She pulled the wooden rod back. It didn't seem any the worse for its experience.

Bork was thinking again about whether he should risk trying his hand when Taz said, "Hello. Company."

He turned away from the white.

Half a dozen of the things like the floating meat loaf with ears moved lazily toward them.

"Looks like felix told his friends about us," Taz said.

"Felix?"

Taz nodded at the floating things. She shifted her grip on the staff, held it like a javelin. "Should we feed 'em?"

"By all means."

She threw the staff like a spear. It arced up and over the floating things, fell into the purple mists, landed soundlessly. The creatures turned and headed that way.

"I dunno how long one staff will satisfy them," Bork said. "What say we find out what's on the other side of this?"

"I'm with you."

He took a deep breath. Well. He'd walked through solid walls a couple times already. In for a demi, in for a stad . . .

Kifo's designs with his walking stick had become more and more complex. He'd progressed to making multiple figure-eights lying on their sides, sketching the sign of infinity in overlapping plates, turning in a quick circle so that he was completely surrounded by the ghosts he created. If he hurried, he could overlay a zigzag pattern before the first eight faded . . .

A big man in dark gray orthoskins came through the wall into Sanctuary. A moment later, a woman followed him.

For a few seconds it didn't track, was meaningless. Then the shock of it flowed over Kifo like ice water from a high pressure hose.

Somebody not of the Few had entered Sanctuary!

This couldn't be!

"No!" he screamed. "You aren't allowed in here!"

Taz blinked at the scene before her. It was right out of a pornoproj—a bunch of naked men and women wrapped around each other, rolling around on the ground, making noises of pleasure. And one guy standing there waving a stick and yelling at them.

Jesu Damn. Whatever she'd expected, it wasn't this.

Bork shook his head. Well. Looks like they'd found the folks they were after. But he'd have guessed all day long and not come up with *this* scenario. Some party.

"Mkono!" a man screamed. "Mkono! Infidels!"

A figure separated itself from the squirming mass of flesh;

he was as naked as the rest, but Bork recognized him even
without clothes. Couldn't be two like him on this world.

A large chunk of supercooled metal formed in Bork's belly
all of a moment. It felt like a boulder. The rock of defeat
and fear.

Bork reached for the hand wand on his belt. Just because it
hadn't worked on the floating thing didn't mean it wouldn't
work on humans. Didn't mean it *would,* either. Only one way
to find out.

"Unclean! Desecration! Blasphemy! Stop them or the gods
will smite us all dead!"

The big man—Mkono, was he?—grew a following as the others on the ground untangled themselves and began scrambling
toward Bork.

The matador wanted very much to toss the wand aside
and meet the giant's charge barehanded. That wouldn't be
real bright, given what happened last time they fought, plus
there were the others, must be fifty or sixty altogether, though
a bunch of them were a couple hundred meters away. The knot
closest to him was made of a dozen, none of them moving too
well save the big one. The wand had multiple charges and at
this distance he could probably knock them all down with two
or three shots. He didn't want to do it, but he had a family now,
and that weighed heavily on him. He had responsibilities.

Then again, a man could be paralyzed if he considered all
the things that might happen to him and stopped to worry about
them. You could get flattened by a hovercab while crossing the
street. Could get caught in an earthquake. Hell, a meteor could
zip along from ten billion klicks away and whack you right
between the eyes. What were you supposed to do, hide under
your bed until you died of old age?

Fuck it. He had to find out something.

Bork stuck the wand back on his belt and went to meet
Mkono.

Taz saw Saval recrow his hand wand. Damn, they must not
be working. Just to be sure, she pulled her own stunner and

pointed it at the group of naked people still scrambling to their
feet. Ten or twelve of them, behind the big one. God, look at
that guy!

Taz thumbed the wand's control, expecting to hear a hum
and have nothing happen. Instead, five of the throng closest
to her collapsed and sprawled on the ground.

Hello?

She took a more careful aim at the others still on their feet,
fired again.

All but one of them went boneless and fell.

She grinned. Hot smoking damn! A third blast took the
straggler out. Three shots, plus the one at felix, that left her
four charges.

She twisted, but Saval and the big man rushing to collide
like planetoids were too close to shoot without hitting them
both. And the one who had been yelling was out of range and
running farther away fast.

Taz stuck the wand to her belt and pulled the fat-bladed
knife. She turned toward Saval and the big man. Grinned
wolfishly. Took two steps toward them.

"No!" Saval yelled. "Get the leader!"

That was all he had time to say before he smashed into the
naked giant.

Kifo ran, panic filling him like his own blood, pounding
into his brain. How could this be? Sanctuary was supposed to
be inviolate, pure, without taint! Why had the gods allowed
those two inside? It went against all he knew, all he had been
taught, all that was right. It was unthinkable.

Another test; yes, that was it, it was a test, but oh, how could
they do such a thing? If the gods could break this, the most
sacred of promises, what else might they do?

Kifo felt sick; his bowels churned with broken glass and
scrap iron. He wanted to stop and vomit, but he could not.
The demons were loose in Sanctuary, and to slow would be to
fall prey to them. The woman—surely she was more than that?
Surely the gods had strengthened her, given her superhuman

powers?—the woman was even now gaining on him as he
ran. He had the hidden stun wand built into the walking stick,
but he suddenly had no faith in it. How could a man trust a
simple machine when the gods themselves had proved false?
It wouldn't work on her, he was sure of it. He had to run! The
gods had betrayed him!

No, no, don't think that! Don't let your faith be shaken! It
is a test, the severest test of all, the final hurdle to be cleared
before . . .

Before . . . ?

The thought was slippery, it nearly escaped him, but he
clamped down on it with frantic haste: before he went to the
center of Sanctuary and spoke directly to the gods!

Yes! Yes! That was it, that was what he had been planning
when he'd been sidetracked by the pleasures of this place!
Could he but get there, he would be safe! He would speak
to the Zonn, he would prove himself worthy by attaining that
place, and they would reward him!

Now Kifo's speed increased, his legs churned like never
before. He was the hot dry wind across an empty plain, a
cheetah pursuing prey. He did not feel fatigue. He flew like the
arrow of time; nothing could stay him from his goal. This body
meant nothing, and did he have to burn it to total exhaustion,
even death, that would not matter. Old flesh meant nothing to
a new god. He would remake himself.

Dedicated to a single purpose, Kifo the Unique ran to find
his gods.

Mkono was bigger but Bork had built up more speed. The
balance of mass and momentum was enough so when they
hit, the impact stopped both of them. They locked arms like
wrestlers and strained against each other. Before, he had been
surprised, taken from behind. Now sucker, let's see what you
can do to a man who's ready for you!

Bork remembered all the times when he had gone beyond
his normal limits, when the machines said he couldn't do it,
when he'd reached deep into himself and come up with just

a little more. Now he went to his depths again, seeking that essence of who he was, demanding everything he had. Now or never, Bork. Let's see what you've got.

He gave himself up to it, knew that he'd tapped energies beyond any he had ever called upon before, knew that every bit of his available strength flowed up from his center and went into this single, simple command: throw or be thrown!

For a heartbeat, the two men stood locked like a quivering statue, tendons creaking, muscles groaning and tearing. Both of them screamed, primal, wordless roars.

Then Mkono lifted Bork from his feet and threw him.

Shit—!

Ahead of her the running man sped up as if his feet had grown power jets. Taz sheathed the knife to keep from cutting herself as she pumped her arms to increase her speed. She zipped past the larger group of mostly naked people who seemed too wit-fogged to get in her way. She had been gaining but the guy's spurt of speed amazed her. She was strong and fast, but she might as well have been walking compared to this guy. What the fuck had happened to him?

She hit her own top speed, thinking that he would have to slow down, he couldn't maintain that for long. After another thirty seconds, she realized she couldn't keep sprinting, either. She eased up a little, still moving fast, but also still outside her breath. He gained further. He was a hundred meters ahead and pulling away.

Dammit!

After another thirty or forty seconds she recovered a little wind, not much. She dug down and demanded more from her burning legs, her aching lungs. She had a stitch in her left side, but if she stopped he would get away. Fuck that.

He must be slowing some because while she wasn't gaining, neither was he pulling away any more. He was maybe two hundred meters away but they were moving at the same speed.

Taz intended to keep running until he stopped. Or until she dropped. One or the other ought to happen real soon.

• • •

Kifo felt his body protesting, screaming for rest, for air, but he denied the demands. He lived from the neck up now, focused on his final destination. The veil Sanctuary had dropped over his mind was gone. He was sharp, a living razor, nothing would fog him. It wouldn't be far, he could feel the power rippling from ahead, emanating like the heat of the sun. There, there ahead was a shimmer in the air, a sparkle only just visible. The center of Sanctuary, it had to be, must be, where a man could claim his reward. He would be there soon. Soon—

Bork had trained too many years in mastering the Ninety-seven Steps to allow himself to be hurt in this kind of fall. He stretched out into a long dive, turned himself into an egg-shaped half hoop, and rolled. He came up facing Mkono. His body moved into a defensive pattern without conscious thought. It wasn't a reflex, but it was close. His body knew what to do even if his brain wanted to force it to do otherwise.

Mkono grinned. "I am stronger!" His already hard muscles tightened yet more and he made fists and crouched to move into another attack.

"Yes," Bork said, finally acknowledging the truth of it. Mkono was physically his better, no way around it. Well. There was nothing to be done for it. That's how it was.

Damn.

Mkono moved in. Reached out to grapple with Bork again, self-confidently, almost lazily.

Bork allowed the bigger man within a hair of touching him, then spun into the second variation of Laughing Stone. He stretched the edge of his right hand into a perfect chop, thumb tucked in just like the boss had taught him, and slammed it into the back of Mkono's head where the muscle met the bone.

Mkono stretched out and went face first into the ground. Bounced.

Oh, *that* felt good.

The bigger man shoved himself up, shook his head, and growled like some huge carnivore. Leaped at Bork, fingers extended into claws.

Bork twisted, dropped sideways, and put the heel of his foot into Mkono's ribs. Heard bones snap wetly as the power of his kick shoved the other man sideways.

Mkono screamed, rage or pain or both, came down hard but stayed on his feet. He lunged again.

Bork put Mkono in the Vacuum Cage; his elbow flattened Mkono's nose with a splat. Blood sprayed as if from an aerosol pump.

Mkono tottered, spun to face Bork again, but held his attack, stood still and gathered himself.

No, sorry, pal. No rest for the wicked. Bork gave him Steel Circle, finished with the optional sweep; his extended leg caught Mkono behind the knees and lifted his feet from the ground. The stunned Mkono fell flat on his back, hit the ground and bounced again, a good eighteen centimeters high.

Bork backed off five steps, whirled his hands in overlapping half moons and stood ready to cast The Flower Unfolding. "Call it stop," Bork said. This wasn't competition, strong as Mkono was. The man had raw power, but it wasn't enough. In that moment, Bork saw himself in Mkono, knowing his strength would always be enough. Wrong.

Mkono growled, the sound bubbling liquidly in his throat. Came in again.

He unfolded the flower. Broke Mkono's left arm.

Mkono came in again. Was bitten by Snake and Spider.

Again. Cold Fire Burns Bright.

Finally, on one leg—the other being broken and unable to support him—Mkono hopped toward Bork.

The man was a murderer, an ice-soul killer, but even so, pity welled in the matador. "You got balls, Mkono. And you *are* stronger than I am. You're stronger, but I'm *better*. Call it stop."

Mkono shook his head. Blood flew in jellied strings from his nose and mouth. He hopped closer.

Bork nodded. He understood. Mkono wasn't going to quit. Bork knew. He wouldn't have quit either.

Teeth bared, Mkono hopped, nothing left but his own Thing in the Cave, fighting on primal rage. He would keep coming as long as he could move, as long as he could breathe.

Bork gave Mkono Mimosa Sleeps Softly, and it was almost a grace note. When it was done, Mkono, who had been stronger, maybe the strongest man in all the galaxy, could no longer move.

Or breathe.

Bork stood over the dead man and shook his head. What a waste. What a terrible waste.

Some of the others still on their feet shambled toward the matador. Now he drew his hand wand and used it.

Kifo felt the power envelop him, drawing him in, filling him. Bright pain flashed over him electrically, then eased. If Sanctuary had been delightful, this place was ten times more so. There came a sense of peace unlike any he had ever known, even in the deepest meditation, the most sound sleep. Here, at last, the center of Sanctuary.

A questing presence touched him.

"?"

Fighting to draw breath, Kifo said, "My Lord Zonn! I am Ndugu Kifo, the Unique of your Chosen Few! Come to claim my promised godhood!"

"?"

"Toy with me no longer! I have earned my place! I have done as you asked. I beg you, please!"

"?"

Kifo wanted to scream.

Taz saw the runner vanish, but damned if she could figure out how. The space ahead of her was clear, empty; she could see to the far wall of wherever this was. He just disappeared as if the air had swallowed him. Another joy of this place.

She slowed to a jog, then a walk. Wait a second; there was some kind of sparkle ahead, kind of like a heat wave. Trying to get more air than her mouth and nose could channel, she moved toward the sparkle.

"In the name of everything holy, I beg you!"
This time the questing presence did not offer any interrogatory energy. Seconds passed. Then it spoke.
Well, not actually in words, Kifo realized. It was inside his head, as the gods had been other times, but different than those had been. This was sharper, clearer, more directed.
AH, I HAVE IT. WHAT ARE YOU? the presence said.
"I am Kifo, your Unique, shepherd to your Few—"
MEANINGLESS, the presence said. DEFINE.
Kifo was stunned, but only for an instance. Another test. Could this be the final one? Was he being asked to respond properly so that the Zonn could be assured of his faith even at this late hour? Was this gate to be strait, narrowed by this Keeper so that only a precise walk could allow passage? He sighed. It must be so. So many trials.
All right. He would pass this test as he had passed all the others. Kifo brought forth the doctrine, the dogma as he had lived it, explained as if talking to a stranger he must convince of the truth.
The presence listened. Absorbed the words.
How long it took the man could not have said, but he spilled it in a flood, a cup overflowing and rising about him until he was immersed in it. The Few. The Faith. His place in it.
Finally, after eons of waiting, the presence replied.
AH, SENTIENT BUT FLAWED. REQUIRING SUPPORT FROM OUTSIDE ITSELF. IGNORANT OF REALITY, FEARFUL, CLUTCHING AT ITS OWN MINDS'S EYE. MUCH DEVELOPMENT NEEDED.
The presence spewed something else, but the meaning of it eluded Kifo like a never-before-heard foreign language.
ADJUST. MILLENNIA YET. MORE.
"Lord—?"

YOU HAVE ERRED, SIMPLEMINDED BEING. THOSE
YOU CALL "ZONN" ARE NOT GODS. THEY NO LONGER
EXIST IN THIS PLANE, IN THIS UNIVERSE.

"Blasphemy!"

AS MUCH TRUTH AS YOU CAN STAND. YOUR
EFFORTS TO EXPLAIN THAT WHICH YOU DO NOT
UNDERSTAND ARE INEPT. YOU ENDOW THOSE
GREATER THAN YOURSELF WITH ESSENCES THEY
DO NOT POSSESS.

"No, I—"

UNDERSTAND WHAT YOU CAN: THIS PLACE
(MEANINGLESS) IS A CONSTRUCT. I ALSO AM A
CONSTRUCT. WE ARE RECORDINGS, (MEANINGLESS)
STORAGE FACILITIES FOR ENERGIES AND EMOTIONS
THE ZONN OVERCAME AND LEFT BEHIND WHEN
THEY DEPARTED FOR (MEANINGLESS). ALL THE
NEGATIVE THINGS THEY NEEDED NO LONGER FOR
(MEANINGLESS) WERE LEFT HERE.

"No—!"

A PHOTO ALBUM, HOLDING UNPLEASANT MEMO-
RIES, A PLACE THEY CAN CALL UP SHOULD THEY
EVER NEED TO BE REMINDED OF HOW LOW THEY
ONCE WERE. CHECKS AND (MEANINGLESS).

Kifo screamed. Too much. This test was too much, he
couldn't endure it! "You lie to task me—!"

POOR CREATURE. SO SMALL. SO DULL. KNOW THIS.
FEEL. TRY.

With that, Kifo's head nearly burst from the flow of sudden
knowledge that filled it. He was a cup under a firehose, a
circuit overloaded with ten thousand times the current it could
safely conduct; his mind burned with it.

Just before it overwhelmed him totally, he felt the truth of
it all, just as the presence had said. His religion was a myth,
based on a mistake, worth less than a handful of hard vacuum.
He had communed not with gods but with the cast-off mental
and spiritual garbage of a race of aliens who had elevated
themselves to another plane before men left the trees. Not

even with demons, but with dregs.

He had looked upon the face of his god and found it was nothing more than a bin full of trash.

The weight of it crashed down upon Kifo.

The air shimmered brightly and the naked man appeared in front of Taz, not two meters away. She snatched at her hand wand, stopped. He lurched at her; too close. He'd get there before she could draw.

She shoved, hit him solidly on the chest with both hands. Saw the horror on his face as he flew backward, spittle spraying. Saw his eyes roll back as he fell. Heard him gurgle as he hit the ground. He spasmed, vibrating rapidly, gurgled again.

"No!" he screamed. He came up, lunged at her.

She sidestepped, hit him a glancing shot with the heel of her hand. Not a powerful blow.

He fell. Screamed, a wordless, horrified cry, the most chilling sound she had ever heard a human being make. It was terror distilled from the beginning of time down to a brew thick as lead, the very essence of fear and betrayal. A sound of despair she would never forget did she live to be ten thousand years old.

Then he closed his eyes and went slack.

Taz did not want to imagine what it was he had seen, wherever it was he had been.

THIRTY

THE NAKED MAN was alive but there was nobody home. His face was locked into a fright mask, his eyes wide, mouth open, features contorted. Taz guided him and he walked when she prodded, but offered nothing coherent. The fear was like a stain. She found his walking stick, picked it up, and saw that it was more than it seemed. There was a short-range stunner built into the handle; a button above the wand's control opened a small compartment inside of which was a sculpted bit of Zonn metal. It had an odd shape and felt like ice in her hand. Carefully Taz replaced the metal and reclosed the compartment's cap. She didn't know what it meant. Let the scientists figure it out.

Ahead of her Saval stood rounding up the others. Even though there were four or five dozen of them, they didn't offer him any resistance. Some of the people were still sprawled from the effects of the hand wands, some were coming out of the shock.

The body of the biggest one lay face down on the ground.

"Taz," Saval said. "You okay?"

"Yeah. You?"

Saval glanced at the big man on the ground. "Yeah. He was stronger than me."

"Didn't matter, though, did it?"

"No. That was all he had." He looked back at her. "What happened to him?"

"Something got him," she said. "He warped in and out of somewhere, I lost him for a few minutes. When he came back, he looked like he'd spent a season in hell. Wonder what could be so scary?"

"Maybe he ran into his god."

"Yeah, maybe. Not somebody I'd want to meet."

"Me, neither. What say we try to find our way home?"

She nodded.

They came out in the ruins, not far from where they'd entered. They were met by a pair of special teams. A command post had been set up, and camp tents erected.

"You guys are pretty quick," Taz said.

The leader of the teams shook his head. "Jesu, Chief, you been gone three days. We could have walked here."

Bork smiled as Taz turned and raised an eyebrow at him. By their own time, they'd been inside maybe half an hour. Another thing to warn the scientific types about.

The teams herded the now-dressed church members toward waiting transports. Some of them were probably connected directly to the crimes instigated by their leader, some of them maybe just guilty of misplaced faith. Bork and Taz watched them go.

"Well," Taz said, "looks like that about wraps it up."

Bork nodded.

"I appreciate your help."

"We're family," he said. "That's what you do."

They smiled at each other.

"Ruul's probably worried about you," Bork said.

"I'll call him. You probably ought to call Veate, too, and see how my nephew is getting along."

"Oh, yeah."

"It'll probably be months before Ruul can shed his exowalker," she said. "And maybe he'll change his mind after having me around that long, but if not, you'll come to the wedding?"

"I wouldn't miss it, little sister."

She reached for him, they hugged, squeezing each other hard; ordinary people would have creaked under the force. But then, the Borks weren't ordinary people. "This was a good thing for me," he said. "I learned something important about myself."

"Me, too."

For a moment they let that rest between them. Life was about motion, Bork realized. You had to keep moving, keep learning, keep growing. On one level he knew that, but it didn't hurt to have it brought home. The big lessons always needed repeating until you got them. Or they got you.

"Come on, brother, let's go get something to eat. Seems like days since we did that. Pickle will have something rigged up, even if she had to cover the hole in her wall with a tarp. And she deserves another shot at you before you go back to your wife."

He chuckled. "You ought to be ashamed, tempting me like that."

"Oh, I am. Really."

They both laughed. Arm in arm, they walked to her flitter.